*THIS YEAR OF YEARS WOULD
NEVER END, LUCRETIA THOUGHT,
AS THEY WALKED BACK TO THE HOTEL
AT DUSK. SHE COULD SEE FROM
WYATT'S EYES THAT HE WAS
BEING SEDUCED BY PARIS.*

In bed that night Wyatt could talk only of the future. The more he thought about it, the less he liked the idea of rushing into the Beaux-Arts, without even looking at other art schools.

"But the Beaux-Arts is the best, and to listen to Duprier, you're as good as in already." Cree turned out the light and slipped her arm through his.

"He's taking over. He's like your grandfather."

"Darling, you're going to keep your appointment, aren't you?"

"Of course."

They fell asleep, but Cree was awakened by loud singing across the courtyard. She thought about their voyage over and how, too often, she had imagined they had been on the Lusitania, and that she was her mother en route to Sweden.

The horror stories of the sinking came crowding back. Nearly four years later, she still missed Daddy and Mother terribly. There were times she thought her heart would never heal.

Wyatt stirred in his sleep. She kissed him softly on the cheek and pulled the comforter up higher. Tomorrow was an important day—for both of them.

The Shackleford Legacy
Book Three

LUCRETIA

Barbara Riefe

PLAYBOY
PAPERBACKS

LUCRETIA

Copyright © 1982 by Barbara Riefe

Cover illustration copyright © 1982 by PEI Books, Inc.

Published simultaneously in the United States and Canada by
Playboy Paperbacks, New York, New York. Printed in the United
States of America. Library of Congress Catalog Card Number:
81–85826. First edition.

Books are available at quantity discounts for promotional and
industrial use. For further information, write to Premium Sales,
Playboy Paperbacks, 1633 Broadway, New York, New York 10019.

ISBN: 0-867-21076-1 (U.S.)
      0-867-21080-X (Canada)

First printing July 1982.

For Alan

First printing July 1982.

Chapter One

Sitting in the back row of the winter-sun-lit room, three
of the walls hung with maps and obscured by black-
boards, the fourth framing ceiling-high windows overlooking Ninety-fifth Street, Cree licked the point of her
pencil and drew a single curving line for the chin of the
profile she was sketching. Studying the drawing, she
shadowed the area beneath the chin with the flat of
the pencil lead and closed her composition book. She
looked up and surveyed the bowed heads, the thirty-one
other girls in the class, who were absorbed in following
Mrs. Cardona reading from their textbook.

"But with the governments who have declared their
independence and maintained it, and whose independence we have on great consideration . . ."

Cree heard, but the words failed to register; her
thoughts were fixed on the hour to come. She glanced at
the octagonal Seth Thomas clock above the blackboard
behind Mrs. Cardona. Almost two thirty.

Mrs. Cardona knew the Monroe Doctrine by heart.
She should, Cree reflected, after stuffing her students'
heads with it for more than thirty years. Mrs. Cardona
knew the Bill of Rights, the Declaration of Independence, and dozens of other important historical docu-

7

ments word for word. She stood behind her desk as rigid as a fence post, her black dress draped like a choir robe down her board-flat chest, her pince-nez straddling the bridge of her aquiline nose, her eyes staring out of her waxen face, her gray hair twisted into little wirelike curls all over her head. On and on she declaimed, her tone and her expression suggesting that she was President Monroe himself addressing Congress.

Cree, too, bowed her head; why invite attention to her absence of interest in the President's concern for the welfare of the hemisphere?

"It is impossible that the allied powers should extend their political system to any portion of either continent without endangering our peace and happiness."

Again Cree's thoughts flew forward. Class would end at two thirty. That gave her twenty-five minutes to get to her locker, into her things, out onto the sidewalk, and uptown by taxi to 125th Street Station in time to catch the 3:04 to New Haven. To be on the safe side, she would have to be out of class at two thirty on the dot.

The taxi worried her. Like umbrellas and waiters and stockings without runs, taxis could be infuriatingly hard to find when you were in the greatest race against time. Missing the train would be a disaster on a par with the sinking of the *Titanic*.

"Lucretia Shackleford."

The sound of her name was like a slap in the face.

"Are you with us today?"

Cree flushed and shrank into herself. "Yes, Mrs. Cardona."

"In body, perhaps, but in mind? Tell us, what would happen if the allied powers tried to extend their political system to any portion of the Western Hemisphere?"

"It would be very bad. . . ."

All eyes were suddenly upon her. Her classmates began to giggle, then exploded into laughter.

"Quiet! It would endanger our country's peace and happiness. Lucretia, please see me after class."

Outside the door, the corridor bell rang tiredly, as if it were its own death knell.

"Class dismissed."

Cree's heart crumbled in her breast. If there was one thing Mrs. Cardona enjoyed more than regaling her classes with recitations of important historical documents, it was lecturing daydreamers and those who caused disturbances. History II, reflected Cree gloomily, really wasn't a class at all. It was High Mass conducted by a priestess in a choir robe. And denying it full attention was a sin.

The girls streamed down the aisles to the door, chattering loudly. The minute hand of the wall clock moved to 2:31.

"Lucretia, what seems to be the trouble today? Spring fever? How can that be? It's the fourth of February."

"I . . ." Monday, February 4, announced the calendar on the wall behind Mrs. Cardona.

"Do you find the Monroe Doctrine boring?"

"No, not at all."

"How refreshing. I'm sure all the other girls do. Is it me, do I bore you?"

2:32.

"No, no, honestly. I guess my mind was just wandering."

Mrs. Cardona's eyes fell on the composition book under Cree's arm. She gestured. Cree handed her the book. She opened it to the picture.

"Who's this, Douglas Fairbanks without a mustache?"

"No, just a man, nobody."

"He's very good-looking. However, this is a class in American history, Lucretia, not drawing practice."

"Yes, Mrs. Cardona."

Mrs. Cardona gave back the book. The hardworking clock hand seemed suddenly to be jumping from one minute to the next, without bothering to make the sixty-second pause. In her mind's eye Cree pictured the passengers boarding the train at Grand Central.

"You may go now, Lucretia, but the next time this happens, plan on staying for one hour, is that understood? Daydreaming is a waste of your time and an insult to me."

"Yes, Mrs. Cardona, I'm sorry."

She walked to the door, raced down the corridor, and breathlessly reached the locker hall. Girls stood about in groups, talking and laughing. Fumbling in her handbag, Cree found her key and removed the suitcase crammed inside. Tossing her books into the locker, she put on her coat, hat, and muffler, and slammed the door shut.

"We seem to be in a great hurry, Lucretia."

She turned. It was Mrs. Cardona. The hall fell silent. Once again Cree found herself the focus of attention.

"I'm in a play," she lied. "We're having dress rehearsal at a friend of mine's house. Excuse me, I have to run or I'll be late and hold everybody up."

"See you tomorrow."

Mrs. Cardona hadn't believed a word of it. Suitcase in hand, Cree ran past a gaggle of girls, down the five steps, and through the double doors that opened onto Ninety-sixth Street.

She was in luck. Almost immediately a taxi turned into the block from Fifth Avenue and came slowly toward her. She waved frantically. It stopped, and she got in.

"Hundred and Twenty-fifth Street Station, please. And hurry."

She glanced out the rear window at the three-story brownstone that took up two-thirds of the block between Fifth and Madison avenues. Miss Barclay's School. Look long, she told herself, fix it in your memory. It's the last you'll ever see of it and of Mrs. Cardona. Her "See you tomorrow" was wishful thinking. They'd never see each other again as long as they lived.

Providing, of course, she made the 3:04.

The streets were rutted with frozen slush, with cars parked on both sides narrowing the way to two lanes. Traffic was heavy and maddeningly slow. When the taxi turned the corner at 125th to cross over to Park, it got behind a huge moving-van, which inched along, its motor sounding as if it might quit at any moment. Cree prayed and crossed her fingers until they began to ache. Halfway up the block, she told the driver to pull over, paid him and ran to the iron stairs leading to the overhead platform.

A clock confronted her at the top of the stairs. Someone had thrown a snowball, which had frozen against the face of the clock, all but obscuring the time. 2:59. Made it!

To the right of the clock was a small metal and glass shed, a windbreaker for the waiting passengers. Attached to the glass were framed posters.

SAVE

1. Wheat—use more corn
2. Meat—use more fish and beans
3. Fats—use just enough
4. Sugar—use syrups

---

and save
the cause of freedom
U.S. FOOD ADMINISTRATION

She despised beans, she thought. Next to it was a war poster.

THE UNITED STATES ARMY BUILDS MEN!

The illustrator had selected four men for building, and at the bottom of the poster was the advice, "To win the war in '18, apply nearest recruiting office."

Alongside the war poster was an advertisement.

HAVE YOU LEFT SCHOOL
WITHOUT A DIPLOMA?

The Chautauqua Institution of Chautauqua, New York, would provide you with one. Cree screwed her eyes shut and turned away. She didn't need reminding. With five months to go until graduation, she was putting school behind her. Good-bye, Miss Barclay, Mrs. Cardona, art classes (which she adored), English and French (which she loved), Latin (which she loathed), the girls, friends and foes, all pushed into the past. Her heart thumped in her chest.

There was a pay phone just up the way near a

stanchion supporting the platform roof. The frozen-faced clock now read three on the dot. There was still time for her to call home. She pictured what would happen. Mrs. Bates or one of the maids would answer. She would tell her she was leaving home for good. Whoever it was would try to talk her out of it, of course, but she would stick to her guns and have to hang up when her train came in. So what would calling accomplish, other than to inflict one more painful stab in her conscience? She could call Grandfather at his office. She pictured flames leaping from the mouthpiece of the phone as he berated her and ordered her to go straight home and stay there.

She wouldn't, she'd committed herself, just as her sisters had. Livvy had married Alec White in defiance of Grandfather's wishes—against his direct orders was more accurate. Julia, too, was leaving. She had been bedridden with pneumonia since early in January, and Dr. Bingham had forbidden her to get up. But after three weeks on her back, during which time she had shown steady improvement, she had confided to Cree only last night that she was determined not only to get up, but to pack up and leave.

Why the mass exodus from 1 East Sixth-first Street? Not just because Livvy had departed. She, Cree, and Julia all had minds of their own, but ever since Mother and Daddy had been killed three years before, in 1915, living with Grandfather had become increasingly difficult, if not intolerable. It was like living under Caesar; he had turned them into three marionettes, his hands holding the strings, virtually controlling their every move. Just thinking about him, his petty tyranny, his inescapable presence, his eternal smothering upset her so much that she promptly dismissed him from mind.

Turning, she moved ten more steps away from the temptation of the phone.

It was early for the commuter rush, but there were at least forty people on the platform, mostly students finished with school for the day and on their way home to Bronxville and Tuckahoe, Crestwood and Scarsdale. Little boys in knitted caps, in sheepskin and horsehide coats, with mufflers teacher-tightened around their necks, shouted and pushed one another, performing for giggling little girls in wool swagger coats with fur collars, who clutched their bookbags and watched the boys.

She herself wore her brown squirrel coat over her navy Barouette satin suit with the box-pleated skirt and dark suede shoes. It was 20 degrees, bitter cold; bonebending cold, Grandfather always called it. She pulled her collar tighter and turned away from the wind.

Not phoning, not leaving a farewell note, might seem cowardly to some, but it made sense, however much her conscience was troubled. After all, eloping wasn't supposed to be a game of hare and hounds. Grandfather would suspect she'd gone to Yale. So? By the time he had found out she wasn't coming home and had sent the police after them, they'd be miles from New Haven.

What choice did she have but to sneak away like a thief? She certainly wasn't about to confront him as Livvy had, voluntarily subject herself to his ranting and raving. Give him the chance and he'd tie her up and lock her in her room. Livvy had been twenty-two when she left, Julia was almost twenty-one. She herself had just turned eighteen and couldn't marry Wyatt without Grandfather's consent either in New York or Connecticut.

But in New Hampshire the age of marriage without parental consent was sixteen for a girl. Wyatt knew; he'd checked.

3:02. Once more her eyes drifted to the pay phone. A woman in a mink coat was using it, then hung up. Cree ran over, got out a coin and dialed.

"Grandfather . . ."

"Lucretia! Where are you, girl?"

"I won't be coming back."

"What do you mean? Have you taken leave of your senses? Never mind, never mind, I don't want to hear. I'm not going to argue with you over the damned phone. Judas priest, if this day doesn't beat all! First Julia running out, now you."

The train was pulling in, its huge black cylindrical body bearing down on the station, whooshing steam from under its wheels, its single eye yellowed with grime, icicles festooning its smoke-box door, snow capping the caps set in a row along the boiler top. The bell clanged a command to board quickly or be left behind. There were miles to be covered and there was no time to squander. The engine panted, and steam billowed into the icy air.

"I have to go now, Grandfather."

"Hold your horses! You listen to me, young lady, you get home here fast as your legs can carry you, you hear? Lucretia, Lucretia!"

"Good-bye, I love you."

She hung up.

"Boooooard . . ."

She entered a car and found a seat. Unsnapping her suitcase, she got out *Carolyn of the Corners* by Ruth Belmore Endicott, then put her suitcase in the overhead rack. She was already halfway through the book. It had started out excitingly with the heroine being kidnapped and spirited away aboard ship. But once she got to sea, the plot bogged down. Cree labored through two pages, then set the book, binding up, on the seat and gazed out the window. Sunday's snowfall still covered the ground and seemed to deepen as the train headed eastward up the coast.

Have you left school without a diploma? her mind asked her image in the window as the train jolted along. One after another suburban stops vanished behind it. Very soon now the train would be crossing the state line into Connecticut. As it rolled on through the gray day, a grayness seemed to collect inside her. Good-bye, Grandfather. Good-bye, I love you. How had she ever gotten up the courage to call him?

That she'd summoned the courage to leave surprised her, now that she thought about it. She could as easily have stayed home under his wing cloistered and protected, dreaming every night of escape.

Not escape. She was eloping, just as Livvy had left to marry the man she loved. More than anything in the world Cree wanted to marry Wyatt—and he wanted to marry her.

Nothing must be permitted to stand in their way.

Chapter Two

The train, a local, arrived in New Haven two hours later, on time. Cree had spent the time daydreaming about Wyatt and trying to ease her conscience. One conclusion refused to be ignored. Leaving Grandfather alone didn't seem fair. She must write him a long letter and try to explain. Would he, she wondered, tear it up unopened or burn it?

Her heart lifted at the sight of Wyatt in his ridiculous raccoon coat, which always looked capable of crawling away under its own power. He wore his muffler pulled taut around his head like a babushka and secured in place with his cap, the bill pulled so low that it hid his face. But there was no mistaking his sorry and abused-looking coat.

He waved and ran to her.

"Sweetheart!" His grin vanished. "What's the matter, you look miserable." He hugged and kissed her. "Are you okay?"

"I guess, just scared. It is scary, Wyatt."

"I'll tell the cockeyed world." He tensed. "You didn't spill the beans to your grandfather, did you?" She nodded. "For Pete's sake, Cree, you promised . . ."

"I had to tell him. When I didn't come home after school, what would he and Mrs. Bates have thought?

17

That I'd been run over by a car or something."

He raised the bill of his cap and furrowed his brow in thought.

"He has to know you're coming up here. We've got to get a move on. Everything's set. Dink Ramsey and his steady, a townie, are coming with us to be our witnesses. You'll like Ginger, she's a real live wire. I drove Dink's Model T over. We have to put the top down and snap on the isinglass windows. They're kind of yellow and hard to see through, but they'll keep the wind out. It's going to be a cold trip, but we'll have blankets and stuff."

He smiled, his brown eyes sparkling, a wisp of dark-red hair sneaking out from under his cap.

"Everything's going to be jake, Cree, you'll see. I promise." He picked up her suitcase and put his arm around her. "Come on, the heap's out front."

"How long will it take us to get there?"

"Who knows? It depends on the roads. Seven or eight hours. As soon as we cross over into New Hampshire, there'll be justice-of-the-peace signs, so Dink says. We'll stop at the first one."

"We probably won't get there until long past midnight. Everybody'll be asleep."

"We'll give 'em a 'Boola Boola' and wake up the whole town."

"Seriously, Wyatt."

"Don't worry about it."

"I can't help it. We're not just running off for a weekend, this is serious. I'm serious."

His smile fled. "I am, too, Cree, you know I am."

"I was thinking, coming up on the train, we have to be out of our minds to do this."

"It's healthy to be a little cuckoo. It's a crazy world;

anybody who's all there is doomed. So maybe we are young, we're old enough to know what we're doing. Lots of kids our age get married and make a go of it. We can, you know we can. Look at the bright side, we don't have to worry about the draft. I won't be twenty-one for a year and almost nine months. By then the war'll be over. We're not doing anything illegal. I'm nineteen, you're eighteen, which means we can marry without our parents' consent."

"Only in New Hampshire . . ."

"What's wrong with New Hampshire? It's a great state. And the snow's only six feet deep up there."

"You think we'll make it?"

"We'll make it if we have to walk, if I have to carry you the last hundred miles. Oh, say, did you remember to bring your birth certificate?"

"Of course. Did you?"

He patted his pocket.

"What about the wedding license?" she asked.

"We get it up there. A Connecticut license wouldn't be legal in New Hampshire. Dink says every justice of the peace has licenses. He just fills one out and notarizes it. Dink knows all about it, his cousin at Dartmouth got married. Everything'll be legal, Cree, please stop worrying."

They approached the car, a tin-lizzie sedan with a double rectangular windshield, a coach lamp on either side of the radiator, headlights the size of stove lids, and fenders turning into running boards that looked to Cree as if a sudden stop would send them clattering to the ground.

"Is this thing going to make it all the way to New Hampshire?" she asked.

"And back. It's no Rolls-Royce, but it goes." He

tossed the suitcase into the back seat, and together they put up the canvas top and began snapping the isinglass windows into place. The car buttoned up, Wyatt swung open the passenger door, got out the starting crank, and waved Cree in. Just as he was about to close the door, he glanced behind the car and blanched. Pulling his cap down another two inches, he pushed the suitcase onto the floor and out of sight.

"Don't look," he rasped.

A black Essex had come up behind them. A distinguished-looking man emerged and helped a plump, heavily furred woman out of the rear seat.

"It's President and Mrs. Hadley," whispered Wyatt. "And Dean Jones driving."

"Isn't he Dean of Students?"

"The Warden. Get behind the wheel and set the spark and throttle levers at ten to three."

Wyatt crouched in front of the car, pulled the choke wire, and began cranking furiously. The engine rumbled into life. Ducking his head, he ran around to the spark and throttle levers and moved them to twenty-five to two.

"Chance! It is Chance, isn't it?"

Dean Frederick Scheetz Jones pursed his thin lips and eyed Wyatt inquiringly.

"Good afternoon, sir." The dean peered inside the car. President and Mrs. Hadley came up beside him. "May I present Miss Lucretia Shackleford?"

"A pleasure to meet you, Miss Shackleford. May I present President and Mrs. Hadley? Miss Lucretia Shackleford. Come to town to visit Mr. Chance, it seems." Dean Jones looked puzzled. "Today's Monday. Is there some social occasion on campus? At the Deke House perhaps? If there is, I haven't heard about it."

"Oh, no, sir," said Wyatt, his voice suddenly thin, almost piping. "Lucre—Miss Shackleford has just come to New Haven to visit her aunt. I offered to pick her up. We're old friends . . ."

"I see. Perhaps I know your aunt, Miss Shackleford."

"Aunt Marjorie," interposed Wyatt. "She lives in Hamden, Spring Glen."

"I see. Well, Miss Shackleford, I hope you'll come and visit us on campus." He stared at Wyatt. "Saturday or Sunday, that is, when young ladies are permitted to visit the first floors of the fraternity houses."

President Hadley tipped his fedora, Mrs. Hadley smiled and nodded, Dean Jones stern-eyed Wyatt, and all three turned and went into the station.

"Aunt Marjorie?" asked Cree. "We once had a cat named Marjorie."

Wyatt blew out a long and labored breath, his shoulders sagging.

"He didn't swallow one word. We'd better get while the getting's good. Dink and Ginger are waiting at the Peabody Museum."

"Marjorie . . ."

"My mother's name, remember? It was the first name I could think of."

They drove up Elm Street onto the campus, passing between Connecticut Hall and the Divinity School building, crossing High Street, and came within sight of the museum. Dink Ramsey and his girl friend were waiting out front with blankets, a lap robe, an overnight bag, and Dink's banjo. They looked cute together, thought Cree. Dink towered to almost six feet four: six inches taller than Wyatt, his complexion darker, not as handsome (in her opinion), not as muscular or as broad, but sweet and funny, especially when he was tipsy. And beside him sat Ginger, barely five feet tall, pink-cheeked and pretty. She wore a coat with an overpoweringly large Baltic Beaver fur collar and a knitted cap with a pom-pom the size of a baseball. There were hurried introductions, and Dink and Ginger piled into the back seat.

"Brother Ramsey," said Wyatt, "how are we supposed to find our way up to the boondocks without a map?"

"Head for North Haven, Sec, old boy. We'll take the least rutted route to Worcester, circle Beantown, and get up to Lowell. Once we cross over into New Hampshire, we have to look for the booming metropolis of Hollis—three houses, a post office, and a one-pump gas station, no doubt. And keep your eyes peeled for justice-of-the-peace signs."

He leaned over the seat, smirking first at Wyatt, then at Cree.

"Are you children sure you want to go through with this? You know what they say, marriage is the best way in the world to spoil a beautiful friendship."

"Oh, hush!" said Ginger.

"Nothing doing, I've got two hundred miles to work on them. Ginger, my heart, don't look at me like that."

"Like what, you boob?"

"With that glazed look. The word 'marriage' always brings it on. Don't you know double weddings are unlucky? We have to wait until I get that old sheepskin. If we jump the gun, Pater'll break my neck. It's none of my beeswax, Sec, but how do you plan to break the news to your old man?"

"Why do you call him Sec?" asked Cree.

"Wyatt Chance the Second, of course. Really, how will Wyatt the First take the good news?"

"Maybe not all that gracefully. Cree and I are both counting heavily on my mother. She's my staunchest ally in times of stress."

"I have just the thing to get rid of those worried looks." He produced a hip flask. "Old reliable Kentucky bourbon, just what the doctor ordered for unfreezing corpuscles and firming backbones."

"Not for me, thanks," said Ginger. "I'll stick to Bevo. How about some?" she asked Cree.

"Not now, thanks."

"I brought along eight bottles and tuna-fish sandwiches and those little grocery pies. They're the berries."

"A toast to the bride and groom." Dink upended his flask and drank and offered the flask to Wyatt.

"Not now. But save me half," said Wyatt. "When this is all over, I'll need it."

"I like that!" snapped Cree.

"To celebrate, of course."

"Don't pay any attention to bigmouth here," said Ginger, glaring at Dink. "You know we're both rooting for you. You sure have gumption. My father'd kill me if he ever caught me eloping."

"That reminds me," said Dink, "did you remember to tell your folks you're staying overnight at your girl friend's?"

"Of course."

"If you think about it, eloping's not exactly the crime of the century," said Wyatt. "We love each other, we're old enough, we want to get married. Why sit around talking about it when you can go ahead and do it?"

"What will your folks say when they find out?" Ginger asked Cree.

"Her parents are dead," said Wyatt.

"Oh . . ."

"They were on the *Lusitania*," said Cree. "I live with my grandfather. My oldest sister, Olivia, left home and so did Julia, the middle one. If I stayed alone with him—"

"She'd end up off her trolley," said Wyatt.

"Grandpa sounds like a monster," said Ginger.

"He's not that bad, he's just set in his ways, like most older people. Living with him is like living on a leash. I just want to be free."

Dink laughed. "So why get married?"

"There's one problem our getting married sure isn't going to solve," said Wyatt. "Cree's grandfather and my dad don't much like each other."

"They can't stand each other," said Cree. "They got into a squabble over some business deal years ago and neither of them has ever been willing to forgive and forget."

She explained that Shackleford Real Estate had tried to purchase the Dorchester Building on Wall Street at a time when her grandfather had been long on assets and short on capital. He'd gone to Wyatt's father's company to borrow the money. His father's people had conducted a routine inspection of the premises, concluded that the building was not in a condition to warrant the designated purchase price, and her grandfather's application for a loan was turned down. He had been furious. Mr. Chance was just as upset, taking the position that by refusing the loan he was protecting Shackleford from an unwise investment. Unfortunately for Cree's grandfather, Chance and Company's decision on the condition of the Dorchester Building was the signal to other lenders to close their doors to Shackleford; he was unable to buy the building and had never again attempted to do business with Chance and Company.

"I'll say this for your grandfather," said Wyatt, "he may not like my dad, but he's never held it against me."

"He's sure going to, after this night's work," said Dink, laughing.

Wyatt was heading along Whitney Avenue between the stately, now leafless, trees that gave New Haven the name the Elm City. It was getting dark, the temperature was dropping, and the wind rising and assaulting the snapped-on windows. Cree snuggled closer to Wyatt, pulling her coat more tightly about her. In only hours she would be Mrs. Wyatt Richard Chance II. Man and wife. Young man, younger wife, but old enough for New Hampshire.

As soon as they had found a cooperative justice of the peace and he had performed the ceremony, they planned to turn around and come back, Dink to the Deke House, where his and Wyatt's beds had been stuffed with pillows to make it look as if they were occupied. When Mrs. Willoughby, the housemother, came around to check beds at ten o'clock, she'd never suspect that two of the brothers-in-the-bond were two states away. And that one would never be back.

"First thing in the morning, before my first class, I'm going to the dean's office and tell him I've moved off campus," said Wyatt.

"Good old Jonesy," said Dink, "he'll be the last to know."

Wyatt slowed the car, pulling up to the curb.

"What are you stopping for?" asked Dink.

"Brother Ramsey, nobody except you and Ginger knows where we're going to be living, right?"

"I won't tell a soul," said Ginger. "Girl Scout's honor."

"I'm not worrying about you," said Wyatt.

Dink frowned, mortally offended. "We exchanged the secret Deke handshake on it, didn't we? What more do you want?"

"Just don't spill the beans, Dink. As far as anybody knows, I'll be living alone, and with no phone. I'll call my folks tomorrow. It's not them I'm worried about, it's Cree's grandfather."

"I'll write and tell him everything," said Cree. "If I call him, he'll only hang up on me. Wyatt . . ."

"What?"

"Once we're married, nobody can get it annulled, can they?"

"Dad and Mother wouldn't."

"Your grandfather can't," said Dink. "At least, I don't think he can, not if you don't go back to New York."

"I won't. Not till I'm twenty-one," said Cree. "If then."

"Get going," said Dink. "It's freezing back here. Why doesn't somebody invent heaters for cars?"

"You'll like our dream house, sweetheart," said Wyatt. "Dream room. I hope you do. We could have stopped off so you could see it, but . . ."

"It can wait, let's just get up there."

"I moved my stuff in. There's furniture, a bed, and two chairs. We'll need other things. There's a second-hand store on Church Street they say has great stuff really cheap."

"I hope we have a stove."

"Only one burner."

"What about the bathroom?"

"It's down the hall, but not too far. I have to be honest, it's a little cramped, it won't be like home."

"That's good news!"

He laughed. "You're a peach, you know that?"

"I'll love it, I will. It'll be our own, we can come and go as we please, we won't have to answer to a soul. It'll be heaven."

"Cut the mush, will you?" said Dink. "Everybody sit back and relax, it's time for Red Hot Ramsey and his Syncopated Strings. Let me get my gloves off." He got out his banjo, strummed it, tuned the E string. "All right, kiddies, request time."

"I request you tune up," said Ginger.

"I request you clam up."

"Play 'Boola Boola,'" Dink said. "With pleasure, thank you."

He played "Boola Boola," segued into "Twelfth Street Rag," and they all sang along with "The Sunshine of Your Smile" and "They Go Wild Simply Wild Over Me."

Cree was finally able to relax and enjoy herself. The wind drummed the top of the car in double time to the faster tunes, the windows shuddered, the banjo twanged, and they sang on. Cree snuggled closer to Wyatt, his right arm encircling her.

My husband, she thought, my husband, my lover, my world, my life.

Chapter Three

Thaddeus Wheelwright, justice of the peace, was almost frightening—his indignation crimson and dangerously close to bellowing at having been awakened at ten of one in the morning. The justice of the peace wore a woolen nightshirt that reached to his well-scuffed boots, a nightcap with a tassel, and roped about his middle, a bathrobe patterned with diamonds in contrasting shades of brown, lending him the look of a bear roused from hibernation. He glared at the four young people on his doorstep.

"What's all the pounding? Who are ye? What do you mean waking a man out of a sound sleep at this hour?"

The wind tore the top off the snow piled on both sides of the approach to the house, sending powder swirling about. Opening the door two inches wider, Wheelwright showed a shotgun in his left hand.

Wyatt held up a folded ten-dollar bill.

"Sorry to wake you, sir, but we've come all the way from Connecticut. We want to get married." Wyatt slipped his arm around Cree.

"Well, why didn't you say so?"

Wheelwright's sleepy eyes now looked somewhat

friendlier. Leaning his shotgun against the wall, he stepped aside and gestured them in.

"All the way from Connecticut, you say? On a night like this? It's four above out there. Get round the stove."

They needed no further invitation, all but falling over one another in their haste to get to the Globe Lighthouse Stove set in the center of the parlor and sending waves of heat from its orange belly.

Cree glanced about. The front windows, glazed with frost, were covered with fancy fishnet lace curtains. The furnishings were holdovers from the last century. An Ansonia Cabinet Clock, badly in need of polishing, sat on the mantel over the woodash-filled fireplace. A Waverly piano occupied one corner of the room, its panels resplendent with lyres and leaves, its once-white keys as yellow as the Model T's isinglass windows. Set about the room were the pieces of a floral-patterned Turkish parlor set: a tête-à-tête, a rocker, a gentleman's easy chair, all heavily upholstered with plush bands and rolls and trimmed with a heavy worsted fringe. A vase tablelamp displayed ten painted bluebirds, and a library lamp hung directly above the stove provided enough light for a good-sized barn.

A coal-black cat came stealing into the room, hissed softly, and leaped onto the back of the rocker. Ginger went over to pet it, but as she approached, it glared and swiped at her.

" 'Pologize for Althea's bad manners," said Wheelwright. "She don't take kindly to visitors, to anyone. She don't even much like her own litter. Cats is ornery beasts."

Footsteps sounded overhead. Mrs. Wheelwright

came down the stairs and through the amber bead curtains separating the front and rear of the little house. She was a tiny woman in a rosebud-covered wool wrapper, her hair done up in little rag knots, her pleasant face distinguished by gray eyes that protruded slightly from behind gold-rimmed bifocal spectacles.

Mr. Wheelwright looked over both birth certificates, then took a marriage license form from the piano bench. He filled it out and stamped it with his notary public seal. Mrs. Wheelwright sat at the piano and played the "Wedding March," first dispatching Wyatt and Cree behind the bead curtain so that they might make a proper entrance. Mrs. Wheelwright did not play very well, and the piano needed tuning. It was all Ginger could do to keep from laughing out loud.

Wyatt produced the wedding ring and placed it on Cree's finger on instructions from Wheelwright. The ceremony took all of forty seconds, not one of which registered on the Ansonia Cabinet Clock on the mantel.

Just like that, reflected Cree. She was married. Wyatt Richard Chance II and Lucretia Anne Shackleford, man and wife. As Wyatt kissed her, Ginger flung handfuls of rice at them.

"Congratulations! Congratulations!"

Mr. and Mrs. Wheelwright kissed the bride and shook hands with the groom, and Mrs. Wheelwright's eyes fell to the rug and the rice grains fast being trampled into it. Mr. Wheelwright accepted the ten-dollar bill Wyatt had held up to him earlier, stuffing it in his robe pocket.

"Where'll you be staying tonight?" inquired Mrs. Wheelwright.

"We're heading straight back to New Haven," said Dink. "Mr. Chance and I have classes tomorrow."

"I doubt you make it afore sunup," said Wheelwright. "You'll be lucky if you don't freeze up on the way."

"We made it up," said Wyatt, "we'll make it back."

"You're welcome to stay."

"Thank you, but we really should be heading back," Wyatt said.

"Sir," interposed Dink, "you wouldn't have any extra gasoline you could sell us, would you?"

"Nope. Got prime white kerosene, though. It's just as good. Draw what you need from the barrel in the barn. They's a bucket sitting top of it you can use. The barrel cost me five dollars. That's ten cents a gallon. I'll let you have it for eleven, fair enough?"

"Fair enough," said Dink.

"And afore you leave, I'll fill you up with some good hot coffee," said Mrs. Wheelwright. "Sears and Roebuck Rio. Bolton Stewart, the mailman, just dropped the sack off this morning. Fresh as a kiss."

Wyatt and Dink put on their coats and went out to the barn. They filled the gas tank under the front seat of the car to within an inch of the top, leaving air space to insure flow to the carburetor.

It was bitter cold. Mr. Wheelwright brought out a teakettle of boiling water and some rags. Dink removed the lap robe and blankets from the radiator and, lifting the hood, wrapped the rags around the carburetor. He then poured the boiling water over them, dumping what remained over the engine itself. Opening the petcocks at the top of the cylinders, Wyatt poured a few drops of ether into each cylinder from the pint can kept in the car's toolbox expressly for winter driving. They added alcohol to the radiator, bringing the level of the liquid almost to the top.

Mr. Wheelwright went back into the house and stood at the front window with the others, watching as Dink got behind the wheel and Wyatt bent over the crank. Dink set the spark and throttle levers and signaled to Wyatt.

"Put a little muscle in it!" he yelled.

"Cross your fingers and pray!"

"She'll start, she'll start at the North Pole!"

"Start, Lizzie, please," pleaded Wyatt, pulling the choke wire and turning the crank once, twice, a third time. The engine came to life reluctantly. It coughed, seemingly possessed of a mind of its own, as though realizing that if it continued turning over, it would have to do so for the next six hours.

"Feed her!" exclaimed Wyatt.

"I am, I am!"

Now the engine was running smoothly.

"We'll let her warm up ten minutes or so," said Dink. "Let's go back in and get some of that coffee."

Cree and Ginger were having coffee and Brown Betty with Mr. Wheelwright. Mrs. Wheelwright was in the kitchen; she reappeared with a milk bottle filled with hot corn chowder.

"I never have seen a Model T with windows afore," said Wheelwright to Dink.

"They're extra, eight dollars the lot. That's what's great about a Model T. You can buy anything for it, even a new radiator for only fifteen dollars."

"I can't imagine coming all the way from Connecticut in a automobile in weather like this," remarked Mrs. Wheelwright.

"I don't blame you," laughed Cree.

"You mean you'd let a little nip in the air keep you from getting married?" Wyatt feigned amazement.

Cree patted Wyatt's cheek. "Darling, I would have gone with you to the North Pole, and you know it."

They thanked the Wheelwrights for everything and trooped out to the car. Off they drove, leaving Mr. and Mrs. Wheelwright grinning and waving good-bye at the front window.

"A wedding up here is only supposed to be two bucks," said Dink.

"Not at one in the morning and four above zero," said Wyatt.

The voice of the engine vied with the singing of the wind, which resumed its attack on the canvas top. The road stretched ahead of them through the darkness, the snow piled high on either side. The moon and stars looked so cold and brittle to Cree that they seemed about to shatter and drop in pieces upon the world. Dink kept the speedometer needle at forty, pushing New Hampshire further and further behind them. The milk bottle of corn chowder was passed around, and the last drop had disappeared by the time they came in sight of the Massachusetts border.

They reached New Haven without mishap—traveling most of the way at top speed, chilled to the bone— rolling down Whitney Avenue into the new day. The gray overhead had turned a pale blue, and the sun brought a hint of springlike warmth to the day.

Dink and Ginger dropped them off in front of the apartment house on Bristol Street, ten minutes' walk from the campus, according to Wyatt. The house looked ancient and abused, thought Cree, lifting her

eyes slowly up the front of it. It had been painted recently, hastily, and cheaply. The porch railings appeared to be all that prevented it from collapsing.

"It doesn't look much like Windsor Castle," said
Wyatt quietly.

"Who cares about the outside. When we finish decorating the apartment . . ."

"Room, Cree."

"I'll find a folding screen and make it into two
rooms, an apartment. You'll see, it'll be beautiful."

"It's small, I mean tiny."

The room was on the third floor in the rear. Wyatt
unlocked the door and carried her over the threshold.
Once on her feet, she looked about. He watched her
intently. She turned slowly around, pushing her upper
teeth against her lower lip and knitting her brows reflec-
tively, considering what she had to work with.

"Didn't I tell you it was tiny?" He was embarrassed.
"I'm sorry, sweetheart. It's all I could find on short
notice. It's hard to find any kind of place this time of
year. People just seem to stay put until spring."

"Stop apologizing."

"You're not saying anything."

"I'm not complaining, am I? I'm just looking and
thinking. I like it."

"You're just saying that."

"I mean it, Wyatt."

"You really are a peach. You wouldn't gripe if we
had to move into a cave."

She laughed. "No caves, please, they're always
damp. I wouldn't be able to dry my undies. Seriously,
this is warm and cozy."

She plopped down on the bed, testing the mattress;

the springs squeaked loudly. Wyatt stood before her, looking down, his expression self-conscious. He was trying to smile, but with little success.

The sun had cleared the horizon. A wide, warm shaft of light spilled through the curtainless window, flooding the floor. The light brightened one side of his face.

She took hold of his hands, placing them together, kissing them.

"I love it," she said quietly. "Home at last, our home. Close the door."

He sat down on the bed beside her and touched her lips.

"Cover the window," she said. Standing on a chair and using thumbtacks, he hung a sheet over the window. They could still feel the sun's warmth through the sheet.

He had made the bed. Anyone could tell a man had made it, she thought: the sheet folded back over the comforter narrowing like a pennant at one side, the edge of the comforter shoved under the mattress, the comforter itself wrinkled. She would not act superior and straighten the bed. She smiled inwardly.

"You did say the bathroom's down the hall," she said.

He nodded. She undressed in front of him, putting on her pink flannel nightdress, her robe, and mules. He turned to look out the window, ignoring the fact that he couldn't see anything through the sheet. She trembled, not from the cold; the room was warm. She had never been naked in his presence before. They would see each other naked from now on. There was nothing indecent about it. It was normal and natural.

Neither spoke. This was the beginning, Cree thought. You say "I do," and the law says you're man and wife, but you're really only two people in love who choose to sustain and nurture their love through the bond of marriage. Getting to know each other as marrieds would take time. But in time everything they did and shared they would learn to take for granted.

Except their love.

The bathroom was a dreary cubicle with half the linoleum-covered floor space taken up by a tub standing on four claws clasping balls. Rust stained the side of the tub in a slender ribbon joining the faucets to the green-circled drain. It needed scouring. Cora, the upstairs maid at home, always used Logans Powder and a good stiff brush. Bathtubs should be white as snow.

She pinned up her hair and drew a tub of water. She lay back, making suds with her Pears soap, luxuriating in the warmth of the water. She bathed, dried herself, put on some Tetlow's Pussywillow Powder, and sprayed on two liberal dashes of Hudnut Three Flowers Cologne. Then she wrapped herself in a dry towel.

She brushed her teeth, combed her hair, put on lipstick, and surveyed herself in the mirror. She looked exhausted. Undoing the towel, she put on her nightdress, robe, and mules and went back to the room.

Wyatt was in bed asleep, his head resting on his right arm, the covers halfway down his chest. His navy pajama tops and bottoms were neatly folded over the back of the straight chair set against the closet door. The room seemed even smaller than before. But straightening it up, putting things in their proper places, would help. They would need a bureau, the smallest they could find, one with a mirror. She couldn't traipse down to the bathroom every time she wanted to look at herself.

She disrobed completely and got under the covers

beside him. The warmth of his body touching hers made her start. He woke up and slipped his arm around her.

"You're trembling. Are you cold?"

"No," she whispered. "Hold me close."

He nuzzled her cheek. "You smell fabulous."

"Tetlow's Pussywillow Powder and Hudnut Three Flowers."

"Neither one, it's you."

His other arm encircled her; he pressed her close. Her heart thundered. She could feel his heart pounding. He seemed as nervous as she.

"I feel funny," she murmured.

"Funny how?"

"Jumpy. Afraid, I guess."

"I won't hurt you, I promise."

"Of course not. I'm not afraid of you, just . . . afraid." He kissed her cheek and nodded, understanding. "What about you?" she asked.

"A little. I love you, darling."

"I love you, my darling Wyatt, my husband." She kissed her ring.

He kissed her soulfully and began to caress her, moving his hand slowly over her small breast, down her body, her thighs. His hand trembled. She quivered under his touch. Her mouth was suddenly so dry that it was an effort to swallow. She could scarcely breathe. He was fumbling now, shifting his body clumsily, his every movement awkward. He was unsure of himself, groping tentatively, almost as if he was afraid to touch her for fear she would shatter.

He would try too hard to please her, she knew. He was so sensitive, so considerate. They both were painfully inexperienced at this. Knowing what to do, how to go about it, how to fan the fires of passion, how to touch and where and when took patience.

"My darling," he whispered. "My Cree, my Cree . . ."

In that instant, her fear deserted her. She snuggled closer to him. It would be all right, she thought confidently, better than all right.

It would be beautiful.

Chapter Four

When she woke up, Wyatt was gone. A note was pinned to the sheet over the window.

My darling wife:

I have Economics at nine and two more classes after that. I'll be through at one thirty and back as fast as I can get here. There's money under the pillow if you want to go out and shop for anything. We can buy the bureau and any other furniture you want this afternoon.

When I get out of Eco I'll have a chance to call Mother. Don't worry, I'll tell her not to contact your grandfather. I know you want to write him, so I'll make it very clear to her.

I love being married to you and hate being apart, even just these few hours. My profs won't get anything into this frazzled brain today. I'll just be sitting in class daydreaming about you. Which is nothing new. Thinking about you, us, our future.

I love you and can't wait to hold you in my arms again.

Love,
Your husband

41

Cree kissed the note, folded it, and put it in the elastic sleeve inside the top of her suitcase. After she washed, she made up her face and put on a wool skirt and her lavender stockinette jumper blouse with the sash. It had warmed up considerably in the less than three hours she had slept. She took the sheet down from the window. By now the sun had risen out of sight on the way to its zenith; its warm rays filled the backyard with brightness.

She looked in the closet and was glad to see that it was quite deep, with enough room to hang all their clothes and a large empty shelf overhead. Wyatt's easel leaned against one corner. On it was a canvas covered with an old piece of cloth that looked as if he had flicked a hundred different colors onto it from his wet brush. His paint box and palette, two rolls of cotton canvas, and three frames had been shoved into the other corner. She brought out the easel, set it in front of the window, and removed the cloth that concealed the painting.

It was a portrait of his mother. She was posed in profile, looking to the right, her beautiful, long wavy red hair—the color of Wyatt's—flowing to a twist at the back of her head. He had captured the flawless texture of her flesh, her face and neck, the faint blush of rose that seemed to lie beneath the surface in a deeper hue. Such exquisite coloring, mused Cree.

Mrs. Chance wore a silk shawl that was slipping off her shoulder and was held closed with the palm of her hand. Her other hand, crossing at the wrist, held a budding rose, the color of the shawl. Around her neck was a single strand of pearls, their whiteness in subtle contrast to the pale tone of her complexion.

Staring at the picture, Cree felt emotionally stirred.

He had such a superb sense of color. Drawing and composition, she knew, could be taught, but not color. That was a gift.

His mother's lips were slightly parted, and her eyes seemed to be fixed on something some distance away to the left. Her eye was bright—a gleam of understanding, thought Cree.

Although Mrs. Chance had an enchanting smile, Wyatt had chosen to give her an almost somber expression. Cree was no art critic, but she understood the artist and knew the emotions that linked him with his subject. He had wanted to extract a subtle emanation of her personality. And he had succeeded.

Or was it that she knew them both too well and was unconsciously reading Mrs. Chance's personality into the portrait?

No, he had painted her as she was: beautiful, pensive, sensitive, and giving. She was always giving of herself to her husband and son, to anyone in need, giving her interest, concern, understanding, encouragement, enthusiasm.

By the criteria of composition, color relationships, and textural application, the drawing was a far from perfect portrait. There was no denying Wyatt's talent, but he needed better instruction than he was getting in Art 102. His technique, his style, his occasional lapses in discipline, would all improve with proper guidance and experience. His God-given talent would grow.

Or would it? His father wanted him to join the company and was steering his education in that direction. Chance and Company, Wall Street: stocks, bonds, money, money. The arena. Wall Street was so cold, a tall cemetery with windows in the stones. His father wanted him to get a liberal arts degree to "broaden him" before he entered Harvard Business School to sharpen his expertise in the business world.

She pictured his talent as a jewel dropped into a velvet sack, the drawstrings tightened, the sack shoved to the furthest corner of a drawer that was rarely opened. There it would lie in darkness, neglected, unappreciated. She sighed. Any fool knew talent is given us to be used. Wyatt's parents had never discouraged him from painting, but to his father it was a hobby, like collecting coins or arrowheads.

Having sat for all but the final touches, his mother had to have seen the portrait. What did she think of it? She'd treasure it, of course, and be flattered, but would she see in it what was there to see: her inner self and how well he had captured it? Would she be as impressed with his abilities as Cree was?

His father would be pleased and proud and insist that it be hung over the mantel in the living room to be admired and made much of by dinner guests and visitors who dropped in. Wyatt would continue to paint; she would never let him give it up, never let his interest flag. But when he finished business school and went to work for his father, how much time would be left for painting? For his "hobby"?

He loved to paint and judge his work severely, criticizing every aspect of it. This was muddy, that was dull. This needed better highlighting, the chin needed work. Like pulling threads from needlework. Would he always enjoy painting, the challenge of the white canvas, the satisfaction of bringing his subject to life, the mistakes, the corrections, the good days, the days when nothing seemed to go right, but at last that moment when he could step back and say done.

He was good.

If only his mother had recognized how good he was and sent him to art school, even if just for a summer. Cree shook her head; she too had a love for painting, though nothing like his talent. How often had she wished she had a fraction of it! At his urging, she had tried watercolors, but everything seemed to come out looking flat and lifeless. She stuck to pencil, pen and ink, and an occasional charcoal. All her subjects were typical, safe—the subjects of every other amateur.

Using her suitcase as a table, she sat at the window and wrote to her grandfather, explaining that she had left because she was in love and wanted to get married, pointing out that she would have done so with or without Mother's and Daddy's permission if they'd still been alive.

> Please try and understand, I'm not deserting you, I'm merely going out into the world to be with him. We love each other, and last night we were married, all very legal and proper. I realize you think it's a sorry way to go about it, to run out the way I did, but you know you'd never have given your permission.
>
> Wyatt and I want to stand on our own feet. Other people our age do, and so can we. Livvy felt the same way when she eloped with Alec.
>
> I know you're upset with me now, but I hope and pray that in time you'll try to see it from our point of view and understand and accept it. I want you to with all my heart. I want you to because I love you.

She stopped writing. Her eyes were misting. She dried them with her hanky and blew her nose.

There was a problem. Should she let him know where they were living? It seemed hypocritical not to, but if she did tell him, there might be the devil to pay. She hadn't discussed the problem with Wyatt, but she had to believe he wouldn't want her to reveal their address. In his note pinned to the sheet over the window he'd said that when he called his mother he planned to ask her not to contact Grandfather.

The more she thought about it, the more convinced she became that even without a return address, if he wanted to hire detectives or send the police after them, he would. He knew they were in New Haven. But he'd never do such a thing. People came to him, he didn't chase after anyone—not for any reason. Livvy's experience was proof enough of that. She had left the country and followed her husband overseas. Grandfather's reaction was to let her go and forget about her. He had intercepted and burned Livvy's letters to Cree and Julia, and had declared her "dead, as far as this family's concerned." Julia, on her way to California, would also be dead in his eyes.

What made her think her own fate would be otherwise? No, he'd leave them alone. Still, she did hope he'd at least read this letter.

Chapter Five

Wyatt's mother and father came to the house on Bristol Street the following day, driving up from the city in their chauffeured Rolls-Royce Silver Ghost limousine. In the back seat was a custom-built bar, and there was a reading lamp and a mahogany cigar box to hold Mr. Chance's favorite Cremo cigars.

Like the Magi of old, the Chances arrived bearing gifts: food and furnishings, including a nine-by-twelve Seamless Tapestry Brussels carpet. More important, they conveyed an understanding and acceptance of Wyatt and Cree's decision to be married, although Cree got the feeling that Marjorie Chance had talked Wyatt's father into swallowing the fish whole, as Grandfather Shackleford described a reluctant approval of anything.

Mrs. Chance was even more beautiful than her portrait. She embraced and kissed Cree, all but ignoring Wyatt, who was busy shaking hands and talking with his father.

Mr. Chance was a head shorter than his wife, broad-shouldered and muscular like Wyatt, but beginning to acquire a paunch. He was a self-made millionaire, but in conversation anyone would have taken him for a somewhat successful insurance salesman. In the rock-ribbed conservative confines of Wall Street, where stuffiness and snobbery abounded, Wyatt Chance, Sr., was an anomaly. He was neither stuffy nor snobbish; on occasion his English put one in mind of a dock-walloper, and he had a marvelous sense of humor.

That afternoon the newlyweds had sought out and bought the smallest bureau they could find: five drawers with a rectangular swinging mirror. Once in position, it left scarcely enough room to turn around. Nevertheless, up the stairs at Mrs. Chance's direction came Reilly, the chauffeur, carrying Wyatt's summer clothes, kitchenware, draperies to match the carpet, even a footstool.

"It's so small, so small," lamented Mrs. Chance. "Rooms this tiny should be against the law."

"You should have an apartment," said Mr. Chance. "At least you'd have your own bathroom."

"This is all I could find," explained Wyatt. "We'll get something bigger in the spring."

"In a building with an elevator," said his mother.

"Mother, this is New Haven, not Park Avenue."

They had dinner at Durfee's on Chapel Street. Wyatt's mother's biggest concern seemed to be that Cree had left school before the end of the term. Cree explained that once they were settled, she would get a transcript of her records from Miss Barclay's and take courses at one of the local private schools to get her diploma.

It was past eight by the time they got back to Bristol Street. A snow sky shrouded the moon and stars. The street lights cast a feeble cadmium-yellow glow over the city, and the cold rose in slender wraiths from the pavement.

Mrs. Chance took Cree away from the men onto the front porch.

"If there's anything you need, call me. Reverse the charges. Wyatt's father is giving him money," she added.

"Was he surprised when you told him about us?"

"Not as much as I thought he'd be." Mrs. Chance half-laughed. "I scheduled the revelation. I was very clever. I waited until he got home from the office, of course. He had his cocktail, and we talked awhile, and he unwound. We were getting ready to go in to dinner. He was in his easy chair, puffing on one of his foul cigars. I told him a joke I'd heard just that afternoon. He told me one. We were laughing. Then I switched the subject to you. You know he thinks the world of you. Wouldn't she make the perfect wife for Wyatt? How could he disagree? He was still nodding when I sprang it on him. He did choke a little, just cigar smoke that went the wrong way. I began piling on all the reasons I could think of why you should get married. I pointed out that you would have waited, that you'd never have eloped if it weren't for your grandfather."

"That's right."

She squeezed Cree's hands affectionately. "I'm glad you did. I'm only sorry we couldn't give you a huge wedding." She lowered her voice. "I know you'll be good for him, my dear, help him grow up. He's still a boy, but you'll make a man of him. It takes a woman to do that, you know. The big thing, the only thing that worries his father, is that he might decide to leave school."

"He won't. I promise he won't."

"His father has plans for him, as you know. It's terribly important that he finish his three years here and go on to business school." She paused and studied Cree. "Lucretia, I did as Wyatt asked me to. I didn't call your grandfather. He won't know about this from either of us." Again she paused. "Do you think if he finds out he'll make a fuss?"

"I think he already knows, but I doubt he cares enough to do anything about it. He's getting used to his granddaughters leaving home. I'm the last in a long line of deserters."

"Still, he loves you, he must. All three of you."

"Deep down he does, but he insists we live our lives his way. It sounds silly, but he doesn't trust us with our own lives. He puts independence on a par with high treason."

"My father was like that, bless his heart. You mustn't let it prey on your mind. All that's important is that you and Wyatt be happy. You love each other and you will be, I know."

"We're happy, we're in heaven."

Wyatt and his father came up the steps.

"What are you two conspiring about?" asked Mr. Chance, puffing on his cigar, sending little blue smoke-wisps into the frigid air.

Mrs. Chance patted his cheek. "Girl talk."

"Wyatt wants us to run back upstairs. He has something for you, dear."

Mrs. Chance gasped, her hands flying to her face. "My painting, you've finished it!"

Wyatt shrugged and smirked. "It's more like I'm done tampering with it."

His mother led the way up the stairs like Teddy Roosevelt charging up San Juan Hill. Wyatt set two straight-backed chairs in front of the easel for them and ordered his mother to close her eyes. He whipped away the cloth covering the picture.

Cree watched her. Slowly she opened her eyes and

stared, her mouth opening; she suddenly seemed to freeze where she sat.

"It's great!" declared Mr. Chance. "Terrific. By the Lord Harry, if it isn't just as good as a real professional job. Better. Say something, Marjorie, you look like a fish."

"Wyatt, it's . . . it's . . ."

"Beautiful," murmured Cree. "Darling, you're so talented."

"Another Rembrandt, that's me."

His mother continued to stare.

"You've made me look years younger."

His father scoffed. "Cut the balloon juice. It's your spitting image, and you know it."

She was delighted with it, thought Cree. They trooped back down to the car, Wyatt carrying the portrait wrapped in the paint-speckled cloth. He set it on the front seat beside Reilly. Moments later, after kisses, handshakes, and repeated congratulations, off they drove, just as the first few snowflakes, the vanguard of the storm, touched down on the sidewalk and the street.

In the weeks that followed, Cree continued to hope for an answer to her letter to her grandfather but received none, in spite of the fact that she had in the end put her return address in the corner of the envelope. She was sure that he'd received it and just as sure that he'd never opened it. She envisioned the letter sitting in the big brass ashtray on the foyer table, his hand holding a lit match, the flame touching a corner of the unopened envelope, the four corners turning up as the fire consumed it.

She received a transcript of her scholastic records from Miss Barclay's School and enrolled in Fairview, taking the trolley out to Hamden three days a week to attend classes. She and Wyatt often went out with Dink and Ginger to the movies, to a little Italian place on Pearl Street for spaghetti, and to concerts on campus.

Throughout spring the tide of war slowly began to turn in favor of the Allies. The Yale ROTC had been officially organized in February of the previous year. Under the law a maximum of two hundred juniors and seniors were permitted to enroll. There were other signs that Yale was taking the war seriously. Ground was broken behind the gymnasium to build Artillery Hall, and an armory was constructed near the Yale Bowl.

Gradually the flow of older students leaving college to join the armed forces increased. Late in the summer of 1918 the draft age was lowered from twenty-one to eighteen, causing immediate concern on the part of the college administration. Yale and all other colleges could lose almost all their students and as a result face a financial crisis, if not bankruptcy. To prevent this and to train men, the government created the Students' Army Training Corps. A training camp was established on campus, and thirteen hundred students, including eight hundred freshmen, joined up. By the time the school year ended in June, the college had begun to resemble an army camp. Osborn Hall became quarters for Red Cross workers, and army cots filled Connecticut and Lawrance Halls. Platoons of artillery trainees marched about the campus, and the Sheffield-Vanderbilt Campus north of Grove Street was converted into barracks.

Various faculty members began contributing their expertise to the war effort. Professor Charles Hastings was assisting the Navy in improving periscopes, telescopes, and other optical instruments; Mr. Woolsey from the Forestry School was supervising the purchase of timber for housing in France; and Professor McClelland was put in charge of evaluating and developing metal to be used in building military aircraft.

Wyatt decided to join the Students' Army Training Corps, although Cree was vigorously opposed. Dr. Simmons, his faculty advisor, and Professor Ransom Colclough, head of the Art Department, agreed with her. Wyatt was a married man, and the college had no shortage of volunteers. He thought it over and changed his mind.

Then, one afternoon in June, shortly after the end of his sophomore year, he came home as excited as a six-year-old on Christmas morning to announce that he had signed up.

Two months before, they had found a three-room apartment on Whitney Avenue almost midway between Fairview and the campus. It was no mansion, but in contrast to the room on Bristol Street, they could open the door to guests, who would not have to pick their way through the furnishings. Their new home was the setting for their first fight, a full-scale shouting match with Cree crying loudly and Wyatt crimson with indignation.

"It's bad enough you do such a stupid thing!" exclaimed Cree. "You don't even warn me."

"You're blowing it all out of proportion. You make it sound like I'm already heading overseas."

"I thought we'd settled the whole disgusting business. You weren't going to sign up because you're married and because they already have enough volunteers."

"That was Dr. Simmons's and Professor Colclough's decision—and yours. Not mine. I just went along with it at the time. But this afternoon I changed my mind.

It's my mind and I've got a right to. Don't you understand how I feel? I've sat by for the last five months, twiddling my thumbs, watching my friends sign up and feeling like a damned slacker. A coward. It's gotten so I can't even look fellows in the eye anymore, not if they're in uniform. I'm fed up. I want to be able to look at myself in the mirror. Dink Ramsey signed up."

"Dink Ramsey's not married!"

"He's as good as."

"He's not, you are. I'm your wife. The least you could have done was to sit down and talk it over."

"I did it . . ." He lowered his voice; suddenly he seemed ashamed, like a little boy who'd broken the front window. "I did it on impulse."

"I'll say. And it's the stupidest thing you've ever done."

"Just shut up and mind your own business!"

The argument waxed furious, bringing a loud pounding on the wall from Professor Wheatley, their next-door neighbor. Wyatt saw the situation clearly but one-sidedly. Cree was a woman, she didn't understand that a man has his pride, a sense of patriotism that stirs him to action, or he has no right to call himself a man. He pointed out that her sister's husband, Alec, had joined up, and without "asking Olivia's permission." He excused his failure to discuss it with her beforehand, insisting that there were some decisions a man had to make for himself.

"Besides, I won't be going anywhere. The war's sure to be over by fall."

"You're sure!"

He continued rationalizing his action; the more he talked, the more furious she became. Yes, she could understand how he felt watching his friends sign up while he stood by idly. But he was still ignoring a very important point. They were single, he was not.

"You can't tell me one married Deke who's signed up. Or anybody else who's married."

He couldn't, which only renewed his fury. The battle might have gone on all night if they had stayed up. But after a supper eaten in stony silence, they went to bed.

They lay side by side in the darkness, each pretending to be asleep, listening to the other's breathing. Since he was so clearly in the wrong, Cree decided that it was up to him to make the first move toward reconciliation. On the other hand, she told herself, bending was a certain indicator of maturity.

Reaching across his chest, she snuggled close to him. He reacted so quickly, sitting up with a jerk and throwing his arms around her, that he nearly pushed her out of bed. Apologies poured out of him like grain out of an elevator chute.

They made love. How different it was now from their wedding night, she thought. They had been so clumsy, fumbling, and apologetic. Their appalling ingenuousness coupled with a desperate desire to please had turned the whole sorry episode into a nightmare of embarrassment.

Now, five months later, they were perfectly attuned to one another, old marrieds. And she found herself loving him more every day, every hour.

At the end of the school year he found a job at Musselmann's Art Store. He marched with his friends and he painted. He did seven nudes of Cree and, despite her protests, painted over six. The seventh, a pose similar to the *Rokeby Venus* by Velazquez, but without the mirror and companion cherub, she hung in the bedroom, warning him sternly that if he ever dared so much as straighten it on its hook, she would claw his eyes out.

He painted scenes in Edgewood Park. He painted the Wrexham Tower in the Memorial Quadrangle, imbuing it with something of the majesty of Notre Dame Cathedral. He did nearly thirty preliminary sketches and then did the painting in less than four hours on a sunny, cloudless Sunday afternoon. But no sunlight bathed his Wrexham Tower; instead, he surrounded its turrets with a violent thunderstorm, lightning, and a downpour that set the face of the tower glistening. To Cree, the tower came alive, defying the storm, pitting its solidity and strength against the enemy from the heavens.

Professor Colclough, who Cree thought looked like Thomas Jefferson in Rembrandt Peale's portrait, saw *Wrexham Tower* and insisted that it be hung in Dean Jones's office, where all Yale could see and enjoy it. Dean Jones was no artist or student of the arts, but he was one of those millions who "knew what he liked when he saw it." He agreed. *Wrexham Tower*, by W. Chance, found a home on the wall behind the dean's desk.

Other paintings by Wyatt and his fellow student-artists were displayed in various buildings about the campus. Cree kept most of his canvases in the apartment, adorning the walls of the living room. Her favorite was a painting of the Second Congregational Church in nearby Foxon. It was a typical white wooden church, differing little in detail from a thousand other New England wooden churches. What endeared the painting to Cree was Wyatt's success in investing such a commonplace subject with such vivid feelings. The steeple did not point to the heavens as much as challenge them, like the upheld lance of a medieval knight preparing to tilt. The church was built entirely of wood, but Wyatt had managed to give it the permanence of Wrexham Tower, an aura of indestructibility.

Cree studied the painting by the hour. There were no figures in the picture, but she could feel the warmth inspired by the presence of the unseen congregation within.

It was, she decided, his masterpiece.

Chapter Six

Wyatt began his junior year in September. Cree, meanwhile, had fulfilled her credits for a high school diploma. In Europe the Germans were on the run. American troops under General Pershing, with the aid of British and French air and ground forces, captured Saint-Mihiel on the Meuse river. Ten days later the Allies launched the Meuse-Argonne offensive. American troops concentrated between the Argonne Forest and the Meuse River attacked the entrenched German forces, pushing them back east of the river and capturing the heights overlooking Sedan.

By October the Germans were in full retreat and Berlin was negotiating for an armistice. The Kaiser and his generals had little choice: Austria-Hungary had already collapsed, and the German army was reduced to a remnant of its strength of 1917. The navy was mutinying, and the civilian population threatened revolt. The Fatherland also faced the prospect of a flood of fresh American troops; two million had already arrived in France.

On October 8 Professor Colclough phoned Wyatt, who was at home working on a term paper. The professor asked if he might bring an old friend to the apartment to meet Wyatt and Cree. Colclough sounded like a man holding back a wonderful surprise.

It was just past seven thirty; Cree had finished serving supper and was cleaning up the dishes when the doorbell rang.

Colclough introduced his friend, a Frenchman recently arrived in the United States. His name was Armand Duprier, and he and the professor had attended the Sorbonne together in 1901 and 1902. Duprier was a small man, inches shorter than Wyatt's father, completely bald. As if to make up for the lack of hair on his head, he affected a flourishing mustache and sideburns. His eyes were black and piercing, and did not look through her as much as they impaled her, thought Cree, as she shook Duprier's hand.

His English was poor, even poorer than her own French. Colclough's French, however, was excellent. Wyatt invited them to sit in the living room.

"We'll have cake and coffee," said Cree.

Colclough translated for his friend, but Duprier dismissed her attempt at hospitality with a wave and a shake of his head. Screwing a monocle into his right eye, he walked to the end of the room by the double windows overlooking the garden and began studying a seascape of Wyatt's. Then, while the other three looked on, Duprier bought a chair up to the painting, took it down from the wall, and sat holding it on his knees. Removing his monocle, he polished it with his handkerchief, restored it to his eye, and resumed his examination. Down came one painting after another as he circled the room studying each work, first from close up, then restoring it to its hook and backing off to appraise it further.

Duprier had just begun when Colclough took Cree and Wyatt to the other side of the room, scarcely necessary considering how absorbed Duprier suddenly was.

"He's a trifle eccentric," Colclough whispered.

"A trifle?" Cree looked at him wide-eyed.

"He speaks perfect English."

"Then why is he pretending not to?"

"Ssssh, don't say anything. He wants to avoid discussing the paintings. Just play along. He's an excellent critic, among the best in all of Europe. There's no one more prestigious in Parisian art circles. He's artistic director of *La Vie heureuse* and before that was editor-in-chief of *Art de Moderne*. Duncan Frisbie, the curator at the National Gallery, invited him to the States. Up to now he was delayed by the war, of course; he got here about two weeks ago. He came up from Washington, stayed overnight in New York, and he's visiting with me for a few more days before sailing for home."

"I appreciate this, Professor. It's great . . ."

"Wyatt, don't get your hopes up. Armand isn't the most tactful individual in the world. He won't hesitate to tell you exactly what he thinks."

M. Duprier grunted. Cree noticed that whenever he finished studying a painting he grunted.

Colclough took hold of Wyatt's sleeve. "Go get the nude of Cree and that scene you did of the two children playing on the lawn near the bio lab. And your sketches for *Wrexham Tower*."

"Right, right."

Cree tingled with embarrassment as M. Duprier stood absorbed by the nude of her. Her cheeks felt as if they were on fire as Duprier went over the painting inch by revealing inch.

"Did he see *Wrexham Tower* in the dean's office?" whispered Wyatt.

Colclough nodded. "He's seen all seven of your paintings around the campus."

They looked on in silence as Duprier set the nude on

the davenport and took up the next painting. When he finished with it, he stretched, restored his monocle to his vest pocket, and rubbed his eyes.

Then he grunted and began chattering in French. Cree managed to catch two words out of at least two hundred: imperfect and lacking something-or-other. Her heart sank. Fortunately for Wyatt, he didn't understand a word.

"What is he saying?" he exclaimed.

Colclough grinned mischievously. "He says he thinks you are in desperate need of competent instruction. Which says a lot for our art teachers. He says he thinks you make far too many simple mistakes, and the same ones over and over. He says any blind man can see that you work too rapidly." He paused and laughed softly. "He says one may dress and eat in a rush, but one does not drink wine, make love, or paint so. He says you are not serious about your painting. A cardinal sin, I'm afraid."

"What's so funny?" asked Wyatt in a hurt tone.

Colclough went on. "If you aren't serious, you should paint houses, not things of beauty. He says you do some things *à mi-chemin*, half-way. He says your knowledge of anatomy is deficient. He says this apartment is no place to work, the light has to be atrocious. The elm trees outside must block the sun. He says you should paint more simply, more directly and less, and sketch ten times as much."

"Does he have anything good to say?" asked Cree wryly.

"Ssssh, let him finish," said Colclough. "Ah, he says you do a hundred things either wrong or poorly."

M. Duprier stopped talking abruptly, throwing up his hands and turning his back on them. Then he resumed lecturing, pounding his fist into his palm for punctuation. Colclough beamed.

"He says for a beginner your brushwork is very good. Your color is excellent. You have a superb inner eye. You have imagination. You are gifted, you lucky devil."

M. Duprier added one final comment, more a declamation than an observation, from the tone of it.

"He says," went on Colclough, "that you should leave this place, Yale, the United States. Go to Paris, take a studio, and study, study, study, sketch, paint— paint until you drop. And maybe, just maybe you will become the artist God and the angels intended you to be. But whatever you are studying at this place is a waste of your time. So don't wait, pack up and go. Now!"

Wyatt started to laugh but stopped abruptly when the little man glowered at him fiercely.

"Sorry," Wyatt said. "I'm very flattered, of course, but I can't possibly leave school. It's out of the question."

"It is if you say it is," said Colclough, in a tone that hinted he didn't agree. His face darkened in disappointment.

Strange words from a faculty member to an undergraduate, thought Cree. No, not at all strange; rather, sincere testimony to his confidence in Wyatt's ability.

Visibly upset by Wyatt's refusal to accept his advice, Duprier rushed through his coffee and raisin cake, and rose from his chair, prepared to leave. Colclough shrugged at Wyatt behind the little man's back and started to usher him out the door. In the hallway, in the midst of good-byes, Duprier suddenly turned about, marched back to the davenport, picked up the nude, studied it briefly without his monocle, shook his head, grunted, put the painting down, and went out.

Colclough paused in the doorway. "Think about it, Wyatt, you don't have to decide overnight."

"I'm really very grateful for this, Professor. It's made me feel, well . . . I don't know how to thank you."

"It's not necessary. We'll be talking." He glanced behind him at M. Duprier wandering up the hallway. Colclough whispered behind his hand. "You say you can't leave Yale. I want you to sit down and discuss . . ."

"Ransom, *pourquoi ce retard*?"

Colclough grinned. "Later."

Wyatt closed the door behind him. Cree leaned against it.

"Haven't I always told you you're a genius?"

Wyatt kissed her, then backed off, raising his arms in triumph.

"I'm gifted, I have a terrific inner eye."

"Superb . . ."

"I have imagination and my color is excellent."

"For a beginner. Let's be serious. Darling, you can become a painter, a great painter, if you want to."

He scoffed, then said, "Don't talk nonsense, I'd have to leave school."

"Is that really impossible?"

"You know it is."

"Why not talk to your father? Tell him all about this. Get him together with Professor Colclough. Wyatt, if he had any idea how talented you are, how good you can be, he'd let you go."

"You make it sound like he has me around the neck. What is this? It's looney. Sixty seconds ago I was feeling terrific. Now suddenly I'm beginning to feel lousy."

"Won't you even discuss it with your father?"

"What would be the point? When I finish here I head straight up to Harvard. It's all decided."

"By him."

"By both of us. We agreed. He let me start here, but I have to go to business school. Get a master's in business. I can't work on Wall Street without it."

"Wyatt, I know you two made this decision long before we were married. And I guess it's right. No, damn it! It's not, it's all wrong!"

"You don't understand. After what he's done for me, for both of us, I can't just up and desert him. I'm not built like that, Cree, I'm just not."

"Listen to me, please. Duprier called you gifted. You heard him. Doesn't that mean anything to you? Do you think Chance and Company will collapse if you don't join the firm?" She held his eyes with her own. "Darling, real talent is so rare. I ought to know, I don't have a speck. I'd love to be able to paint, there's nothing in this world I'd rather do. Me and a million others. You seem to have no idea how much I envy you."

"You never said a word . . ."

"Of course not, you boob. I love you, I admire what you can do, I encourage you, as much for me as for you. I paint through you, can you understand that? It's true, in my ego your talent is my talent. It's make-believe, but it relieves my frustration at not having any talent."

"I can't do it to him, Cree."

She sighed and looked away. "I'm sorry, I guess I got carried away."

"Let's not talk about it anymore, okay? I'm going to go back to work on my paper."

"Go ahead, I'll just clean up here and put the paintings back in the bedroom."

A twinge of guilt tugged at her heart. She had promised his mother that she'd never let him leave school. And here she was all but begging him to. Perhaps he was right. They shouldn't even think about leaving the United States. They should forget about Paris.

As if she could.

Chapter Seven

On November 11, in Senlis in northern France, Germany formally surrendered and the armistice was signed. The world exploded with joy. The great day fell on a Monday; all classes were cancelled, and Yale joined the world in celebrating. A fire engine commandeered by the Zeta Psis screamed up and down Whitney Avenue for six hours. Parades wound through the city and left the campus littered with toilet paper, empty bottles, and other debris.

Wyatt and Cree threw an all-day party that lasted into the night. They invited fifteen friends and forty showed up. Dink Ramsey got drunk, passed out at eleven, slept until three in the morning on a pile of coats on the bed, then woke up and proceeded to get drunk a second time.

Classes were cancelled the following day, when no one, not even the professors, showed up. Cree and Wyatt slept until five o'clock. The doorbell awakened them.

It was Dink and Ginger, come to help them clean up the apartment. Dink looked as if the fire engine that had kept Whitney Avenue awake the night before had run over him. The whites of his eyes were solid red, his cheeks were ashen, and he was unable to speak above a hoarse whisper.

"Cree, come look at death upright!" Wyatt yelled, welcoming them at the door.

From the bedroom where she was dressing, Cree called, "You get back in here and get something on."

"Your underwear is wrinkled, Brother Chance," whispered Dink. He would have fallen into the apartment, had not Ginger and Wyatt caught him. Ginger looked about and groaned.

"This place looks as if they fought the last battle here."

They began to straighten up the place, the boys lugging carton after carton of bottles out to the trash barrels behind the house, the girls washing walls, waxing furniture, replacing broken light bulbs. The kitchen had been hardest hit. The Bevo and Moxie, ginger ale, beer, and hard liquor spilled on the floor created an almost solid layer that required three moppings before the black-and-white linoleum's shine was restored.

Cleaning up took four hours, after which Dink and Ginger left, and Cree and Wyatt went back to bed. Lying beside him, listening to his heavy, steady breathing, Cree raised herself on one elbow and, leaning over, kissed him on his bare shoulder. And thanked the gods for ending the war.

Now that it was over, there would be peace for the rest of their lives.

She fell asleep savoring this optimistic assumption and dreamt of a battlefield shrouded in stillness under a high sky bright with sunshine. Abandoned, without combatants, without corpses, without discarded weapons or any of the other refuse of conflict, only empty trenches carved in the earth and tangled and trodden barbed wire indicated that a battle had ever taken place.

In the distance, recognizable at once by its turrets, finials, and pinnacles, stood Wrexham Tower, the solitary building in the entire broad, flat landscape. The tower moved closer, and as it did she could see that it had suffered damage. A figure appeared at the centermost embrasure, a man. She could not make out his face. He began waving. The tower moved closer; he continued to wave. She still could not see his face, but she recognized his build. It was Wyatt.

To her horror, the instant she identified him, the tower began to collapse, disintegrating slowly and soundlessly into rubble, bringing him down with it. Dust wafted upward. She ran to it and with astonishing strength began pulling stones away, great heavy chunks of granite; she worked feverishly to clear the way to him. The stones rolled silently left and right down the sides of the pile. She dug and dug until she came upon a highly polished mahogany casket. It had not been marred by the stones piled upon it. Continuing to dig, she finally exposed it entirely.

Wyatt!

The meaning was suddenly clear. The war wasn't over. The armistice was a hoax or another war had begun, and he had been involved in the fighting, shot and killed, and his body returned to her.

The seam separating the two halves of the casket lid was clearly visible. Slowly the top half began to open to reveal a mound of beautiful flowers. Bending over, her hands trembling, she began picking them away one by one, hyacinths, gardenias, lilies. With each one she flung aside, she died a little more. The corpse lay underneath. The face . . .

She gasped. It was Mr. Chance, his hair neatly combed and parted, his mustache newly trimmed, his face waxen, his eyelids sealed.

She awoke, sitting bolt upright, drenched with perspiration. Wyatt stirred beside her and switched on the lamp.

"What's the matter?" he asked sleepily.

"Nothing, go back to sleep. I'm sorry I woke you."

"You're soaking. What was it, a bad dream?"

"Yes."

"What?"

"Nothing." Her hand crossed her forehead; she brought it down, her palm glistening with sweat. "I dreamt I was being chased through a tunnel, snakes, monsters . . ."

He laughed. "Not very original. Are you okay? Do you want me to get you a drink of water or some aspirin?"

"No, I'm okay. Turn out the light. Let's go back to sleep."

He had a nine o'clock class in Art History. They got up at seven thirty and she made breakfast—eggs over, the only way he liked eggs, a bowl of Force, fresh orange juice, and coffee.

"I guess I just turn in my uniform," he said. "I told you I'd never make it to France."

"Thank the Lord."

He reached across the checkered oilcloth and took her hand.

"You look kind of down in the dumps. Are you okay?"

"I guess." She brightened consciously. "I wonder what happened to Professor Colclough's friend, Duprier?"

"He went home. What do you think?" He had his coffee halfway to his mouth. Pausing, he lowered the cup slowly. "Cree, we're not going to start arguing about that again, are we?"

"We didn't argue back then. We discussed it; you asked me to forget about it. I did, didn't I?"

"Did you?"

"You can't expect me to stop thinking about it. I haven't been harping on it. This is the first time I've brought it up."

He glanced at his watch. "I've got to get a move on. What are you doing today?"

"Shopping this morning. Do you want anything special?"

"No more Force." He spooned up his half-eaten cereal and let it fall back into the bowl. "How about changing over to Cream of Wheat? And we're running out of Sozodont. And get some Moxie, okay?"

She saw him out the door, then wandered back into the living room, where she flopped onto the davenport and thought about M. Armand Duprier. Study, study, study, sketch, paint—paint until you drop.

"And maybe you will become the artist God and the angels intended you to be," she said aloud.

It was so sad and so wrong. She should be furious with him, as furious as she'd been over his joining the SATC. But she'd be wasting her breath challenging him and his parents. Still, she wondered how Marjorie felt about it deep down.

Professor Colclough had been a disappointment. He could have supported Duprier with a little more enthusiasm right then and there. Not that it would have done any good. If she herself couldn't sway Wyatt, if she couldn't even get him to talk to his father about it, why should she expect Colclough to have any better luck with him?

Mr. Chance. Her nightmare came back to her. She banished it from her mind and went to the double window overlooking the backyard. The campus, the Green, practically every patch of grass in New Haven, lay under a skin of sere and motley leaves. The breeze set a few of them whirling, dancing. Did the chestnut trees litter Paris in the same lovely way every fall? she wondered.

She went into the kitchen to clean up, washed and rinsed the breakfast dishes, and left them to dry. She was sitting down to make out her grocery list when the phone rang.

It was the long-distance operator for Wyatt.

"Mr. Charles Crowder of New York City wishes to speak with Mr. Chance."

"He's not in at the moment. He'll be back at twelve. He'll be here until two o'clock."

She could hear mumbled conversation at the other end. Mr. Charles Crowder, whoever he might be, was discussing the situation with the operator.

"My party will call back after twelve o'clock," said the operator. "Thank you."

Cree hung up.

Charles Crowder? The name sounded familiar, but she couldn't place it. Did he work for Mr. Chance? Why would he be calling Wyatt? Maybe she should call Marjorie and ask her. No, it would make her look nosy. Crowder, whoever he was, hadn't asked to speak to her. Perhaps it had something to do with the business. Charles Crowder . . .

She put on her heavy red sweater with the five buttons down the front and her white knit cap. Harvard colors in Yale's town—risky, risky, she thought, smiling.

Toilet paper and other litter could still be seen along the avenue. The trolley clacked to a nearby stop, but she preferred to walk. It was a brisk, bright, beautiful day.

A sign in Nystrom's window proclaimed the bargain of the week: sirloin steak, thirty-five cents a pound. Down from thirty-nine, but still high, she decided. She was watching their budget closely; she didn't want Wyatt's parents to think their son had married a spendthrift. He had augmented his allowance during the summer with the twelve dollars a week he had earned at Musselmann's Art Store, but once school started again he had had to give it up. Classes, painting, and the SATC all but filled every weekday.

The grocery store was crowded. There was only one counter, hemmed in by shelves and crowded with barrels and customers. Cree waited her turn. Mrs. Nystrom, a motherly little woman who always managed to look cheerful despite her endless catalog of ailments—never the same one twice—waited on her. They were out of Sozodont, so Cree settled for Colgate's toothpaste. She bought Wyatt his Cream of Wheat and two large bottles of Moxie. She also bought cocoa and some Swift's Bacon and a few other items. She saw Cremo Cigars and immediately thought of Mr. Chance.

Prices were discouragingly high. Milk had gone up to eighteen cents a quart, butter to thirty-five cents a pound, eggs to fifty-seven cents a dozen, bread to twelve cents a loaf.

She spent almost four dollars, a third of what Wyatt earned in a week behind the counter at Musselmann's. She took the trolley back to the apartment and was putting her groceries away when he came in. He kissed her and flung off his cap and corduroy jacket.

"What's for lunch?"

"There's leftover hamburger or bacon, lettuce, and tomato sandwiches. Take your choice."

"Bacon, lettuce . . ."

"How did Art History and Eco go?"

"Okay and lousy. I hate Economics. It's all theory; it's like trying to catch steam in your hand. You either have a knack for it or you don't. Dink eats it up. I'm lucky to pull a C."

"There was a call for you from New York. Charles Crowder."

He looked surprised. "Charley Crowder called me?"

"Who is he, Wyatt?"

"He's the family lawyer. You've never met him. He looks like a funeral director, bald, no chin. Remember the fellow who played Dr. Scapinelli in *A Bargain With Satan*? On second thought, he's not that bad."

"He'll be calling back."

Wyatt had finished one sandwich and was starting his second when the phone rang. Cree stood at the kitchen door looking on.

"Yes, operator, speaking." There was a pause. "Mr. Crowder. Yes, sir, how are you? What?"

Cree watched his cheeks pale as he listened. For an eternity he listened. He looked stunned, as if he'd been suddenly struck.

"How is she taking it? Yes, yes . . . We're on our way. Sometime late this afternoon. I don't know the train schedule. Wait, on second thought, we'll drive up. I can borrow a car. Yes. Good-bye, sir."

Hanging up, he turned to her slowly.

She ran to him. "What is it?"

He sank down onto the davenport. "My father. He's dead."

"No . . ."

He nodded slowly, the shock of it striking him and taking hold.

Chapter Eight

The manner in which Mr. Chance had died was as bizarre as Cree's prescient nightmare. According to Crowder, the Chances had been crossing Forty-fifth Street on their way home from the theater the previous night when, according to two women who had witnessed the incident from across the street, a cornice had dropped from the facade of a building and struck Mr. Chance. Falling against Marjorie, he had sent her sprawling across the sidewalk. Apart from skinning her knee, she was unhurt. He had been killed instantly.

Wyatt borrowed Dink Ramsey's car, and they drove hurriedly down to New York. He was very worried about his mother.

"You said Mr. Crowder said she was taking it beautifully," said Cree.

"Beautifully. At least, up to when he called me. Who knows what's going on now?"

"She's very strong, Wyatt. Are you all right?" she asked.

An unnecessary question, she thought, regretting it the instant it was out of her mouth. He was far from all right. He was crushed and clearly showed it.

"Do you mean am I going to fall apart? I don't know, I've never had anything like this before. I feel numb. How could such a crazy thing happen? Crowder told me the two witnesses said there was no sound, no warning. He never knew what hit him. You hear that all the time, but it's true. One second he's alive, the next, dead. Forty-three years old, in the prime of his life, healthy as a horse. Dr. Stabler gave him a thorough physical exam every year, Mother saw to that. Every year. He always said his heart was made of cast iron. He never had a sick day, except maybe a cold. He was so healthy and vigorous."

He slowed the car, turning to her, his eyes filled with grief. She wished he would cry, let it out.

"A cornice, a piece of stone. How could it get loose?"

"I don't know," she said softly. "What did Mr. Crowder say?"

"I don't think he knows. It must have been cemented on, a piece added. The cement dries out over the years, weathers, cracks, and the weight of it . . ." He brought his fist down sharply. "It drops, the very instant he walks under it. What are the odds against that, a trillion to one? Ten trillion? A hundred?"

She had no answer. He drove on in silence, his eyes fixed on the road ahead, his mind obviously churning.

"An accident. It makes you wonder, doesn't it? Could such a thing be foreordained? What's to be gained? Nothing—he loses his life, she loses him, and so do I."

"And I."

"Yes."

He pulled her closer to him.

"Wyatt, I can't say if it's an accident or it was pre-destined. Who knows the answer to that? Who can— oh, Lord, listen to me prattle. I'm sorry. I want to help, but I'm not helping at all."

"You are. You're here with me. We'll get through it, the three of us. We'll stay at the house until we can be sure Mother is okay. No matter how long it takes. I'll run the car back after the funeral. We can live at home."

He paused. Again he looked at her; there were tears in his eyes.

"It's just so goddamned unfair! Things like this don't happen, they can't, the odds are all against them."

He slowed the car, pulled over onto the shoulder of the road. He gripped the top of the wheel, lowering his forehead against the backs of his hands.

"He's dead. We'll never see him again, his smile, his bad jokes, his cigars. I loved him so much. Just seeing him walk in the door, I could feel my heart swell inside me like a balloon. I remember when he taught me how to ride a two-wheeler. The front wheel waggled back and forth. He caught me before I fell. He was always catching me. He taught me how to swim. I hated it. To this day I can't stand the water, but of course I made him think I wanted to learn. And I did, thanks to him. He taught me how to catch a fly ball.

"When we lived on West Seventy-second Street we used to go to Central Park on Saturdays and Sundays to play catch. Baseball, football. He had a great arm, but wild. We'd yell back and forth and laugh. All week long I'd wait for Saturday afternoon and Sunday. If it rained, we'd stay in and build things with my Erector set, play with my steam engine, my Lionel trains. . . .

"He knew all about sports. He could remember thousands of names. He never missed the baseball box scores in the papers. He loved the Giants—Christy Mathewson, Rube Marquard, Fred Merkle. . . . Oh, Cree, I miss him like hell already. It's like part of me is torn right out of my body. It hurts, oh, damn, it hurts!"

"Of course . . ."

"But I've got to shake this off before we get there. Mother will need me to be strong, able to take it, not be babbling on like an idiot." He stiffened and shuddered, trying to drive the incubus of grief out of him. "Do you have a handkerchief?"

He wiped his eyes and blew his nose. Then he took a deep breath and straightened his shoulders. Shoving his foot against the low-speed pedal, he drove back onto the road, let the car into high gear, and roared off.

Chapter Nine

The living room was sumptuously furnished. Against the wall stood a late-seventeenth-century twelve-panel coromandel screen: rocky ledges, streams, trees, and shrubs alive with beautiful birds. It was set behind a divan against Clarence House velvet wallcovering.

In the middle of the room an ornately carved, exquisite baldachin fabric-covered table stood on an antique Turkish carpet of soft browns and subtle reds. Louis XV *fauteuils* were covered with matching soft red fabric. Against the wall opposite the coromandel screen a pair of antique French chinoiserie figures were positioned left and right of the portrait of Mrs. Chance hanging above the fireplace. A large, oblong, Flemish-style ebony and hammered-metal mirror occupied the wall across from the picture.

A fire burned in the grate, curling up and around a single massive oak log.

Marjorie Chance, preceding Cree into the room, drew off her gloves and handed them to the maid with her wide-brimmed black velvet hat.

"We'll have tea, Janice."

The girl nodded almost imperceptibly and withdrew. Wyatt's mother was dressed entirely in black in deference to tradition, but black was much too severe for her beauty, reflected Cree. She looked paler, more haggard than she would have normally—years older than her portrait. Despite her apparent exhaustion, she seemed to be bearing up magnificently, struggling to put on if not a pleasant face, at least one that was not too gloomy.

Wyatt and Cree watched her sink into a chair. Tilting back her head, she studied the ceiling without seeing it, her mind miles away. Cree went to her and placed a hand on her shoulder. Marjorie covered it with her own.

"There must have been four hundred people," said Wyatt, breaking the silence.

"He had so many friends," murmured his mother.

"I'm glad they didn't come trooping back here."

Marjorie straightened in her chair, smiling thinly at him. "You couldn't walk down the street with him and get to the corner without bumping into someone, wherever we went in town. And he'd never just say, hello, how are you. He would always stop and chat and have a cigar. Where's Janice with the tea, I wonder?"

Wyatt went to ring.

"Don't, she'll be here."

"Can I get you anything?" he asked.

"Would you like to lie down?" suggested Cree.

Marjorie shook her head.

"Maybe you ought to," said Wyatt. "Go in and lie down, and we'll come and keep you company. Unless you'd rather nap. A nap would do you good. We can have tea anytime."

"Wyatt, please don't coddle me. I don't need to lie down. Let's just talk. You know, I really think now that we've gotten through the funeral I'm going to be able to muddle through all the way, by hook or crook. Every-

one's been so supportive, your Aunt Meredith and
Uncle Gene, Cousin Erica, Cousin Vivian, all our
friends. The trouble is no one knows what to do. Nor
do I. Lucretia, do you know what I'm talking about? I
mean they want to say comforting things, but they're
hesitant—I guess for fear of bringing my mind back to
it. As if it could ever let go in such a short time. Not
even three days. Where's the tea?"

Wyatt rang for tea. Marjorie lowered her head,
touching the corner of one eye, her resolve briefly flagging. She patted Cree's hand, which still rested on her
shoulder.

"He did have so many friends. So many people loved
him. We were married twenty-four years, Lucretia. He
started out with next to nothing and worked and built it
all up, the company, all we have. For you and me,
Wyatt, certainly not for himself. I think in all the years
we were married the only thing he wanted for himself
was the Rolls. He had his heart set on it, and when he
got it, his toy, it swelled him up so with pride. . . ."

There was an awkward pause. Cree sighed inwardly.
The sadness surging through her was no stranger. She
could remember feeling the same way when she, Olivia,
and Julia had finally accepted the fate of the *Lusitania*
as fact and realized that they would never see their
father and mother again.

"Mother," said Wyatt, "Cree and I have been talking
about how this changes everything. It does, you know.
I've decided to quit school."

Marjorie glanced at Cree with accusing eyes. Wyatt
caught her expression.

"Cree's dead against it, but my mind's made up."

"I see," said his mother. "You want to leave Yale.
Then what do you plan to do?"

"Go into the business right away, of course."

"And do what?"

"Learn it from the ground up. Keep it going and healthy, with Mr. Steglio's help and Redican's and the rest of the executives. And Mr. Crowder."

"You haven't even started business school."

"There's obviously no time for that now. I'm going to work."

The maid wheeled in the tea cart. There was silence as she poured the tea. Then Wyatt began to press his case. He readily conceded that he knew nothing about business and finance at present, but with the help of Chance and Company's vice-presidents and treasurer he could learn quickly. His mother let him go on without interrupting until he began to flounder and repeat himself. She sat sipping her tea and gazing at him, a suggestion of a smile playing about her lips.

"I get the feeling you think that the company is suddenly on the verge of collapse. It's not. I know that for a fact. Charles Crowder, who is very well informed, has already reassured me. And your father was never secretive. He arranged everything so that nothing catastrophic could happen. He was shrewd. He had the foresight to spread the responsibility among Mr. Steglio, Mr. Redican, and the others. I'm in charge now, but they'll take good care of things, so your leaving Yale to go to work won't really accomplish much for you or the company."

"I think I should discuss it with Mr. Steglio and Mr. Crowder."

"Do, by all means. I simply want to allay any concern you have about the company's future or my own."

"There's something else I want to do with Mr.

Crowder, sue the company that owns that building. They murdered Dad."

Cree glanced at Marjorie and watched her shake her head slowly. Wyatt went on.

"They have a responsibility to keep their property from falling apart."

"Wyatt, I don't want to sue anybody. What would we gain? We could get some money, I suppose, but do we need it? One thing we don't need is for your father's name to be all over the newspapers, reporters flocking about the front door. A suit would only keep this terrible, terrible thing alive. What do you think, Lucretia?"

"I agree."

He looked from one to the other. "I guess I'm out-numbered. But I still intend to get Crowder's opinion."

"You stand to inherit a great deal of money," said Marjorie. "The bulk of the estate . . ."

"Mother, that's the last thing I want to talk about, honestly."

"Then let's go back to your dropping out of Yale." She stirred her tea, sipped, then turned to Cree.

"Lucretia, do you remember a conversation you and I had on the porch of that ramshackle house where you two had that tiny little room? I mentioned how important it was that Wyatt stay in school. You promised you'd never let him leave."

"I remember."

"Wyatt, do you mind us talking about you as if you weren't here?" Her tone of voice and her expression grew serious. "My dear, that promise you made me has outlived its usefulness."

"I don't understand."

"Mother, what are you talking about?"

"You, your future." She turned to survey her portrait over the fireplace. "I love my portrait. Vanity, vanity. Your father was so proud. People would come here and look at it and ask who painted it. He'd carry on so. Proud as a peacock, as I am myself. Remember Mr. Fabian?"

"Of course, my art teacher at Horace Mann."

"I never told you this. At the time it didn't seem right to, I guess, because I didn't think it would sit well with your father. He was so fired up about you following him into the business. But on graduation day—they held the ceremony out on the lawn—you remember how we mingled with the other parents and the faculty and the headmaster and his wife. I never can remember his name . . ."

"Dr. Bigelow."

"Like the carpets. Your father was talking to somebody else, and Mr. Fabian came up to me. We talked about you, naturally. I'll never forget what he said: 'That boy could be a crackerjack artist.' " She laughed, a tinkling bell. "It seemed a funny way for an art teacher to describe talent. Nevertheless, he did think you had talent, a great deal of talent. That was three years ago." She stared at her portrait. "I wonder what he'd say if he saw this? Wyatt, I want you to leave school."

He scoffed and turned away.

"I'm serious. I want you to go to art school here in New York—even better, abroad. The war's over. You can go anywhere in Europe you please. You know you'd love to. Say you will."

Cree felt her heart quicken.

"I can't. I mean I don't want to. I'm just not that

interested in painting, not like I was. It's a lot of fun, but to make it your life's work . . ."

"Stop pretending. You're still worrying about the business and me. Do you think we're both so helpless we can't survive without you? You're very wrong. Oh, I went along with your father and his plans for your future. Why wouldn't I? It seemed right. For a time I'm sure you even thought so yourself. But deep down you know you're not inclined toward business. He was, but you're not. And no matter how hard you work at it, you can never be what he was. Be honest, you agreed only out of loyalty and duty."

"Mother, what's happened doesn't change anything. If anything, it makes it even more important that I follow through. I'm not about to run off and six months from now, a year from now, pick up the paper and read that Chance and Company has become Pickwick and Company."

"Let me tell you something about your father. This is a true story, cross my heart. You were twelve, and we were out at the house in Westhampton that summer. I think it was a Friday night. You were down on the beach playing football with the Williams boys and that short boy who growled when he talked, I can't remember his name. His father was in steel. We were sitting on the veranda watching you. Your father had just come back from the city. Wyatt, that Friday he'd had lunch with Dr. Stabler, who was terribly upset. His son Jordan, who was in his sophomore year at Johns Hopkins in premed, had just that day quit school and run off to Maine to become a lobsterman."

Wyatt laughed. "He must have been upset. I can imagine what Dad said."

"What do you think he said?"

"That Jordan Stabler was a jackass, or something equally complimentary."

"You're wrong. He said he could understand how Dr. Stabler felt and he sympathized with him. But he told me later, 'Better a good lobsterman than a medi-ocre doctor.' "

"You don't have much faith in me as a businessman, do you?"

"I have faith in you in anything you attempt, whether it be business or trapping lobsters." She grinned. "Any-thing. But my faith isn't all that important. What we're talking about is your artistic talent."

His face darkened. "Cree, have you been talking about this behind my back?"

"We have not talked about anything behind your back," snapped his mother.

"Never mind. Mother, if you don't mind, I'd like to end this conversation. Let's talk about Aunt Meredith. She looks tremendous."

"May I say something?" asked Cree.

"Not about painting."

"Yes." She began telling Marjorie about Armand Duprier's visit. Wyatt tried to interrupt; he was furious. But she got it all out in few words.

"Thanks," he said tightly. "I appreciate it." He got up.

"Where are you going?"

"Back to New Haven. I have to return Dink's car, remember? I'll be back on the train sometime tonight." He glared at Cree. "Or maybe tomorrow."

"I'll come with you."

"I'd rather you didn't. We could use a few hours away from each other."

He walked out. Cree settled back unhappily in her chair. Marjorie did not seem at all disturbed.

"He'll simmer down," said Marjorie. "Know what I think? He wants to go to Paris so much he's turning upside down inside."

"You're so right."

"You may find it hard to believe, but this has been at the back of my mind for years. Lucretia, what's the answer? How do we bring him to his senses?"

"I don't know that we can. He makes up his mind, and it's like the steel door of a mausoleum closing."

"I think there's somebody who can open his mind. Charles Crowder. Wyatt's like every other male, my dear. Because I'm a woman, he refuses to take my word that the business is just fine and will go on being fine. But he respects Charles. He'll believe it, coming from him."

"He might, but I doubt if Mr. Crowder or anybody else is going to change his thinking."

"Maybe the three of us working together?"

"It's been on my mind ever since that night Professor Colclough brought M. Duprier to the apartment. I can only think of one possibility. What if we could get him to try it for, say, a year? He knows what his potential is, no matter how much he downgrades his talent. He knows for sure now Duprier has talked to him. Let's assume we did go to Paris for a year, and he worked and worked, knowing that the business was going along fine and that he could hold off making his decision until the year was up."

Marjorie brightened. "A year over there would be the same as taking his junior year here. It wouldn't be wasted. The reason he started with liberal arts was because his father thought it would broaden his outlook before the business world narrows it. I shouldn't say that, it makes me sound like a traitor. But I find all this so frustrating!"

"Yes, I've been living with it every day. I almost get a sore throat from holding back."

Wyatt reappeared in the doorway with his jacket on, his cap in hand.

"I'll be back tonight or tomorrow. I'll decide when I get there."

"Drive carefully," said his mother.

Cree rose from her chair and went to him, Marjorie following her.

"Do I get a good-bye kiss?" asked Cree.

He kissed her and his mother. Marjorie turned her back on him and winked at Cree. He left still smoldering.

"I was saying," said Marjorie, "that if he does come back, if he hasn't come to his senses by the time the year's up, there'll be no need for him to continue with liberal arts. He could go straight to business school and forget about Yale."

She was oversimplifying the situation, thought Cree, in her eagerness to get them across the ocean. The odds appeared depressingly long against it.

"He'd have a terrible time in business school," said Marjorie. It would be a disaster. I hate to say it, but it could make your marriage . . ."

"Uncomfortable."

"Perhaps even intolerable."

Cree was pacing. "Up to now I've been the quiet little helpmeet, minding my own business, never saying two words about that night with Professor Colclough and Duprier. But now that I know how you feel, I'm going to work. I'm going to break him down. If it comes to it, I'll threaten to walk out."

Marjorie smiled and shook her head. "If it comes to it, he'll let you."

"Probably. Still, I'm fed up standing by and watching him go bulling off in the wrong direction when it's so obvious he should be painting. One year is all I want. I'm going to get it."

Chapter Ten

Late in the evening it began to rain, a downpour that pummeled the front windows for nearly two hours before it let up, leaving Park Avenue glistening. Wyatt phoned to say that he would not be back until late the next morning. There were things they hadn't had time to do before rushing off, he explained to Cree; he planned to stop in and see Dean Jones and tell him that he wouldn't be able to resume classes until next week at the earliest. He also wanted to see his professors and leave the key to the apartment with Dink.

His mother also spoke with him. No sooner did he hang up than she dialed Charles Crowder at his home and asked him to come to the apartment at eleven thirty the next morning.

"Charles and I have talked about this problem of Wyatt's," she said, hanging up, "anticipated it. He's on our side."

Cree shook her head and lowered her eyes.

"What is it, Lucretia?"

"He's getting it from all sides, isn't he? Maybe trying to change his thinking shouldn't be a group effort. I wish I could do it by myself. At least it wouldn't look to him as if everybody was ganging up on him."

"I wouldn't worry about that. Charles is clever with words. Besides, Wyatt wants to speak with him. It might be all he needs. I have a feeling he's teetering on the brink."

"I wish I had the same feeling."

Cree went to bed in the Cambridge Bedroom, her favorite guest room. On one wall was an exquisite seventeenth-century Brussels tapestry, a sylvan scene somewhat reminiscent of one of her mother's tapestries at home. The other three walls displayed plaster garlands in the Grinling Gibbons style, and opposite the tapestry was a large giltwood mirror of inverted triangle shape above a matching giltwood console. The Chippendale four-poster was huge, with Genoa cut-velvet hangings in a colorful feather and flower pattern. The mattress and pillows gathered her up cozily as she lay back and thought about Wyatt. She would be sleeping alone for the first time since their marriage, their first night apart. How she yearned to feel his arms around her.

Perhaps Marjorie was right. Perhaps Mr. Crowder would be able to buttress their arguments and break down his stubborn resolve. Crowder was a lawyer; his powers of persuasion had to be well honed. All she could do was cross her fingers and pray.

Her thoughts drifted to Marjorie. She was giving every indication of coming out of all this intact, she decided, scarred but surviving, and able to pick up the pieces of her life and put them back together. There would be periods of depression, long sleepless nights, reminders everywhere of her loss, and above all loneliness. But time would pass, the phantoms would fade.

Marjorie looked rested and refreshed in the morning. She had put on her Doeuillet dress: navy-blue serge with a pleated tunic over a little blouse of white satin and a candy-striped belt. It was an ensemble that determinedly defied gloom.

They had breakfast, talking like long-separated old friends. A large bouquet arrived while they were having their coffee. The card identified the sender as Laura Mathes, Marjorie's roommate at Skidmore. She had learned of the tragedy only the day before, having been away in Montreal.

Marjorie and Cree were in the living room arranging the flowers on the table when Wyatt walked in. He looked tired, he hadn't shaved, but he seemed relaxed and his scowl had vanished. Cree ran to him, kissing him affectionately. His mother hugged him warmly.

He held her at arm's length. "You look better, Mother. That black outfit was . . . ."

Marjorie smiled. "Lady Macbeth."

Cree took her by the arm. "We're going shopping today and out to lunch."

"Good for you." He pursed his lips in a small yawn. "I can take a nap. I told everybody up at school I wouldn't be back for classes until next Monday at the earliest."

His mother glanced at Cree. "Wyatt, there's no need for you to sit around here holding my hand. I'll be all right."

"There's no need to rush back. For what? To finish the semester?" He flicked a dismissive hand. "Why bother? I'm quitting anyway."

His mother was about to disagree when the doorbell chimed.

"That will be Charles Crowder," she said.

Wyatt looked perplexed. "What's he here for?"

"I asked him to. You did say you wanted to speak with him."

He looked from one to the other. They could hear Crowder being admitted, Janice and he speaking in low tones as she took his things.

"I see you two have been busy while I was away. Don't get your hopes up. I'll talk to him, but he's not going to change my mind."

Crowder came into the room. He smiled a greeting, somewhat icily, but undoubtedly his best effort, Cree decided.

"Marjorie, Wyatt . . ."

"Charles," said Marjorie, "I'd like you to meet Mrs. Wyatt Chance. Lucretia, this is Charles Crowder."

Crowder scrutinized Cree as he extended his hand. "Delighted to meet you. I didn't have a chance to congratulate you over the phone. Congratulations indeed, oh, my, yes. Lucretia . . ."

"Shackleford," said Cree.

"Of course, Hiram Shackleford's granddaughter. Now I remember. Wyatt, your father mentioned that you two were smitten. And now you're married." Again he shook Cree's hand. He had fastened his smile on her, holding it there even as he spoke to Wyatt.

"Let's go into the study, shall we, sir?" said Wyatt. "Would you like me to ring for some coffee?"

"No, thank you," said Crowder, "coffee's poison to me. Always has been."

Marjorie and Cree went back to fussing with the flowers in the vase. There were nearly twenty they were unable to make room for.

"Lucretia, there's a vase with dying geraniums in it on the console in the hallway just outside the study. Be a dear and arrange the rest of these in it. You're so much better at it than I. Where would you like to have lunch? How about Gilbert's, on Seventieth? Geeeelbert's. *Très* French and tiny, and none of the waiters

speak English, except behind the customers' backs."
Cree gathered up the remaining dahlias, hollyhocks,
and other flowers. "They have those little pink Normandy sausages and a delicious carp à la chambord.
It's like a café in Paris." She winked. "It'll give you a
taste of what's to come."

"You're optimistic."

"You should be." She patted Cree's cheek. "If persuasion doesn't work, there's always force."

Cree went out to the hallway with the flowers. She
took the faded geraniums into the kitchen, where the
cook, a heavyset, no-nonsense Swedish woman with
braided blonde hair roped about her head was sliding a
roast into the oven.

They nodded to each other, the cook's expression
suspicious. If a man's home is his castle, thought Cree,
his cook's kitchen is the inner ward, where even members of the family are considered trespassers.

Having disposed of the geraniums and replaced them
with the fresh flowers, Cree brought the vase back to
the console. She was walking by the study door on her
way to the living room when the muffled sounds of
Wyatt's and Crowder's voices inside the study stopped
her. Tiptoeing to the door, she pressed her ear against
it.

"Isn't that like calling war an act of God?" asked
Wyatt. "I don't see it. To me it's an act of man. Somebody put that damned thing up there in the first place,
and it should have stayed up."

"It should have, but—"

"I really think we should sue. It might make whoever
owns that building and all the other landlords in town a
little more conscientious about taking better care of
their property."

"It was a freak accident. How do you prevent such a

thing? Hire human flies to crawl up and down buildings to check projecting stones? My boy, if you're determined to sue, we'll do so. But frankly, I see little hope of winning, and no hope at all of getting some sort of watchdog law enacted. Besides, didn't your mother tell you?"

"What?"

"Suing the owner could be a bit awkward, since he happens to be your wife's grandfather."

Cree moved quietly away, telling herself that when you eavesdrop there's always the risk of hearing something you would rather not know.

Marjorie was at the window taking her hair down. She turned to Cree as she entered the room.

"What's the matter?"

"My grandfather owned the building the cornice fell from, didn't he?"

Marjorie nodded, averting her eyes. "I suppose I should have told you. But even if he didn't, I couldn't see suing, for the reasons you heard me give Wyatt yesterday. Are they almost through in there?"

"I don't know."

"The longer they keep at it, the better, don't you think? I'm going upstairs to get ready. I'll stop by your room. You're going to adore Geeeelbert's."

Cree and Marjorie got back at five thirty, arms filled with packages, mostly hats, stockings, and underclothing. Lunch at Gilbert's had been as delicious as Cree had been led to expect.

On their way home in a taxi, Marjorie asked, "While you're in town, will you phone your grandfather?"

Cree reminded her that she had written him months before and was still waiting for his answer. He expected her to phone him, and she had no intention of doing so.

"If I did, he'd only think I'd suffered a change of heart and was paving the way to come crawling back."

"You couldn't now. You're married. He knows that."

"That letter was my first and last gesture, overture, whatever you want to call it. The trouble is nobody ever makes peace with him, except on his terms. Which means you scrap your principles, then surrender. Livvy didn't, Jule won't, and neither will I."

Marjorie laughed. "Telephone him from Paris when you get there."

"If."

They had consciously avoided any discussion of Wyatt and Charles Crowder's success or failure in changing his thinking. The two of them had still been at it in the study when Cree and Marjorie left.

Twenty minutes after they had walked in, the phone rang. Assuming it was Crowder, Marjorie took the call on a phone at the other end of the house, just in case Wyatt came wandering in.

She was on the line for more than half an hour. She came to the dinner table with a somber look, at the sight of which Cree's appetite all but deserted her.

After dinner, while Wyatt was on the phone to the Deke House at Yale, Marjorie took Cree aside.

"Charles said he did his best but it was like talking to a lamp post. He tried to argue that Wyatt's willingness to do as his father wished certainly made sense at the time, but now everything's changed. He's no longer under that obligation. He pointed out that I'm the head of the household now and that I should be entitled to the same consideration and cooperation he gave his father."

Cree shook her head. "The trouble with that is Wyatt doesn't see any less a need for him to join the company. If anything, it's even more important now that he do so. I must say I'm a little disappointed in Mr. Crowder."

"He did try, Lucretia, all the arguments you and I brought up: how well established and healthy the company is, that there's no earthly need for Wyatt to drop everything. He didn't say too much about his having talent and what a pity it was to waste it. His opinions along that line wouldn't carry much weight anyway. Frankly, I don't think Charles knows John Singer Sargent from Sergeant York. Lucretia, what are we going to do?"

"I'll have to go to work on him." She took Marjorie's hand. "Either I'll bring him to his senses or one of us'll be filing for divorce," she said with a short laugh.

"Good heavens!"

The clock at the end of the hallway outside their bedroom door timidly struck ten thirty. Wyatt stood with his back to her at the foot of the bed putting on his slipover pajama top. She loved to watch the muscles rippling under his skin when he raised his arms. Pulling down his top, he turned to her. She sat on the edge of the bed in her ecru silk pongee nightgown embroidered with organdy medallions, brushing her hair and judging the result in a hand-mirror.

"I'm getting old-looking. It must be married life."

"The Witch of Endor, that's you."

"What did you and Mr. Crowder find to talk about all day?"

"It was only an hour. Yes, he's on your side, as if you didn't know. And no, I didn't give an inch. But you didn't think I would, did you?"

"Certainly not."

"You think I'm an obstinate idiot, don't you?"

"Yes."

"Everybody's right and I'm wrong."

"Do you think I might say something without you going through the ceiling?" He shrugged and looked away. Permission granted, she thought. "A suggestion. What if you were to go to Paris and study for a year? One year out of your whole life. At least give it a try."

His reaction told her she had touched a tender nerve. Not that he hadn't expected her to mention Paris, but trying it for a set length of time made sense. Was it possible he'd even thought of it himself?

"If when the year's up—"

"No. I'll say it again, I've already decided."

She threw down her mirror and brush, shooting to her feet and glaring at him.

"You're ridiculous! Colclough, Duprier, your own mother, even your father—yes, I believe every word of that story about Westhampton, even if you don't."

"Did I say I didn't?"

"Everybody whose opinion you'd respect if anything else was the issue tells you you're wrong. And to top it off, along comes Mr. Crowder. If there's anybody on earth you could expect to be on your side, it would be Crowder, right? But he's not."

"Is it possible he's just being sympathetic toward her?"

"What are you talking about?"

"My mother. He knows how she feels, so he's siding with her to make her feel good."

"That's absurd."

"Why, because you don't happen to agree?"

"Do you know what I think's at the bottom of this? Your ego, pure and simple."

"Of course."

"Seriously, Wyatt, I think you think everybody's dead against your going into the company because they're afraid you'll gum up the works and bring the walls tumbling down. But you're going to fool 'em, you're going to prove they're wrong. Even if you have to destroy yourself doing it!"

"Can we talk without raising the dead? It happens I don't think any such thing. I, little girl, simply think that this is what I have to do."

"Have to?"

"Want to."

"No, you did mean have to. And don't call me 'little girl.' "

"Then quit carrying on like a six-year-old."

"What about you? Have to, want to—it's all a lie, an excuse to play the martyr. And you know it. You don't want to at all. Just the thought of it makes you sick to your stomach."

"What's making me sick is that nobody wants to let me make my own decision."

"Our decision. I'm your wife. It affects me just as much as you."

"You know what your trouble is, Cree? You refuse to look at the picture as a whole. In the first place, I have no intention of quitting painting. I'll go on, I will. I'll paint, and better and better. I'll get myself an excellent teacher right here in New York—"

"Do you think that working all day and every other night down on Wall Street, there'll be any time left to paint? Do you think you'll have any energy left, any desire? Real artists don't have time for anything but their art. As if I had to tell you that." She studied him stonily, her hands on her hips. "One thing I'll tell you, keep this up and there's one thing you'll be painting all right —a pretty dark future for you and me."

"I had a hunch we'd get to threats sooner or later."

"Call it what you please, that's what it'll come to. I know you. You're going to love strolling into that office day in and day out, paperwork piling up on your desk, lunches with your fellow-businessmen, decisions, decisions. Oh, you'll love every minute of it. And end up taking it out on the world. It's what happens to people who spend their lives working at jobs they despise. It's even worse for those who know what they want to do and can't—or, as in your case, won't. You'll take your frustrations out on me, because you're only human. You'll become very hard to live with, and I'll get sick of trying to please you, trying to be a good wife. So go right along with the big lie you call making a living. That's what it is, a lie. But let me tell you something, husband. I have certain rights in this marriage of ours—"

"The right to tell me what to do with my life?"

"Hardly. But the right to an opinion. And a right to happiness. And I'm not going to get anything like happiness in the direction you're taking us."

"Cree . . ."

"You're setting a course to disaster. What galls me is that both of us can see it coming. Disaster—that's the word, all right—for our marriage, our future, everything. How in God's name can you be so stubborn? All I'm asking is one year. When it's over, if you come to me and say I tried it, it didn't work out, we're going home, Wyatt, I promise that you'll never hear me say the word Paris again. I'll never mention art, Duprier, Colclough—nothing."

He had a strange expression on his face, she thought,

like that of a man tempted to reach out and steal something he had to have but holding back, fearful of being caught.

"Not a word," she went on, and went back to brushing her hair. "You come back, take whatever you need in the way of courses, get your degree, or go right to work. Either way I'll never bring the subject up again, so help me God!"

He stared at her a long time without speaking, the battle visibly raging within him. She held her breath, conscious only of her heartbeat.

"Wyatt . . ."

He looked away at the giltwood mirror above the console.

"What do you say?"

He continued to stare at himself.

"Say something, for heaven's sake!"

Turning toward her, he took her by the arms. "Cree, I just don't know. You've got to give me time to think."

"You've thought about it too much already. All last night, all the way to school and back here. With Crowder and since then. By now it's spinning around in your head like a top. Wyatt, you know I'm right. You know I'll never let up on you." She held his face tenderly between her hands. "One year, yes or no?"

"You're a bitch, a she-devil."

She brightened. "That's yes."

He rolled his eyes ceilingward, looking away from her. But she glimpsed in them what looked suspiciously like relief.

Chapter Eleven

Having been persuaded to change his mind, overnight Wyatt became possessed of the idea. To Cree, he seemed like a man released from confinement. So eager was he to get to Paris that he had to force himself to concentrate on his schoolwork. But he finished the semester at Yale, and the two of them went back to New York for the Christmas holidays and to spend their last week with Marjorie.

On January 3, a Friday morning with the temperature eight above zero and the wind sweeping through the city like an Arctic gale, they sailed for Europe aboard the *Ivernia*, a sister ship to the ill-fated *Lusitania*. Cree determinedly refused to let the coincidence resurrect old thoughts of the tragedy that had claimed the lives of her father and mother four years earlier. Instead she concentrated on Wyatt's change of heart and planning the year ahead. She never dared tell him, but almost from the moment he had capitulated, in her mind the year became the first year of forever, rather than merely a trial year.

The *Ivernia*'s captain was under orders to save coal; the crossing took thirteen days. It was the heart of the winter, the mornings indescribably bitter. A pale sun ascended the sky but sent down little warmth. The wind never tired. With the exception of a handful of hardy souls who in Wyatt's opinion must have had hides like walruses, the passengers stuck to their staterooms, venturing out on deck to get a breath of air for no more than a few minutes at a time.

Arriving in Calais from Dover they traveled by train to Paris and took a taxi, sitting buried under their luggage, to the Hotel Montelembert on Rue Montelembert in the shadow of the Church of St.-Germain-des-Prés. Professor Colclough had contacted Duprier to tell him of Wyatt's decision. In his return cable Duprier had congratulated Wyatt on coming to his senses and suggested that M. and Mme. Chance register at the Montelembert. He had even gone to the trouble of selecting their room for them. He also advised Wyatt to look for a "decent but reasonably priced" studio in the neighborhood of St.-Germain-des-Prés. Duprier had been away on business when they arrived and had still not returned.

Discussing the war with the desk clerk at the Montelembert, they were told that on Good Friday the year before, a shell had struck the Church of St.-Germain-des-Prés when it was crowded with worshipers, killing nearly a hundred and wounding twice that number. The area surrounding the Palais de Justice had been particularly hard hit by the enemy's Big Berthas, entire blocks having been reduced to rubble. The railroad yards were also a favored target.

But now the war was over, and the lights were on again in the City of Lights, in the streets, in the people's hearts, in their eyes. The death and destruction, the separation from loved ones, almost all the painful cankers of war except the food shortages and steadily rising prices, were now in the past.

* * *

The apartment, 110 Rue du Bac, was located in the heart of the city. Cree and Wyatt went through a porte cochere by the concierge's box and down a narrow tunnel, emerging between high, water-stained walls into a courtyard with several doors, a fragment of an old frieze, and a brass drinking fountain. The door to the apartment was painted blue and displayed a brass horseshoe knocker.

Inside, three steps below the courtyard, was a landing no more than a yard square and a monster of a settee with a desperately shabby-looking mohair cover and crooked legs. Cree caught a faint whiff of mildew.

Opposite the entrance a door opened into a spacious room painted in simple, flat tones of blue with white doors and windows. It was furnished with three Empire chairs, a couch, and a table. The furniture and the blue mat on the floor were littered with pages of *Le Figaro* and the *Journal des Débats*. On the far side was a glass door, framed outside by a rose trellis, which was part of a garden. Away it stretched to several catalpa trees, beneath which were seats. It was a country estate in miniature in the heart of St.-Germain-des-Prés.

To the right of the drawing room was the dining room. It too was done in blue, with blue-and-white china in a cupboard and a large blue-and-white porcelain stand in the center of the room. Suspended from the ceiling directly above it was an empty bamboo birdcage, and to one side stood a dining table surrounded by more Empire chairs.

Nodding at each other, Cree and Wyatt decided the apartment was near-perfect. Fantastic, thought Cree, far better, despite the mildewed settee, than any other lodgings they had seen in their week of searching.

The concierge who showed Cree and Wyatt through

the studio was in her fifties. Her face was long and thin under straight gray hair that slanted down her forehead in an inverted V. Even when she smiled, only her upper teeth showed; the corners of her mouth seemed unable to turn upward.

She might have been taken for a professional mourner but for one feature, her extraordinary eyes. Delft blue, they were mirrors of her emotions, sparkling when she laughed, clouding when she felt put upon or concerned, brightening like jewels when what was said aroused her interest.

Cree translated for Wyatt. The concierge's name was Mme. René Cecile Boulette. Her husband had been killed in the war, one of more than six million French casualties. The woman rattled on as fast as Duprier. Cree did her best; she had been working to improve her French since the morning after Wyatt had given in and agreed to "try it for a year." On the ship coming over, she had spent hours building her vocabulary and polishing her pronunciation. She was getting better and teaching Wyatt.

"Do we want it?" she asked him.

"*Oui.*"

"*Quel en est le prix?*"

The woman beamed as broadly as her mouth permitted and, smoothing her oversized apron, loosed a stream of French.

"Twenty-five hundred francs a year," said Cree, "payable on the first of every third month. She calls it the quarter day."

"That's what—five hundred dollars? *Madame, d'accord . . . d'accord . . .*" he began.

Cree rescued him. "*D'accord, nous la prenons.*"

The concierge's eyes glittered. She spoke again.

Cree's head bobbed up and down with understanding. "The first three months is due immediately, six hundred and twenty-five francs."

"It's almost the end of January."

Cree explained this to the woman as best as she could, and in return was informed of the landlord's policy.

"I guess we've only ourselves to blame for getting here a little late," said Cree. "I read up on renting on the train coming up from Calais. The tenant is supposed to pay on the quarter day. If you rent between quarter days, you evidently get stuck for the whole quarter."

"I'm glad we didn't get here the last week in March."

"Under the law she could ask for six months' rent instead of three: half for this quarter, the other half payment for the last quarter."

"We can afford it. It beats everything else we've looked at by a mile." He counted the correct number of francs into Mme. Boulette's hand. The three of them started out the door to the little garden. The concierge resumed talking. Cree translated.

"This apartment was Veesler's." She crinkled her forehead questioningly at Wyatt. "What's that?"

"Veesler? You mean Whistler?" he asked. The concierge nodded. His face lit up. "James McNeill Whistler, sweetheart, Whistler's mother's son. I'm going to be working in Whistler's studio!"

"Congratulations. It's an omen."

Cree glanced about the garden, then looked in through the open door of the apartment. She was already falling in love with the place, although it was in desperate need of sweeping and scrubbing. And furniture, a bed before anything else.

The breeze came alive in the garden, scattering the dead heart-shaped catalpa leaves. Over the low wall paralleling the street came a voice.

"Coco, coco."

They went back through the tunnel to the gate. An old man in a ragged velveteen vest was passing. Around his neck was a bright-red neckerchief, and he wore a gownlike leather apron that reached to within two inches of his thin ankles, visible as he passed the iron gate. Strapped to his back was a polished brass tank trimmed with copper bands; an array of goblet-shaped cups hung from hooks at the bottom, with two flexible pipes extending forward under his arms. The pipes were fitted with brass cocks to discharge the chocolate water contained in the tank. He rang his bell and called out:

"A la fraiche, quii vient boise!"

"Whistler's studio," murmured Wyatt, "I don't believe it."

Cree didn't hear him. The vendor still held her attention. Almost everything they'd seen since arriving seemed colorful, different—from the street vendors and sidewalk artists braving the biting cold to the clothes the Parisians wore, their food, the crooked little streets lit with gas lamps, the beautiful churches, the bridges clasping the banks of the Seine as it meandered through the city.

They had gone to Île St.-Louis the afternoon of their second day in Paris, crossing the old Pont des St. Pères, stopping halfway across to watch the fishermen and workmen scrambling over the lighters moored to the quay. They had looked down at their reflections in the greenish-blue water strewn with ripples of rose and gold.

And they had looked up at Notre Dame; the sight of it had taken Cree's breath away. She recalled Émile

Zola's description of the apse as a colossal stone monster crouching amid its flying buttresses like paws in repose.

This year of years would never end, she thought, as they walked back to the hotel at dusk. The shining roofs of the houses were softening to violet, the chimney pots and gables glowing orange, the narrower streets plunged into shadow, their lamps turned on even before the sun had set. It would stretch into a lifetime. She could see from Wyatt's eyes that he was being seduced by Milady Paris. Everywhere he looked he discovered something to frame in his thumbs and upraised forefingers.

"What a scene, what a face, what color . . ."

They moved into Whistler's studio at 110 Rue du Bac. They went shopping for furniture and bought an ancient unpolished brass bed and a foot-thick goosedown mattress. They bought a second-hand wardrobe of varnished birchwood, three small tables, linens and tableware, and a pair of lovebirds for the cage in the dining room. They called the birds Heloise and Abelard, the names, Cree was sure, of half the lovebirds in Paris.

Two days after they had moved in, Armand Duprier returned to Paris from London. Checking with the Hotel Montelembert, he was given the address on Rue du Bac. He sent a messenger around inviting Wyatt and Cree to call on him—at once.

Chapter Twelve

M. Duprier's house was across the river near the Place Vendôme, on the other side of the Tuileries Gardens. As Cree expected, it was beautifully furnished, with Empire gilt furniture by Bellangé, several excellent paintings, including one of the Marquis de Poyanne on horseback, a portrait of Princess Palatine, and various other nobles. Duprier's taste in art appeared to be firmly entrenched in the eighteenth century. His lone concession to the nineteenth century, at least in the room in which he welcomed them, was a crystal chandelier with legions of candles intricately arranged.

He greeted them warmly in perfect English, not in the least embarrassed by his pretended inability to speak it the last time they had met. Cree watched Wyatt as he shook hands with the little man. His eyes were over Duprier's head and drifting from painting to painting.

"Sit, sit, sit. Ransom Colclough cabled me and told me you had taken my advice and registered at the Montelembert. And now you've found a studio in Rue du Bac."

"The same studio Whistler had when he was here twenty-five years ago," said Wyatt.

"A talented mountebank. That's what my friend the art dealer René Gimpel called him. He wasn't bad for an American. Eccentric. Still, working in such illustrious surroundings should motivate you. Tomorrow you will go to the École des Beaux-Arts and initiate the process of enrolling. It is, as I'm sure you have heard, the finest art school in the world. Tuition is free, but there is an entrance examination and red tape, which can be cut." He pantomimed scissors. "You will find the work hard, not like New Haven with the raccoon coats and ball playing and other foolishness." He took a small notebook out of his pocket, scribbled on a page, ripped it off, and handed it to Wyatt.

"Go to the receptionist at nine o'clock and ask to see the director, Adelbert Vachon. He is a close personal friend of mine. He will take you under his wing."

"I appreciate your doing all this for me, sir. I know how busy you are. . . ."

"Very busy. I have a great deal of catching up to do. Every time I go away I come back to a pile of work." He paused, fixing his dark eyes on Wyatt. "Is something the matter?"

Wyatt cleared his throat. "Well, to tell the truth, I was planning to look around a little . . ."

"Look around?"

"At different schools."

"The École des Beaux-Arts is the only school for you. Any other would be a waste of your time. Oh, there are one or two in the Luxembourg Gardens that are not too bad, but not nearly as good as the Beaux-Arts. Remember, tomorrow morning at nine sharp. Be prompt. Don't bother to bring any of your work. First you'll talk with Adelbert, then the next time you get together you'll show him what you've done. Before then I will help you select what to show him."

He stood up. The meeting was over.

All the rest of the day, during supper and in bed that night, Wyatt could talk only of the future. But for all his enthusiasm, Duprier had raised doubt in his mind. The more he thought about it, the less he liked the idea of, as he put it, rushing into the Beaux-Arts without even looking at other schools.

"When I said good-bye to Professor Colclough we talked about schools. He got me some information."

Colclough had told him about the various ateliers scattered about the city, where men like Henri Matisse, Piet Mondrian, Raoul Dufy, Pierre Bonnard, Pablo Picasso, and other giants taught.

Cree turned out the light. Heloise and Abelard cooed softly in the other room, then were silent.

"It just seems a crime not even to look into the smaller schools and at least a couple of the studios."

"But if the Beaux-Arts is the best . . ."

"It's also the biggest. Over a thousand students. I read someplace that only about one out of four applicants passes the entrance exam."

"Is that what's worrying you? To listen to Duprier, you're as good as in already." She found his arm, slipping her own through it.

"He's taking over. He's like your grandfather."

"Darling, all he's doing is getting you started. Isn't that what you want?"

"I suppose."

"You're going to keep your appointment, aren't you?"

"Of course."

They fell asleep, but Cree was awakened by loud singing across the courtyard—one of Mme. Boulette's tenants coming home in his cups.

Cree got up and made tea. She sat at the table thinking about their voyage over. Too often on the *Ivernia*, lying in bed at night or standing at the rail in the freezing wind, she had imagined that it was the *Lusitania* and that she was her mother *en route* to Sweden to visit Aunt Marta, who had been seriously injured in an automobile accident and was in a hospital in Stockholm.

The horror stories of the sinking, the last desperate eighteen minutes, came crowding back. Now, nearly four years later, she still missed Daddy and Mother terribly, painfully. There were times she thought her heart would never heal.

"Happy birthday, Lucretia!"

The family was at the table—Mummy, Daddy, Grandfather, Olivia, and Julia, all eyes on Cree seated at the head in Grandfather's chair as Mrs. Bates came in with the cake, which she set in front of her ceremoniously, the six candles glowing.

"Happy birthday, Lucretia, happy birthday to you!"

Mummy, young and beautiful, her long blonde hair, her aquamarine eyes so full of love, her smile, which seemed to illuminate the room, dimming the candle-glow.

"Six years old, darling," she said. "Aren't you excited?"

"She's still the baby," said Julia, infuriatingly proud of her two-year advantage over Cree.

"You were the baby, Julia, before the stork brought Cree," said ten-year-old Livvy. "So there."

"She's got you there, dumpling," said Daddy, laughing at Julia.

"*Julia, don't be jealous,*" *said Mummy.* "*You have a birthday coming up. You'll be princess for a day. Will somebody please turn out the lights?*" *Mrs. Bates obliged.* "*Lucretia, take a deep breath, de-e-e-ep, hold it. . . . Blow!*"

She blew with all her might. Five candles flickered and died. The sixth flickered; the flame righted itself and continued glowing.

"*She doesn't get her wish!*" *shouted Julia.*

"*Quiet!*" *said Mummy.* "*Behave yourself or you'll go straight to your room.*"

"*I'm sorry,*" *said Julia, subdued,* "*but she doesn't. She can't. You can tell your wish now, it's not going to come true anyway.*"

"*I won't. It's a secret. I'll keep it till my next birthday, next month.*"

Everyone smiled, even Grandfather. Julia laughed. "*You only get one birthday a year, silly.*"

"*I know!*"

Daddy was nodding. "*Thank the Lord, otherwise everybody would be sixty starting kindergarten.*"

"*Nothing wrong with sixty,*" *muttered Grandfather.*

With Mummy guiding her hand, she made the first two cuts in the cake and set the piece on a plate herself. Then Mrs. Bates cut everyone else's piece. Mummy held Cree's hand to keep her from starting to eat before the others were served. Daddy was last. She attacked her piece. It was scrumptious, chocolate layer, her favorite. When the last crumb had vanished, she salvaged the candle that had refused to go out, slipping it under the edge of her plate.

"*What are you saving that for?*" *Mummy asked.*

"*Next birthday it'll be the first one I blow out,*" *she said seriously.*

"Listen to your little sister, girls, she's going to get even with that candle," Daddy said.

Olivia and Julia laughed.

"Don't listen to any of them," said Mummy. "Keep it in your button box, and next year you'll blow it out easy as blinking your eye."

Six years old. Piles of presents. Skirts and summer dresses, a squirrel muff to replace her old one that she'd accidentally caught and torn on a spike on the fence outside, a Mother Goose board game, a zoo-animal coloring book so big she could hardly lift it, and crayons and paints and brushes. And regular books—no more picture books now that she could read like a whiz, as Daddy said. Two more Jimmy and Jane books, a series by Bertha Elwood Carey that she loved and already had seven of.

From Grandfather a doll mansion, too big to call a doll house. White, with a blue shingle roof and white-fenced widow's walk circling the two chimneys. The back was open. The walls of the rooms were papered, and there were miniature chairs and tables and beds and even tiny toys made of sticks and wheels, beads and sequins. A family: a sea captain, whom she immediately named Captain Shipwell, and his wife, named Maggie, because she looked a little like Maggie Conklin, Mrs. Bates's friend.

Her favorite piece in the entire house was the cradle by the upstairs fireplace. If you touched it lightly, it rocked. Mummy promised to keep her eye out for a tiny baby for it. All the bureaus and cabinets had pulls painted to look like brass, and some drawers could even be pulled out.

It was the most beautiful doll house-mansion in the world, and she spent rainy days rearranging the furni-

ture and figures, the rugs, and even the tiny plates and bowls of food on the dining room and kitchen tables.

The last present she opened was her biggest present from Mummy and Daddy. Her hands trembled as she tore away the paper.

"Oh . . . They're beautiful!"

Two old-fashioned dolls, a boy and girl. They stood ten inches tall, their arms held stiffly at their sides, the boy in a linen shirt, silk vest, and sturdy woolen coat trimmed with metal braid and buttons, lace collar and cuffs, and knee trousers with white silk stockings. His hair was auburn, like Julia's, and on his head he wore a black velvet tricorne hat.

The girl wore a delicately embroidered brown and beige dress with a lace collar and over it a crepe shawl embroidered with pink and green flowers. Her bonnet was muslin sewn over reeds. She held a painted fan. Her slippers were brown-and-white-striped taffeta, and over one wrist she carried a flowered and tasseled reticule.

Cree named them Jimmy and Jane on the spot, and took them to bed with her that night, leaving her favorite doll Annabelle, abruptly relegated to second place in her affections, sitting on the windowsill. Mummy came to tuck her in and kiss her good night. She sat on the edge of the bed.

"Did you have a happy birthday, darling?"

"The best ever, except . . ."

"You didn't get your wish."

"I'll get it next year. I will."

"You'll be bigger and stronger. If you're not careful, you'll blow the candles clear off the cake."

"I just didn't aim good." She peered past her mother to the door. It was closed.

"Can I tell you my wish?"

"Do you think you should? If you don't keep it secret, it won't come true."

"But it's all right to tell now, because it'll be a whole brand-new wish by next birthday. Besides, I have to tell or I'll burst. Can't I just whisper it?"

"I suppose. If you really want to."

"Promise you won't tell Daddy or Julia or Olivia; it'll be our secret of my secret."

"I won't tell a soul." She crossed her heart and bent over.

Cree slipped her arms around her mother's neck. "I wished that I'll always stay like I am. Never ever grow up."

"Like Peter Pan."

"I mean it."

"That's a curious wish."

"It's a wish for all of us, don't you see? If I don't grow up, then Julia and Olivia won't either. And you and Daddy and Grandfather and everybody else in the house won't grow older and get wrinkles and bent over and all."

"Are you sure you want to stay six years old?"

"Seven next year. Yes, more than anything."

"Maybe you should think it over. Think of all you'll be missing—high school, new friendships, a boy friend, college, parties, dances. Your wedding. Becoming a mother, with a little boy as handsome as Jimmy and a little girl as pretty as Jane."

"I'd give all of it up to keep things just the way they are now, with all of us."

"Darling, are you afraid to grow up?"

"Not exactly."

"Afraid of what, then?"

"Of going to heaven. I heard Mrs. Bates on the telephone. A lady she knows is very sick in the hospital and Mrs. Bates is worried about her. She said she was afraid her friend was going to die and go to heaven. Was Grandfather terribly sad when Grandmother died?"

"Yes."

"And did it break your heart?"

Mummy nodded.

"See? That's what happens."

"When it happens to one you love, it's very painful, because you love the person so. But you do get over it."

"You think my wish is silly, don't you?"

"Not at all. I think it's a very thoughtful wish, a wish for all of us, as you say."

"Because I love you all, even Julia, even though she says mean things sometimes. I just don't want everyone to grow up and go away."

Mummy hugged her. "I wouldn't worry about that for years and years, if I were you. It's getting late, darling, the sandman's waiting." She pulled back the coverlet so that Cree could get up. "Prayer time."

She got up, picked up Annabelle, and put her on Jimmy's other side. Then she knelt and said her prayers.

". . . and God bless Mummy and Daddy and Grandfather and Olivia and Julia and Mrs. Bates and everyone. And please forget my wish, I'll just grow up. Maybe it'll be fun. Thank you. Amen."

"Amen," said Cree to the darkness framed by the window. She could hear the bed creak as Wyatt stirred in his sleep. She went in to him and, bending over, kissed him lightly on the cheek. Then she pulled the comforter up over his shoulder. She hoped he'd sleep well. Tomorrow was an important day.

Chapter Thirteen

Satisfying Paris's appetite was a gargantuan and somewhat grisly task, reflected Cree, as she made her way through the cattle market of La Villette in the great Central Market, Les Halles. According to the City of Paris information book she had picked up at the Hotel Montelembert, more than seven thousand steers, ten thousand calves and pigs, and thirty thousand sheep were slaughtered at the market every Monday and Thursday to feed the city.

On the advice of Mme. Boulette she had come early, as soon as Wyatt finished breakfast and left for his appointment. She had crossed the Pont Neuf and the pedestrian bridge over the railroad tracks to find herself confronted by a group of old iron pavilions built, according to the book, during the reign of Napoleon III.

An extraordinary sight met her eyes: three thousand stalls spread over twenty-two acres. Every night the supply carts from the market gardens came rumbling through the streets, heaped with fruits and vegetables and edible creatures, alive and dead. Behind her stretched the great wine market with its castellated terraces of barrels lining the wide quays, enough wine to quench the thirst in every throat in Europe, so it appeared.

She wandered about, her shopping basket over her arm. The babble surrounding her rose like the thunder of Bishop Alphege's gigantic organ at Winchester when its four hundred bronze pipes played simultaneously. She made her way through the rapidly growing crowd to the nearest of the six pavilions. It was a city within a city. Each pavilion, separated from the others by wide streets, sat under its own enormous roof supported by a forest of pillars and crisscrossed by stanchions. Daylight filtered into detached galleries through large windows with slatted venetian blinds.

The incessant clamor in the fish market, the vegetable market, the flower and fruit markets intensified as the morning wore on. No one talked, everyone shouted. Strange odors came at her from every side, some distasteful, even disgusting, others delicious. In the fish market were large sacks packed with shiny black mussels and snails, and there was tier upon tier of oysters in crates fetched fresh from Cancale in Brittany. Fish of every variety were displayed on wooden slabs—mackerel, tunny, wrasse, cod, haddock, flat fish, herring, sardines, squid, skate, all pink and pearly white and gray, their teeth and widely separated eyes all too visible for Cree's taste. An army of men and women was bringing in and arranging great masses of food: mountains of potatoes and cauliflower from Brittany and Normandy; eggs, butter, cheese, poultry, nuts, prunes, asparagus from Yvelines, Essonne, and Seine-et-Marne.

Women and girls selling flowers and plants from the south of France sat behind big square baskets packed with roses, violets and dahlias, chrysanthemums, hyacinth—splashes of pink, vivid scarlet, orange, white, a vibrant palette of colors.

The delicious scent of geranium and moss rose

erased the pungent smell of seaweed and fish as she began shopping. She bought fresh mussels, potatoes and onions and other vegetables, salt, sugar, tea and coffee, and a potted geranium, which displayed a single bud valiantly struggling to blossom. On her way back across the Pont Neuf she stopped at one booth after another to inspect the *articles de Pont Neuf*, mostly toys and imitation jewelry. And she paused to watch the mimes and jugglers. Reaching the opposite side, she turned for a last look at Les Halles and the succession of twelve round-headed arches and the massive cornice crowning the bridge. And beyond it the tightly packed ancient houses and gables overshadowed by the gray towers of Notre Dame.

On her way home she passed old men in shabby coats and berets and velour hats, their faces buried in their *Le Soir*. She stopped to buy fresh gingerbread from a fat, mustached woman hawker, her wares balanced on a tray as big as a table suspended from her shoulders. She also bought two sticks of bread, each a yard long and no bigger around than her fist, from a raggedly dressed, scrawny, but unusually polite little boy in front of Bon Marché. Arriving at the front gate of the house, her basket and arms overloaded, she set the basket down long enough to buy birdseed for Heloise and Abelard from a man in striped overalls and a caved-in top hat, his nose red from the cold and the contents of the bottle in his back pocket.

Mme. Boulette met her at the gate, her apron dusty with flour, her hands and arms looking as if she'd thrust them into the barrel. In her hand was a bottle.

"Pour le cuivre jaune du lit," she said, handing the bottle to Cree. It was a moment before she understood it was for the brass frame the dullness of which had

refused to yield to soap and water. In the bottle, the concierge explained, was her secret formula: white vinegar, salt, and lemon juice. Cree thanked her.

"Won't you come in and visit?"

After Cree had put her purchases away, they had tea. The birds began calling. She fed them and gave them fresh water, and they ignored each other long enough to fill their little stomachs.

Mme. Boulette only stayed twenty minutes. She explained that she had to clean out one of the apartments. It had recently been vacated and prospective tenants were coming later in the day to look it over.

When she left, Cree went into the bedroom and worked on the brass headboard. She had expected Wyatt home by noon at the latest. She couldn't conceive of the director of the Beaux-Arts giving him more than fifteen or twenty minutes. Then he'd probably turn Wyatt over to someone else for a tour of the place. When he didn't show up for lunch, she assumed that he'd gone from the school straight to M. Duprier's to tell him what had happened and to discuss the situation. If he didn't come home soon, he would call; he was reliable, he had never yet let her wait and worry.

At one o'clock she sat down to write to Marjorie Chance, her first letter from their new address. She described the apartment and what they'd seen of Paris so far, writing four pages on Les Halles alone. She told her about their visit to Duprier and Wyatt's meeting with the director and repeated Duprier's praise of École des Beaux-Arts. It was almost three by the time she had finished the letter, thirteen pages, both sides. She had been so absorbed in writing that it wasn't until she was moistening the flap on the envelope that she realized she'd skipped lunch. She brewed a fresh pot of tea and

buttered two slabs of bread. Then she went back to
work on the bed. She polished the headboard until it
glowed, making the rest of the bed even more tarnished-
looking in contrast. But Mme. Boulette's formula, powerful enough to dispose of thirty years of neglect, was
beginning to affect her hands. She decided to wait until
she could buy a pair of rubber gloves before she resumed the task.

When Wyatt didn't show up for supper, she began
pacing. It wasn't like him to stay away without at least
calling. They had yet to have a phone installed, but
Mme. Boulette had one. The least he could do was call
to say that he was all right and give her some idea
when she might expect him home.

She hesitated to begin steaming the mussels for fear
he might not show up until very late. At six fifteen she
went out to post the letter, telling herself that when she
got back he would be there, all apologies and with an
explanation. With or without, she'd tell him what she
thought of his thoughtlessness.

Coming back from the corner mailbox, she hurried
her steps to the gate, down the tunnel, and into the
house.

"Wyatt!"

Heloise and Abelard cooed a welcome. She went into
the kitchen and reheated the tea. She thought about
calling the Beaux-Arts school, but it was too late; besides, he had to be long gone from there.

Three possibilities faced her. He'd gone straight from
the school to Duprier's house. They had talked and
then gone out together to celebrate. Without her? No,
that didn't make sense. Besides, Duprier wasn't the sort
to celebrate such a success. It was a *fait accompli* in the
little man's mind. She'd never met anybody so arrogant,

egotistical, demanding. Even her grandfather, as imperious as he was, let the other person get in an occasional word. Still, if Duprier was willing to help Wyatt get started, that was all that mattered.

Second possibility: He'd made friends with someone at the school, maybe a fellow American. They'd gone to his place or they were roaming the city.

Third, something had happened, something dreadful—he'd been hit by a car and was in the hospital, or worse.

He walked in shortly after eight, a bottle of Pouilly under each arm, bubbling with excitement, a victory smile stretching across his face. At the sight of him, she was too relieved to be angry.

"Wyatt, where have you been?"

He had been drinking, but he was not drunk, only comfortably tipsy on a cold night and still coherent. Setting the bottles on the table, he whipped off his hat and bowed so low she was afraid he'd bump his head on the floor.

"Greetings, my darling, my love, my Rokeby Venus."

"I've been worried sick. Why didn't you call?"

He looked abashed. "I should have, I know. I apologize, darling. So much happened, I got so involved, I lost track of time. When I saw a clock in a store window and it was almost eight, I couldn't believe it."

"Didn't it occur to you it was getting late when it started to get dark?"

"I'm afraid not, but when I saw that clock across from St. Sulpice, I turned around and headed straight home. I ran. Feel my forehead. I'm sweating. It's the truth, you can ask the *gendarme* on the corner. I nearly bowled him over." He kissed her. "Can you forgive me?" He dropped to his knees, begging.

"Get up, you idiot. I suppose I forgive you. But don't ever do it again! I was terribly worried! I still feel like a stranger here. I love Paris, but it's foreign territory, and when you leave me alone without any idea of where you are . . ."

"Cree, I have stupendous news!" He had set both bottles on the table. "Get some glasses. This is the biggest thing that's happened to us since we got married."

"You saw the director."

"Sure. The school's only a couple blocks from here. I got there about ten of nine. He was very charming and very busy and didn't bother to hide it. We talked. He asked a hundred questions."

"When are you taking the entrance exam?"

They sat at the table. He poured the Pouilly. It danced in the glass in the glow of the overhead light.

"I don't think I'm going to be taking it."

"What?"

"Cree, let me tell you what happened. Only promise you won't hit the ceiling."

"You're not taking the exam because you're not going to the École des Beaux-Arts. You went someplace else, the Luxembourg Gardens."

"Please, just listen. I answered all his questions, and he turned me over to one of his assistants. He showed me around the place."

"You didn't like it."

"It's like Yale. Studios as big as barns, filled with students, practically shoulder to shoulder, everybody slapping away at their canvases. It was like overtime in Santa's workshop."

"Wyatt . . ."

"I walked around the place with him, and then we

went back to the director's office, but I'd already made up my mind. I said to myself, this is not for me. I don't care if it's the best in the universe. Did you know that when Whistler first came to Paris his father wanted him to go to the Beaux-Arts, but he didn't?"

"The devil with Whistler!"

"Aren't you even going to taste the Pouilly? It's dry and really light. When you had it back home you liked it."

"If you're not going to the Beaux-Arts, where are you going?"

"Be patient. I left there and went to the Luxembourg Gardens and talked to a second-assistant-somebody at one of the schools. He was ice-cold. I had the feeling it was because I was an American. Can you imagine? The war's been over, what, three months? Talk about a short memory.

"Cree, sweetheart, you've got to feel right about something like this. Feel it's right for you, that you're going to fit in. I couldn't feel it at either place. I left there and just walked around for a while, thinking, and about four o'clock, I guess it was, I was on the other side of the river on Rue St. Denis, where it crosses Rue Réamur."

"Wyatt, I don't know where that is. Will you get to the point? And stop drinking."

"Okay, okay. I looked up, and there was this little two-story building. The front was painted lavender. And the door was gilded. The Studio Gleyre. I saw the name out front on a bronze plate and recognized it immediately. Cree, the Studio Gleyre was Whistler's first school in Paris. Gleyre inherited the studio from the painter Hippolyte Delaroche, then later handed it on to someone named Gérôme, who in turn gave it over to its present owner, a Professor Simeon Lacroix. Lacroix retained the brass plate with Gleyre's name on it.

"He's little and very old, close to eighty. His skin is as yellow as a chicken's, and he has this preposterous mustache six inches long on each side and twisting up at the ends. He wears pinch glasses that keep falling off his nose. He doesn't even look through them—he looks over them."

Wyatt stood up, his head to one side and his face screwed into a ferocious scowl, imitating Lacroix.

"Monsieur, you are slap-dashing! If you will be so kind as to clean your brush. On second thought, cover your canvas with white. Better black. Even better, burn it. You there, longshanks, look at this line. It is supposed to be the lady's breast, no? Not an extension of her belly."

"He sounds like a martinet."

"He is and he isn't. It's all a little bit of tongue in cheek. Cree, he doesn't miss a thing. There was a hair from the brush in a daub of alizarin crimson on one canvas. I stood right next to him and didn't see it, and neither did the student. But *he* did. And he has all these wild rules, his controls, he calls them. They sound ridiculous, but if you think about them, they make sense. Step back after every brush stroke. *Every* stroke. He says it's the only way to work. Keep an eye on your light; when the sun moves, you move. It goes without saying, right? Only nobody ever said it to me. That's what's so exciting. He takes nothing for granted! Listen to this—he says varnish yellows a painting. Varnish has turned all of Rembrandt's canvases yellow. Then he tells how sixty years ago, when he was a student, he used to go to the Louvre and put his shirt cuff up close to the collars in Rembrandt's portraits. When they were painted they were just as white as clean linen. But you could see they'd turned yellow with age—from the varnish.

"He personally favors the spectrum palette, which is what the Impressionists prefer—red, orange, yellow, green, blue, indigo, and violet. And white.

"But he also likes Monet's arrangement. Cobalt, ultramarine blue, violet, vermilion, ocher, orange, dark green, another very clear green, and a yellow. In the center a double-size pile of white."

Wyatt went on to explain how, according to Lacroix, arrangement was all. The optical properties of oil were all. Experimentation was all. Proper use of light was all.

Everything seemed to be all, reflected Cree, as she sipped her wine.

"Don't reproduce a prototype, use it. Make it unmistakably your own. Every touch of pigment, every nuance of glaze, every stroke, combine to produce the total effect. Cree, I watched him haranguing his students, and you should have seen their eyes. It was as if they were all Moses getting the Ten Commandments from God."

The professor spoke French and fluent English and Italian, and every instruction, every criticism, every observation, was delivered *basso profundo* in the three languages in succession.

Wyatt grinned. "For twenty-five francs a month, you get language lessons along with art."

Lacroix's purpose was clear. Everyone in his atelier learned from everyone else's mistakes. Not to mention their own.

"He believes embarrassment is very good for the

memory. Nobody takes it personally. They love him."

"He sounds worse than a martinet, more like Simon Legree."

"He is, only without the whip. He carries a stick. He points with it; he impales your mistakes on your canvas. When I first got there and introduced myself, we talked for about ten minutes, then it was time for a life class. He let me stand and watch."

"Was she pretty?"

He laughed. "She looked like Hélène Fourment, Rubens's second wife. She was his favorite model. Big." He held his hands out as if measuring a fish. "You know how Rubens painted women, big everywhere. But this girl has a beautiful skin." Again he laughed. "Lots of it. He wants to see my stuff tomorrow. Everything—good, terrible. I'll bring my sketch book and a few paintings, what I can carry. Help me pick them out. I want him to see whatever is halfway decent, except the nude of you."

"You don't like it?"

"It's too much like the *Rokeby Venus*, only without the cherub and the mirror, and of course your hair's light. I primed the canvas with white lead in oil and covered it with deep red, except under you. Exactly the way Velazquez did it. He'd spot it in a second."

"I want him to see it. Aren't you supposed to be able to copy the Old Masters?"

"Sure. But I have plenty to show him. There were only thirteen in the life class. Cree, that's practically private instruction."

"I wish we'd brought along *Wrexham Tower* and the Foxon church."

"I have enough."

"You must be starving. I bought mussels; it'll only

take a few minutes to steam them. I went to Les Halles. What a madhouse!" She touched his cheek lovingly. "Wyatt, you have a problem."

"Don't I know it. After I left Professor Lacroix and came down to earth, I walked around thinking about it. I decided I should go straight over to Duprier's house and tell him. Then I changed my mind."

"You have to tell him."

She had filled the sink and was washing the mussels.

"I will." He sighed. "I didn't do this on impulse, Cree, honestly. I just felt the Beaux-Arts wasn't for me and just as strongly that Studio Gleyre is. I'd be lost at the Beaux-Arts. Besides, I'd have to wait to take the exam, and what if I didn't pass it? Think of all the time I'd be wasting."

"Darling, you're rationalizing."

"I'm not. I'm just trying to explain. Do you think I'm wrong?"

"No."

He poured more wine. She took the bottle from him, corked it, and put it in the cupboard along with the unopened bottle.

"Cree, I never admitted this, but there's something about him I don't like."

"He's a tyrant."

"Still, he did go to all this trouble . . ."

She lit the flame under the pot of mussels. Another nettle showed its prickles: Whatever the two of them thought of Duprier, the man was Professor Colclough's long-time friend.

"I'm going to have to write and explain," continued Wyatt.

"You're going to be too busy, I'll take care of it first thing tomorrow."

She sprinkled oregano and salt and pepper on the mussels. One by one they opened. They smelled delicious. She scooped them out of the pot into two bowls, then melted some butter.

"I remember a cartoon once in *Judge*," he said, "this big Wall Street tycoon type at a cocktail party. He was penning a fellow into a corner with his arms up on either side of him. The caption was, 'You wanted to see me?' It's not hilarious, but it fits. Duprier makes me feel penned in. He never asks, he demands. He doesn't advise, he orders."

"How are you going to explain it to him?"

"I'll tell him the truth." He sighed, his breath whooshing out. "Okay, I walked out of the Beaux-Arts for another reason, because he steered me there. Because I don't want to be his protégé. I don't want anybody's collar around my neck."

"Talking about him is ruining my appetite. I wrote your mother today. We should be hearing from her. By way of the Montelembert."

They talked about Marjorie, home, how different in every respect Paris was from New York. They reminisced about Yale. It began to snow, huge flakes tumbling down from the black sky, settling on the dead leaves in the garden, some of them melting, some beginning to form a cloak of white velvet over the city.

It was after nine thirty by the time they had finished eating and done the dishes. They were preparing to go into the studio to select paintings for Professor Lacroix when a sharp rap sounded at the door.

"Who do you suppose that is at this hour?" asked Wyatt.

"Who do you think?"

Armand Duprier looked like a bearded Emperor

penguin. He leaned his cane against the door. Taking off his top hat, he shook the snow from it, handed it to Cree, removed his cape, shook it out on the floor, and began pulling off his gloves.

"I can't stay long. I'm meeting friends for dinner at the Cafe Flore on Boulevard Saint Germain. Not my favorite restaurant, but the snails are incredible. Everyone takes them with garlic butter, but I insist on à la Chablaisienne. Ahhh!"

He bunched his fingertips and kissed them. "I will take you two one evening."

"Won't you sit down?" asked Cree, sneaking a sidelong glance at Wyatt. He seemed nervous.

Duprier sat with his cane upright between his knees.

"Well, how did it go? I've been running around like a cat on fire all day. No chance to call Adelbert. And there was no message from you, my young friend. So? When do you take your examination? What were your impressions? Did you like what you saw? Oh, Mrs. Chance, do bring out his sketchbook and some of his paintings. We shall have to make a selection. The nude definitely."

"Duprier," said Wyatt quietly, "I'm afraid I'm not going to enroll at École des Beaux-Arts."

"And that one of the little tykes playing on the lawn. I like it, it's charming, if a little trite."

"I've found another school, smaller, a studio."

Duprier looked shocked as Wyatt's words finally sank in. His eyes bulged, then the lids closed slowly, pushing them back into their sockets. His lips moved soundlessly.

"Let me explain," said Wyatt. "I went to the Beaux-Arts this morning and looked the place over . . ."

"You have found another school?"

"Yes, sir."

"I sent you to Adelbert. You saw him, you two spoke?"

"Yes."

"And you're telling me you walked out? To another school? I don't believe it."

"If you'll just let me tell you what happened."

"Would you like a glass of wine?" asked Cree, then felt like a fool as she realized how ridiculous she sounded. Duprier flung out his hand, dismissing her. His eyes were beginning to smolder.

"By any chance, does insanity run in your family?"

Wyatt bristled. "Wait just a minute."

"Are you utterly mad?"

There followed a torrent of French, Duprier sputtering, spitting, spewing insult after insult. He had risen to his feet and was pointing his cane at Wyatt like a duelist *en garde*. Wyatt stood barely an inch from the upraised ferrule.

"Have you the vaguest idea how many aspiring artists are turned down by the Beaux-Arts each year? How many of your countrymen? They come straggling over here by the hundred and the door is closed in their faces. Just as it would close in yours, were it not for my speaking up in your behalf, using my influence, requesting a favor of an old and dear friend. Which he did not hesitate to grant."

"I know. I know it looks like I'm ungrateful, but . . ."

"Ungrateful? Treacherous. Perfidious. And stupid." He tapped his temple with his forefinger. "Stupid! Where did you go, what school?"

"An atelier."

"Which one?"

"Studio Gleyre . . ."

"Simeon Lacroix. I know him. He's a doddering crank fifty years behind the times. Next month, next week, he'll be in his grave."

"If you'll just let me tell you what happened. . . ."

"Haven't you already? It's all very clear. I open the door for you, and you slam it shut." He stood up, his face crimson with anger. "But then, what else am I to expect from a spoiled rich American?"

"I think you'd better leave." Wyatt took Duprier's cloak down from its hook by the door. Duprier put on his hat and gloves. He smiled icily.

"Nothing would please me better than to leave. But one last word, Mr. Wyatt Chance. I have an excellent memory, and in it from now on I will have a special compartment for you and your ambition. The circle of art is surprisingly small. And I know everyone in it. We are a very special breed, very close."

"Get out!" shouted Wyatt. Striding past him, he jerked open the door.

Duprier spun about and vanished into the curtain of falling snow. Wyatt slammed the door.

"Goddamned son of a bitch!"

Cree groaned. "He didn't take it very well, did he?"

"He's all mouth, he can't hurt me. Let him try."

There was a long, heavy silence. The snow was piling up on the window frames, slender bands of it filling in the corners of each pane of glass.

"You think I did it deliberately, just to spite him."

"Don't be ridiculous. Wyatt, it's done and it's right. If *you* think it is, that makes it right. Don't let him make you have second thoughts. He can take his pride and ego and go to hell."

"Such language."

He grinned, held her close, and kissed her.

"Let's go to bed," she whispered, as he softly kissed her closed eyes.

"My darling Cree," he answered, and led her to the darkened bedroom.

Chapter Fourteen

In the morning Wyatt sat down and wrote a letter of explanation and apology to Duprier. It would never be read, he was sure, but it had to be done, he told Cree. His conscience demanded it.

Together they selected nine paintings to show Professor Lacroix. They decided to wrap them in newspapers, tie them in groups of three, and take a taxi to the studio. Wyatt wanted Cree to go with him to meet the professor.

"You could sign up yourself. You'd love it."

"No, thank you, you're the artist in the family. I'll stick to doodling."

Less than three inches of snow had fallen during the night, and when the sun rose the temperature began to climb. By the time they were ready to leave, the streets were awash with slush.

Professor Simeon Lacroix fitted Wyatt's description of him perfectly. He was certainly eighty, thought Cree, if not older, but he acted like a man half that age. When Wyatt introduced them, Lacroix shook her hand as if he were working a pump handle. Then he took Wyatt's sketchbook and walked down the crimson and white hallway, muttering to himself. Stopping, he turned.

"Bring your paintings, come. A pleasure to meet you, madame. Good day."

She left, smiling to herself. The plots of Charles Dickens were peopled with such characters. She stood outside surveying the gaudily painted building. So this was to be where the gifted amateur was to be converted into the recognized artist. How well recognized? How good an artist? How good could he become? she wondered. Were the limits of his talent defined in his genes? Could he be another Whistler, Picasso, Matisse, Renoir?

Wouldn't it be marvelous! How proud his mother would be, and Professor Colclough, Dink Ramsey, everyone who knew him. Except, of course, Duprier. She walked to the corner and turned down Rue Réaumur. Halfway up the block two *gendarmes* stood talking, one towering over the other. As she approached them they snapped their hands to the peaks of their kepis in salute.

"Pardon. Pouvez-vous m'indiquer la direction du bureau télégraphique?"

"Oui, madame, c'est au bureau de poste. C'est là-bas sur la Rue du Louvre."

"Merci."

The main post office proved to be a somewhat smaller version of Pennsylvania Station in New York, with a lofty ceiling and wrought-iron chandeliers. Mobs of people surged up and down the marble staircases. She stood at a table writing on the form given her by the clerk.

PROFESSOR RANSOM COLCLOUGH
YALE UNIVERSITY
NEW HAVEN CONN USA

UNFORTUNATE DISAGREEMENT SELECTION
SCHOOL DUPRIER STOP LETTER EXPLANATION
FOLLOWS

LUCRETIA CHANCE

She paid for the cablegram and started home. The
sun shone brightly, melting what was left of the snow.
The roofs and vehicles and boulevards glistened.

"Unfortunate disagreement." How long a memory
did Duprier have? she wondered. Was there the dim-
mest possibility he'd read Wyatt's letter, and gotten
over his anger?

No. In her effort to be optimistic, she was merely
being naive.

Chapter Fifteen

Wyatt was accepted as a student at Studio Gleyre. He went to his first class, Color and Composition, the next morning, following it with four hours of drawing in the afternoon. He came home exhausted but full of praise for the studio and Professor Lacroix and the other faculty members. The tuition was twenty-five francs—five dollars—a month.

On the days when he had no classes he stayed at home and sketched and painted. Occasionally he and Cree went to the Louvre to wander through its seven museums. Often he would bring along his easel, paints, and a canvas and reproduce a portion of an Old Master. Attracted by Jean-Baptiste-Siméon Chardin's expression and casual attire in the artist's self-portrait, Wyatt copied it entirely. In his opinion, Chardin had never had the recognition he deserved. Cree disagreed; to her, anyone with three paintings hanging in the Louvre could be classified as famous.

Wyatt tried to duplicate Chardin's technique, using thick layers of color one over the other with the overall impression filtering through from underneath. The original had a magical quality that Cree found intriguing. At times she saw it as if through a cloud of smoke; at other times it glistened as if it had been spattered with water.

Wyatt was disappointed with his attempt to duplicate it and gloomily announced after a week of trying that it only proved how far he had to go.

In the Grande Galerie there was a Cranach that he particularly admired, *Venus in a Landscape*, a sylphlike Venus wearing a wide-brimmed hat, a necklace, and transparent veil. Her wavy blonde hair fell to her thighs. There was about her an ephemeral quality, a gossamer lightness. Viewing her for the first time, Cree was surprised that her slender feet were touching the ground.

Unfortunately the more Old Masters Wyatt studied, the more pessimistic he became over his future. But he was working steadily, heedless of the clock, of mealtime, now and then even of bedtime. Study, study, study, sketch, sketch, sketch, paint, paint, paint. He would have worked eighteen hours a day if she'd let him.

In early February two letters arrived from Marjorie. Both began with the assurance that Chance and Company was doing splendidly. An exaggeration, perhaps, but they knew that she would never deliberately mislead him. Actually, although Europe was in economic chaos, the United States had emerged from the war financially healthy and anticipating prosperity.

Heloise and Abelard continued their courtship, the geranium flourished, and African violets filled the four bowls in the porcelain stand in the dining room. A telephone was installed. Wyatt got an answer to his letter to Professor Colclough. He had written him the evening of the day Cree had sent the cablegram. He explained in detail his falling out with Duprier, assuming the blame for the incident. Colclough wrote back to tell him that he understood and urged him to forget about it. The professor avoided criticizing Duprier, but reading between the lines, they realized that the incident did not surprise him and that his sympathies were with Wyatt.

Wyatt made friends with his fellow students. Roland Robays was a young Belgian from Antwerp who lived with his wife in a garret two blocks from 110 Rue du Bac. On mornings when their classes coincided, Roland would pick Wyatt up at the front gate and together they would take the metro.

Roland was small and swarthy, with tousled black hair and a knowing smile. He had a marvelous sense of humor and was forever crossing swords, usually in fun, with Professor Lacroix and the other teachers. Roland was married to a girl from Lorraine, who had also come to Paris to study art but had decided that her talents were too limited to pursue a career. She helped support Roland's preparation for his career by working at the Jardine Art Supply Shop around the corner from the studio. It was at the shop that Roland and Giselle had met; they had fallen in love and married only one month to the day before Wyatt had enrolled at the studio.

The Robays invited the Chances to dinner one Friday night. It was a bitter-cold night, the wind belligerent, the streets and sidewalks patched with ice, and the sky threatening a storm. Cree and Wyatt bundled up and brought along two bottles of a good Beaujolais. The Robays' house was a battered block of a place, the front door giving the impression of having been sealed for centuries, the roof missing shingles here and there. A gate clinging by one hinge opened onto an alley. At the rear, wooden stairs led up to a landing and a door just under the eaves.

Giselle opened the door, her large blue eyes glistening and beautiful, her hair a mass of tight blonde curls. She greeted them warmly. Roland was at the far end of the garret setting out biscuits and cheese. Thin blankets tacked to the rafters divided the garret into four rooms. Canvases and posters pasted to heavy cardboard were suspended from the rafters at varying heights. Four candles burned in old wine bottles set on an upended orange crate. The only other illumination came from two bare bulbs protruding from the ridgepole and a small lamp in the improvised bedroom. There was a window at each end of the garret, the panes opaque with ice. The wind howled outside, setting the chestnut trees creaking; a small coal stove glowed fiercely, challenging the cold and defeating it.

As Cree took in the place she was impressed by the ingenuity with which their hosts had turned a gloomy attic into a home. The warmth and love was as pervasive as that which had filled her own home at 1 East Sixty-first Street in the happy days before the *Lusitania*. Wyatt had not exaggerated in describing the couple's poverty. The few francs Giselle earned at the shop paid their rent and Roland's tuition and their daily metro fare during the winter. From late March through the summer they planned to walk the almost three-mile round trip between school and work and their home.

Roland supplemented their income by painting signs, canvasing the shops in the neighborhood with his samples, getting orders and dashing off *À louer, À vendre* and other such signs, anything any shop owner wished.

But the Robays did not permit their poverty to impoverish their lives. They were obviously very much in love, optimism reigned, their happiness obliterated every inconvenience and deprivation. Money was of minimal importance. He could not talk to her without taking hold of her hands, without touching her face or arm. If she spoke to him from across the room, he would come to her so as to be able to touch her when he answered. She was animated, gay, and refreshing and she had marvelous eyes, which reminded Cree of Mme. Boulette's. Both had learned English in secondary school.

Cree helped Giselle finish preparing dinner, keeping the *pastilla*, a sweet, flaky pigeon pie, hot on a small grill set on the coal stove. There was also *Jésus de Morteau*, liver sausage, a *salade verte*, and *mousse au chocolat* for dessert.

Wyatt opened one of the bottles of Beaujolais and poured it into wide-mouthed tumblers to let it breathe properly and to take the wind-chill from it. There were two cheeses, a *bleu de Bresse*, tangy and perfect with Beaujolais, and a modestly mild *reblochen*. Cree was somewhat saddened by the sight of all the relatively expensive food; it was apparent that Roland and Giselle had spent much more than they could afford. A shame, she thought at first, but soon recognized that it was a matter of pride. Roland knew that Wyatt had money, an unusual situation for an art student in Paris. But rather than look upon him with awe he probably appreciated the fact that Wyatt never flaunted his wealth, decided Cree. They lived frugally, and most of what they spent went for art supplies and food. This evening was Roland's chance to show his friend that the occasion was important to him and to Giselle. Instead of feeling sorry for them, Cree thought, she should relax and enjoy herself, like Wyatt.

Roland had taken him to his "studio" at the far end of the garret in front of one of the two windows. There his easel was set up, on it an almost completed sketch of an old man done in Hardtmuth pencil and colored pencils. In his lapel was the red rosette of the Legion of Honor. He wore a soiled, greasy-looking cap, his jacket was shabby, his self-respect seemed to have deserted him. His eyes were doleful, all but empty of feeling. His sagging shoulders and sunken chest reinforced the impression. He was plainly a hero of the past, fallen victim to the present. Cree and Giselle listened to Wyatt and Roland discussing the picture.

"I don't like it, because looking at him I got to feeling sorry for him and lost my objectivity," said Roland. "You're not entitled to pity anybody, no matter how pitiful they may be. It degrades you both."

"You're right," said Wyatt.

"I stumbled into a trap."

"But you draw what you see."

"Objectively, objectively. I can't do faces anyway."

"Better than I can."

"You can do anything. You and Picasso. I only do portraiture because old Simeon stays on my neck. I like landscape. You know who I really admire?"

"I can think of about a hundred names."

"Think of the greatest. Corot, Wyatt. A genius, the greatest of his century, the greatest landscape painter who ever lived. A giant. You've seen the *Cathedral of Chartres* in the Louvre. Tell me it isn't the greatest landscape ever painted."

"It's terrific, but I like the *Road of Sin-le-Noble* better."

"Careful, my friend, somebody will accuse you of having taste."

He threw his arm around Wyatt's shoulder affectionately.

"Roland thinks the world of him," Giselle said.

"You two make a lovely couple. You're beautiful, I envy you."

"Not me. My sister Julia's the family beauty."

"Is she in New York?"

"California."

"Are there just the two of you?"

"There's our older sister, Olivia. She was over here during the war. Her husband was with the American Second Division. I expect they're back in America now," she added wistfully.

"You miss her. Don't you keep in touch?"

Cree explained that the three of them had left their grandfather and none knew where the others were.

"It is hard living at home," said Giselle. "It was for me. I have nine brothers and two sisters. Hard and crowded."

"Twelve of you?"

"I *had* nine brothers. Edouard and Fernand were killed in the war." She ticked them off on her fingers. "Which leaves Marcel, Louis, Antoine, Adolphe, Raoul, Gustave, and Jacques. And Elizabeth and Marie."

"Where did you live?"

"Up north, a little bend in the road about ten kilometers from Carleville-Mezieres. Do you know the Ardennes?" Cree shook her head. "It's where the forest is, where two big battles were fought. The *Boche* massacred our soldiers in the first one, but in the second, the Battle of Meuse-Argonne, just before the end of the war, we won, with the help of the British and the Americans."

She was silent for a long moment, staring down at the stove and the heat waves rising from the pigeon pie. Then she brightened.

"You should see our village; you could tuck it in a

corner of St.-Germain-des-Prés. My father has a farm; why else have nine sons? We raise sugar beets. By the time I was twelve I couldn't stand the sight of them. Do you know what a sugar beet looks like?"

"No."

"It's the dullest-looking vegetable growing. Even homelier than the potato. See these hands? They have sketched a thousand sketches and pulled a hundred thousand sugar beets. Hey, Monet and Manet," she called to the men, "time to eat."

Cree found that she and Giselle had one thing in common. While Wyatt and Roland talked about Professor Lacroix and his behavior in class, every story concluding with loud guffaws, their wives discussed their common plight. Both had a little talent for drawing, but not enough to paint seriously. Giselle had left home as much to get away from the sugar beets as to study. But she had no confidence in herself, only in Roland. Cree felt the same way about her own limitations and Wyatt's potential. Wyatt had evidently told Roland of his father's death and the necessity for him to make a decision. Giselle was curious as to how serious he was and how far Cree thought he would go.

"I don't ever bring it up," whispered Cree, leaning close. "Let's talk about it later, okay?"

For all Armand Duprier's criticism of Lacroix and the Studio Gleyre, the little atelier had an impressive history.

"I never heard of Gleyre," said Wyatt. "Who was he?"

"A Swiss," said Roland. "Charles Gleyre. He came to Paris to teach drawing at the École des Beaux-Arts back in the eighteen-sixties. He didn't stay long. He opened his own studio and started teaching drawing at ten francs a month. All the aspiring artists were as broke back then as we are today, but in spite of the charge and the fact that the Beaux-Arts was free, soon some very familiar names followed Gleyre out the door —Renoir, Monet, Sisley, Bazille. Next time you're in drawing class, stop a moment, sit very still, and let the walls whisper to you. The ghosts of all the dead Impressionists will tell you stories."

"I keep running into coincidences," said Wyatt. "It's uncanny. First we land in Whistler's old studio. Then, out of all the schools in Paris, I end up at his, and in between I too walked out of the Beaux-Arts."

"You, Renoir, Monet. You wouldn't like it there. It's too tight. No fun. You have to have a few laughs in this life. At the Beaux-Arts you work in a mob and it's no nonsense. At the Studio Gleyre it's no sense." Roland laughed.

They finished every speck of food and emptied both bottles of wine. The wind continued to howl and punish the eaves; the chestnut trees in the courtyard threatened to split and cast off their boughs. Cree and Giselle did the dishes while the two men continued their one-track conversation.

"Is he serious?" asked Giselle, the moment they were out of earshot. "I'm sure he must be, to come all this way, but there is serious and serious. Take Roland. If he stopped painting for a week, I think he would die."

"Wyatt is trying it for a year. To find out if he's good enough."

"Roland says he's very good."

"He's very demanding of himself. I don't think he's painted a single thing that's really satisfied him. He always finds something wrong."

"Roland's the same. To be an artist and be satisfied with your work is fatal. Are you afraid he'll give it up after the year?"

"I don't know. I don't think so."

"What does he say?"

"He doesn't talk about it. Sometimes I try and tell myself he's forgotten all about it. Of course he hasn't; still, there are good signs. He loves it here. We both do. He loves the school. He's making friends. Giselle, I want him to go as far as he can, never mind one year. Whatever I can do to help, I'll do willingly."

"The same with me. What is the matter with us women? Where is it written down that we have to be the martyrs? Saint Giselle, Saint Lucretia."

They stayed until very late. Walking home, heads bowed to the wind and the slender shards of frozen rain pelting them, they talked about the Robays. Wyatt had sunk into a dreary mood.

"I pay five dollars a month tuition, the same as he does. To me it's like buying a candy bar. For him it's like giving a pint of blood. Especially this time of year. And yet did you see the feast they laid out? It must have cost her thirty, forty francs. They scare me."

"What do you mean?"

"If she got sick and was laid up for two or three weeks and couldn't work, they could starve to death."

"Wyatt . . ."

"It happens. Artists starve to death because they'd rather put their last centime into a brush or cadmium yellow than eat. Roland owns one suit—not even a suit, a pair of trousers and a jacket two sizes too big for him. No winter coat. He wears a scarf wrapped around his neck about ten times and a cap big enough so he can pull it down over his ears. It's a crime, Cree, he has real talent. He can draw ten times as well as I can, but between staying alive and buying supplies the two of them are wearing themselves out."

"Wyatt, they're young, they're healthy."

"I don't care, it's unfair. We have so much, and they don't have anything." They ducked into the metro entrance out of the cold. "You know what I wish? That something would happen. He couldn't get any sign-painting jobs, she got laid off for a time, and they couldn't come up with the rent, and their landlord threw them out. That way they could come and live with us. We have plenty of room. Mme. Boulette wouldn't care; if she squawked, I'd just slip her a few extra francs every quarter day."

"Do you think they'd want to live on your charity?"

"Cree, I'm living on my charity. We are. I haven't spent a dime I've earned since I worked behind the counter at Musselman's."

They resumed walking; the rain hurtled down from the sky, propelled by the wind.

"It all has to do with the distribution of wealth in the world. It's not even distributed, it's just a few people grabbing the lion's share. It stinks. Maybe that's why I always hated Economics."

"Maybe that's why you'd never make it in business."

"You're probably right," he said with a cheerful grin.

Chapter Sixteen

In Paris it is said that the month of March behaves as it does out of frustration, because it is incapable of deciding whether to carry on with winter or banish it and begin to warm the world in preparation for spring. By the time it solves this perennial problem, it is April.

Cree was at home one afternoon, sketching. The breeze blustered about the garden, playing with the last of the leaves. Clouds raced down a slate sky. Three more days, and it would be April, their first April in Paris.

Wyatt came bursting in.

"Cree . . ."

He stood loosening his scarf, his cheeks ruby, his eyes watery from the cold. She had never seen him so excited.

"Wyatt, what is it?"

"Where's the checkbook?"

"Where it usually is, in the night-table drawer. Why?"

He ran into the bedroom. She could hear him opening and closing drawers.

"It's not," he called. "I know, in my *tabouret*."

He came dashing out and into the studio. She stood in the doorway watching him.

"Here it is. I stuck it here last time I bought supplies."

"Wyatt, what's going on?"

"Darling, I found a Cranach in a little antique shop on Rue Lafayette. Roland and I were browsing, poking through this and that. I turned over a bunch of prints, and there it was. Can you imagine, a genuine Cranach!"

"Are you sure it's genuine?"

"It's signed, Cree. The frame covers most of the signature, but you can make it out. It's one of his early things, very early, a crucifixion. He did dozens. Roland's there keeping an eye on it for me."

"Just because it's signed doesn't make it genuine."

"It is, and the fellow who owns the place is only asking ten thousand."

"Francs or dollars?"

"Francs! It's a steal!"

"If it's not a forgery."

"It's not. Every once in a while gems like this pop up. It's probably been hiding in somebody's attic for a hundred years."

"Two thousand dollars is a lot of money."

"For a Cranach? One of his sketches would be worth twice that, let alone a painting. Cree, it could be worth fifty thousand dollars, seventy-five."

"Why is he selling it for two thousand?"

"He's not an art dealer, he doesn't know its value. He wants payment by note drawn on the Bank of France. We can get one at our bank. Get your coat on. We've got to get there before it closes."

The Banque Nationale de Paris was located at 37 Avenue Champs Élysées. Their taxi pulled up, and Cree paid the driver while Wyatt leaped out and raced to the door, wedging himself inside and holding it for her under the glare of the guard, who had been two seconds too slow to close it.

The guard muttered as Cree squeezed past him. The teller was just as annoyed. He kept looking up at the clock every few seconds, his way of mutely upbraiding them, as he made out the note in the amount of ten thousand francs.

Back outside, Wyatt hailed another taxi, directing the driver to 115 Rue Lafayette. Ironically, the antique shop was located next door to an art dealer: Art Ancien—Paul Chamborn. It seemed strange that a genuine Cranach was destined to be found by an art student only one door away from an expert.

"*Bonjour encore,*" the storekeeper said to Wyatt, saluting him.

"*Bonjour. Apportez-le nous.*"

The man rubbed his fingers together. Wyatt produced the bank note. Cree caught his arm as he was about to hand it to the storekeeper.

"*Un instant,*" she said, and asked the shopkeeper if he was prepared to authenticate the Cranach in writing.

"*Certificat d'authenticité, s'il vous plaît.*"

He shook his head. "*Je suis désolé.*" He couldn't do it, he explained. He was no art expert. It was clearly a case of take it or leave it. Cree was inclined toward the latter and said so to Wyatt.

"But it's genuine," he insisted.

The man produced the painting from under the counter. Wyatt held it up to the front window; the rays of the setting sun brought the colors to life. It was lovely and it appeared genuine, but without x-raying it, how could they be certain? She'd read about forgeries —what art student hadn't?—but she was no expert, nor was Wyatt or Roland. Wyatt was beginning to lose patience, especially since Roland wholeheartedly agreed that the painting was authentic.

"It's Cranach's signature," said Roland.

She began to argue with them. The shopkeeper stood with his hands on the counter looking from Wyatt to Roland to her. Finally she threw up her hands.

"Pay him." She wandered over to a pair of dusty imitation Louis XV wall sconces and a broken set of small terra-cotta portraits laid out on a table, dutifully ignoring the transaction behind her. Picking up one of the portraits, she examined it briefly, put it down, and turned around. The shopkeeper was wrapping the painting in brown paper, tying it with a piece of knotted cord. The bank note lay on the counter in front of him. It was all too easy, an unbelievable bargain, she thought, as Wyatt and Roland said good-bye and the three of them left. But it was all over; there was no point in any further discussion.

Wyatt seemed almost disappointed that she had nothing more to say about it. They walked down the Rue Lafayette, Cree watching traffic, looking for a taxi to take them back across the river.

"Sweetheart, it's authentic. You can tell by the paints he used, the canvas."

"You know better than I that paints and canvas can be aged. Styles can be copied, any style. The world is overrun with forgers. Counterfeit Old Masters hang in the Louvre, in just about every museum in the world," she said.

Roland nodded. "Cranach himself made a copy of Hieronymus Bosch's triptych of *The Last Judgement*," he said, drawing a quick scowl from Wyatt and hastily adding, "but I really think this is genuine."

"You think, but you don't know. It's your money, Wyatt, I won't say anything more about it."

"You could show it to Simeon," suggested Roland. "He could get it x-rayed."

"Isn't it a little late?" asked Cree drily.

"You don't think he'd let us take it out and have it x-rayed?" snapped Wyatt. "Maybe I am taking a chance. Hey, how about if we call Professor Lacroix and ask him to supper tonight? He can examine it."

"If you want to. Roland, you and Giselle come too, please."

Roland's hand slapped against his heart, momentarily caving in his narrow chest. "For a second I thought you weren't going to ask us."

Cree had not seen Professor Lacroix since Wyatt had introduced them the day before he'd started school, nearly two months before. In that interval the professor had not only not aged, but actually appeared to have grown younger, as if he'd found and was frequenting a fountain of youth. He was the most sprightly old man she had ever met. Coming in, he flung off his cape and hat, twisted the ends of his preposterous mustache to make certain they were in balance and, seizing her hands, kissed them loudly.

"Good evening, madame, good evening, good evening. It has been ages. You look positively radiant." He looked about. "So this is the famous Studio Chance? I have heard so much about it. Impressive, very. And what is for dinner?"

Wyatt and Roland laughed, and Giselle, coming out of the kitchen, rolled her eyes.

"Blanquette of veal with calvados, carrots, and strawberries Melba, and a Médoc Bordeaux."

"That is not dinner, that is a banquet. Except for the wine. Médoc Bordeauxs are uniformly watery, tasteless. The most impoverished of grapes. Cleverly anticipating such an eventuality . . . *voilà!*" Out of his back pocket he pulled a bottle of white wine. "Su-duiraut. Delicious."

Cree and Giselle worked at the sink and sideboard preparing dinner while Wyatt brought out the Cranach, and set it against a stack of three books on the table directly under the light. Professor Lacroix put on his pince-nez and proceeded to study the picture. From his inside pocket he brought out a magnifying glass and, properly adjusting his glasses, peered through it. The women stopped working and watched Wyatt and Roland lean over, both hypnotized by the painting, Wyatt holding his breath.

"The canvas is very old," said Lacroix. "But canvas is old in fifty years—less. The synthetic paints Prussian blue and Chinese white were not even introduced until the eighteenth century; synthetic ultramarine, cobalt blue, and cadmium yellow came in in the nineteenth. Yes, yes, it looks like a fifteenth-century canvas, and the brushstrokes do resemble Cranach's. The way a man lays his paint on is almost like a fingerprint."

He paused and straightened.

"There are four general tests for any work of art. First, style. Did the artist paint in such a style? Does the painting show his personality and the characteristics of his other works? Then content. Is everything in the painting in harmony with its time? Are there departures from that harmony? The other two tests, provenance, the history of ownership, history of exhibition, and documentation of the work is unavailable, of course."

"Other *two* tests?"

"Yes, the technological tests, scientific examination. An x-ray. That is the acid test. It shows up the characteristics of a covered image, if there is one, the painter's change in the positioning of a head, the removal or repositioning of an object, hidden changes, how many different hands worked on the painting, many things. If you wish, I can take it to my friend Étienne Tresicq and have it x-rayed." He smiled warmly, tilting his head from side to side. "It is possible I am being premature, but in my judgment, Mr. Chance, you have bought yourself an authentic Cranach."

Everyone cheered except Wyatt. A wave of relief passed over him. He glanced at Cree with I-told-you-so in his eyes.

"For how much did you say?"

"Ten thousand francs."

"Amazing. It could easily be worth twenty times that. Not being a dealer, I don't know prices. You found it in an antique shop, you say?"

"On the Rue Lafayette."

"Professor," interrupted Cree, "will you tell me something? Why would anybody sell a genuine Cranach for a fraction of its value? Certainly not out of stupidity or ignorance."

"Sometimes. There is another possible explanation." He looked at Wyatt, his expression apologetic. "It could have been stolen."

Wyatt winced. His eyes and Roland's met. "We never thought of that, did we?"

"Of course not," said the professor. "You thought, three cheers, I am now the proud owner of a Cranach crucifixion."

"Do you know of any Cranachs that have been stolen?" asked Roland.

"Not in Paris, but it's hard to say. There are robberies you never hear about unless you're a dealer. It need not have been stolen. I only say it's possible. It could have been lying in somebody's cedar chest for ages or in a frame behind a picture of their great-grand-father. I will speak to a dealer I know, have him look over his lists. If a Cranach crucifixion shows up on one of them, well . . ."

"When can you find out?" asked Wyatt.

"Not tonight. Tonight is dinner, tomorrow is for Lucas Cranach."

Cree ran to the stove. The veal was slightly over-done, but not so that anyone with an appetite would have refused it. The dinner and the evening were enjoy-able. Teacher and students smoked cigars and sipped brandy around the table while Cree and Giselle washed the dishes and left them for Wyatt and Roland to dry.

Professor Lacroix got up from the table and called to Cree.

Mme. Chance, when you are done, may I prevail upon you to show me the studio?"

"Of course. I'm done."

Inside the studio he closed the door behind them. Cree's face fell.

"It's a fake, isn't it?"

"No, no, no, at least, I don't think so. That's not what I wanted to talk about." He nodded toward the closed door. "He's working very hard."

"He tells me he finds it hard. He's becoming pes-simistic about his progress."

"So I've noticed. He's a smiler and lately he doesn't smile so much."

"Is he right to be pessimistic?"

"Of course."

She stiffened. "I see."

"That way he won't become overconfident. Forgive me, I shouldn't treat such a serious subject so lightly. .

He finds it hard because it i hard. He is going through a period of harsh self-evaluation, but he will come out of it—they all do—and before long sink into another one, perhaps even deeper. It's all part of the battle; he is making progress. He's talented and he's intelligent. And just as important, he's responsive to instruction. You would be surprised at how many are gifted but fail to progress because they are incapable of breaking old habits or too sure of themselves, unwilling to listen and learn, even too stupid to learn. But you need have no worry about him. He and Robays have a bright future. Both should go very far." He smiled benignly. "I hope I live to see their success. It will be my success, too."

He wandered about the studo, picking up paintings and sketches, examining them, commenting on the studio, the east window. It was evident to Cree from their conversation that he was unaware of the circumstances that had brought her and Wyatt to Paris. She was tempted to tell him, eager to point out that Wyatt did not have to paint to survive, that he was doing it out of a love for painting. But she said nothing; it would sound like bragging, it was unnecessary. It was just that she was proud that he could work as hard as the poorest student, as if his whole life depended on it. And perhaps it did.

At the end of the evening, as their guests were about to leave, Cree took Giselle aside.

"Do you know a good doctor?" she whispered.

"Dr. Chabot in Rue St. André-des-Arts, just up from the corner of Rue Dauphine. He's old and can bore you to distraction, and his office looks like a windstorm struck it, but he's an excellent doctor, bright, conscientious. Aren't you feeling well?"

"I think I'm pregnant."

"Cree!"

"Ssssh. My breasts hurt, and in the morning . . ." She touched her stomach and made a face.

Roland leaned in at the door. "Are you staying?"

"Just a second," said Giselle. "Cree, call me after he sees you."

"I haven't said anything to Wyatt. I don't want to until I see a doctor. Don't tell Roland."

"I won't." A smile brightened her face. "You do want a baby? Or don't you?"

"I do, and I think he will. We've never talked about having children. It sounds strange when you think about it, but for us it just seemed like something we could put off for a while, at least until this year is up and he decides if we're staying or going back. But I do want a baby. It would make us complete, a family."

"I think it's wonderful. Some day Roland and I will have dozens of children. Now it would be very hard, but for you two . . ."

"Giselle!" called Roland.

"Remember, call me as soon as you find out."

"Bon soir," Cree said, giving a warm hug.

She was pregnant. Dr. Chabot confirmed it. He was as Giselle had described him, overweight, a confirmed droner who chuckled at his own jokes. Giselle's comment on his office was an understatement. The place was an absolute disaster, not dirty, but incredibly untidy, folders piled on the desk and on the floor, records and patient files in total disarray, practically every inch of space taken up by furnishings or equipment. It made Cree think of their room in the house on Bristol Street in New Haven.

The baby would arrive the first week in November.

Dr. Chabot was required by law to take down certain information. When he inquired what her husband did for a living and she told him that he was studying to be a painter, he laid his pen down and rolled his head on his neck, as if to relieve stiffness, then pointedly asked if they could afford another mouth to feed. She assured him that they could and left, with instructions to return in two weeks for a check-up. He gave her pills for morning sickness and a prescription for more if she needed them.

She shopped for an hour or so and did not get home until late in the afternoon. She called Giselle at the art shop and told her the news. Wyatt came in moments after she had hung up the phone. He kissed her; taking him by the hand, she led him to the settee.

"What's up?" he asked.

"How was school?"

"The same. Hey, remember Roland's sketch of the old soldier? He brought it in. Simeon liked it and sent him out the door to see what he could get for it. He went across the river and offered it for fifty francs to the big dealers. Then he went back to the left bank and offered it for fifty and forty, then back to the right bank for forty and thirty, then back for thirty and twenty. He finally got seventeen for it from an old woman in Place St. Michel. She just stopped him, asked him where he was going with it, and bought it from under his arm. Cree, you're not listening. Why are we sitting down?"

"Because I love you."

"I love you, too."

"Guess what?"

"What?" His face burst burst into joy. "You heard from Professor Lacroix about the painting! His friend who is x-raying it was going to get back to him after four. We know it wasn't stolen, it's not on any dealer's list . . ."

"No, no. Wyatt, we're going to have a baby."

He froze, his mouth open. Slowly his jaw dropped. "We . . ."

"A baby. I went to Giselle's doctor today."

"A baby!"

"In November."

He threw his arms around her. "Cree, Cree, Cree, that's wonderful! Tremendous!"

"That's a relief, I thought you might be upset."

"Are you kidding? It's beautiful, you're beautiful, the world's beautiful."

He kissed her lovingly; she clung to him, her head against his chest.

"My husband, my love. How you've changed."

He straightened, holding her at arm's length. "Oh?"

"No more raccoon coat, joyriding, party-party, no more live for today. You've become a man, darling, a husband. Now you're going to be a father."

"I guess I have grown up in some ways. Maybe it was getting married, that and what happened to Dad, and all of a sudden I'm the man in the family." He grinned, then became serious, infusing his voice with tenderness. "But you're the main cause; because you grew up. I didn't have any choice but to."

"How have I changed?"

He laughed. "For one thing, you don't read all those mushy romances anymore—*Carolyn of the Corners*, *Love's Greatest Mistake*."

"Every girl reads romantic novels until the real thing comes along." She pecked him on the cheek. "How else have I changed?"

"When we were first married you couldn't boil water, now you're a good cook."

"You could say excellent."

"You're sure getting there; the veal last night was a little overcooked, but that was Lucas Cranach's fault. You never shopped for food, never cleaned house, never got down on your knees and scrubbed a floor in your life. What poor little rich girl has?"

"I'm not talking about that, I mean my personality."

"The wide-eyed, naive, and oh-so-cloistered schoolgirl disappeared and a woman took her place." He stroked her hair and made love to her with his eyes. "We've both grown up. We don't get lost in the dark anymore. We know our way by heart, isn't that so?"

She nodded.

"I love you, my darling," he said. "I love you, love you, love you, love you, love you, love you, love you."

She stopped his mouth with a kiss, then drew back. "Practice what you preach, mister."

He kissed her eyes, her cheeks, and the arc of her neck from one earlobe to the other. And her lips, warm and willingly given. The phone shrilled. He groaned. Again it rang and a third time. He picked it up.

"Yes? Oh, Professor . . . That's great! Whatever it cost, I'll give you the cash. Right, and thanks again, thank you. Good-bye."

He hung up and immediately began to cough, a hacking sound from deep in his chest.

"Darling . . ."

She ran and got him a glass of water. He downed it and stopped coughing, but his cheeks were crimson from the effort. She felt his forehead.

"You have a fever. How long have you been coughing?"

"Just the last couple hours."

"I'm not surprised, running around with your jacket unbuttoned, your scarf loose. Half the city's down with colds and flu, and you carry on like you're immune. You're not, you know." Again she felt his forehead. "You're sweating. I want you to take aspirin, take a nice hot bath, and get right into bed."

"I'm all right."

Obviously he was not all right. He took the aspirin, but stubbornly refused the hot bath and bed. They had leftover blanquette of veal, vegetables, and a salad for supper; he had little appetite, pushing his food about his plate, smothering his cough in his napkin. She made him drink cup after cup of tea with lemon, but his cough refused to be quelled, and, she noted, he was sweating more profusely and losing his color, his cheeks taking on a waxen look.

"I'm calling the doctor," she said.

"I don't need any doctor. Let's just go to bed."

He coughed during the night. She put an extra blanket over him, doubling it in hopes he might sweat the culprit out of his system, but in the morning he was worse. He complained of feeling exhausted, and his fever lingered. His nose ran and his throat was raw.

"Wyatt, I'm calling Dr. Chabot."

"Why bother? I'll just stay in bed for a couple of hours."

Two hours later he was much worse, in spite of more aspirin and hot tea. Chabot came shortly after ten o'clock, his necktie askew, his stethoscope protruding from his bag. He slipped it around his neck. Cree stood in the bedroom doorway while he took the patient's temperature and examined his throat with a tongue depressor.

Getting up from the edge of the bed, he said, "Where is your telephone?"

He saw it before she could answer. He dialed.

"Jacques Chabot, oui. La grippe." Turning his back to them, he added something of which Cree could distinguish only one word: *ambulance*. He hung up.

"An ambulance will be coming shortly," he said, looking from one to the other. "You're going straight to the hospital."

"For a lousy cold?" Wyatt was annoyed.

"I say it's influenza. It comes on very fast." He gestured. "Witness. Very soon now the other symptoms will follow: aching in your back and legs, fever rising, coughing up more and more sputum. If we don't get you into the hospital, it could turn into pneumonia. Pneumonia can kill. People are dying all over the city. You start spitting up blood, your nose bleeds uncontrollably, your skin begins turning blue. No arguments, please, we must get your fever down and keep it there. And the best place for that, the place for you to be so your wife doesn't catch it, is the hospital. Before it gets any worse and it becomes dangerous to move you."

Chapter Seventeen

An ambulance arrived at 110 Rue du Bac, the familiar military olive drab in color with a large red cross on white painted on each side. Wyatt was taken to Hôpital St. Louis on the other side of the Seine in *arrondissement* St. Laurent. The hospital commanded the north end of Avenue Parmentier. Its main building was huge, the facade scarred and neglected-looking, with windows boarded up here and there and sections of the roof in want of repair. The interior had not been painted since the turn of the century; the walls were laced with cracks and discolored with water stains. The corridors were poorly lit, and doctors and nurses moved about like weary automatons. Only the marble floor, recently polished and smelling of wax, offered respite from the dreariness.

Wyatt was assigned to a bed in Ward 6 in the west wing on the third floor. Dr. Chabot introduced him to Sister Phillipa, who would be looking after him. Sister Phillipa spoke some English with a slight lisp. She went about her work with relentless energy.

There were forty beds in the ward, three of them concealed by screens. Dr. Chabot told Cree that screens indicated that the patient was dying, and if nothing else, his departure would be in privacy. A large crucifix adorned the otherwise bare wall over Wyatt's head.

They still have many *poilus* here," said Dr. Chabot to Wyatt and Cree, looking about. "Some casualties, but mostly flu victims. So you're in good company, M. Chance. I must be on my way now. Sister Phillipa will take excellent care of you. Take your medicine, stay in bed, and cooperate, and you'll be out of here in ten days."

"Ten days!"

"Perhaps a week."

Wyatt's response was a scowl.

"I'll look in on you this evening, if I can get away from the office at a reasonable hour."

Chabot took Cree by the arm and walked her to the door.

"He's annoyed because he'll be missing school," she said.

Chabot nodded. "The artist burning to create, eh? I'm afraid we must let the fires simmer for a couple of days. Maybe the day after tomorrow you can bring in his sketch pad, when his fever gets down to normal and his throat clears up. He's much better off here. You, too. It's highly contagious; in your condition you must stay healthy."

Cree went to the hospital early the next morning. She was the first visitor in the ward after the examining team made its rounds. She brought a letter from Dink Ramsey, and she sat at Wyatt's bedside as he opened the letter and read it aloud.

Hi, Sec:

Boola boola! Got your gay Paree address from old Eli's dauber-in-chief, your friend Ransom

Colclough. Expect you're b.z. dashing off Old Masters by the dozen. Every time Dean Jones calls me on the well-known carpet, I stand in front of his desk and look up at your painting of Wrexham Tower and wonder why it took you so long to come to your senses. I'm sure the little lady had oodles to do with it. Speaking of the fair sex, Ginger and I have said our official ta-ta's. She gets all hot and bothered when I keep ducking her lasso, and I get all h. and b. when she throws it. Finally got really piffled and told her to go pound sand. Met a curvy little sophomore from Barnard in N'Yawk last weekend, a real live wire. Her pater's in coal or something. Family's got more do-re-mi than Rockefeller.

Well, Sec, the old corneas are starting to glaze over. We party-partied until the wee small hours last night. I got gassed as usual, and this morning my head feels like the Sousa band is marching around inside. No real dirt to shovel your way anywho, although there's a rumor that Brother Beta is shortly to become a papa, without the jingle of wedding bells. Stand by for further reports. School is still as fascinating as a funeral, I'll tell the cockeyed world. Can't wait to get out of here for good. You don't know how lucky you are being over there with all those curvy mamselles. Oo-la-la! Whoops, hope Cree doesn't read this.

The brothers all send their chercest regards. Write if you can. Ta-ta for now. Ouch, my head feels like the *Stars and Stripes Forever* fortissy-mo!

Yours in pain,
Dink

"Same old Dink," said Wyatt. "Did I really talk like that?"

"Sometimes."

"It seems a hundred years ago, doesn't it?"

"A lot has happened since. Tell Mother the truth, how are you feeling?" She took hold of his hand. "You're getting your color back. How's your throat?"

"Better. I ate breakfast."

They talked and talked and had lunch together, then Cree read while Wyatt napped.

Roland and Giselle came to visit late in the afternoon, after Giselle got off work. In the days that followed, other students dropped by. Professor Lacroix brought Wyatt a book on forgeries. First he read it, then Cree. She decided that her education at Miss Barclay's and Fairview in Art Appreciation and Art History had disregarded some of the more interesting aspects of the business side of art. The book dealt chiefly with counterfeiting in many of its more bizarre manifestations, but there were two chapters devoted to appraising authentic works of art, which artists fetched the highest prices, and why. She decided that in the future she would read everything she could find on forgeries and appraising. She would thus be better able to advise Wyatt on any "finds" he might come across.

He improved steadily after getting over his sore throat. Being confined to a hospital bed was good for him, Cree told him; if he'd stayed home to recover, he would probably have been in and out of bed for the next six months. Why some people thought they were indestructible was beyond her understanding.

At the end of the week Wyatt was discharged. As he was paying his bill at the cashier's counter just inside the main entrance, Dr. Chabot, who had dropped by to sign the release, took Cree aside and whispered to her.

"You see, we were right to get him in here. It's always easier to avoid complications than treat them. Pneumonia can be vicious."

His words lingered in her thoughts and affected her appetite at Wyatt's welcome-home dinner that night. Roland and Giselle and two other couples came to the apartment to celebrate the patient's recovery. Wyatt sensibly did not overdo it. The party was loud and enjoyable but broke up very early.

Spring arrived in Paris on the golden wings of the sun, erasing the grayness, banishing the chill, stilling the winds, bringing the city to life. Under the sightless gaze of the gargoyles of Nôtre Dame, leaf buds sprouted and brought shade to streets, gardens, and parks. Horse-chestnut candelabra lightened the masses of glistening green along the boulevards. Like beggars seeking alms, legions of tulips raised their crimson cups in a thousand places. Overnight the parks and gardens became host to hordes of children, laughing and shouting happily with hoops, skipping ropes, and balls of all colors and sizes.

Along the boulevards the warming braziers around which people had clustered all winter gave way to green tubs of pink hydrangeas. Along the Seine ragged laborers stripped to their waists for their first sunbath, and vagrants along the quays lay for hours on the warm stone stairways, dismissing the dreary discomforts of winter from their minds. Toy boats appeared in the fountains and pools, their sails as white as the winged caps of nuns. In the Tuileries Gardens bees droned and disported themselves, tiny yellow flashes weaving an invisible tapestry in the air. Under the trees the statues, suddenly outnumbered by people, stood robed in shadows ragged with sunshine. The lilacs filled the air with fragrance, and the jessamine struggled to compete.

Paris seemed to be the wellspring of the season, whence it spread over Europe and the world. Cree welcomed the warmth and wonder, especially because Wyatt's cough returned occasionally, and she hoped the sun would banish the last, lingering effects of his disease. Dr. Chabot gave him a syrupy concoction that Wyatt insisted tasted like rotten raspberries. She had to remind him continually to take it. Apart from his cough, however, his health was excellent. Although she still suffered from morning sickness, she felt well otherwise.

Wyatt continued to work much too hard, in her opinion, but she did not badger him about it. She could see the improvement. He did a nude of her sitting by a candle, her chin resting on her palm, her mood pensive. It was after *Mary Magdalen with Oil Lamp* by Georges de La Tour, he declared. It was original as far as she was concerned, despite the similarity in the interplay of light and shadow. It turned out to be the first of his nudes that Professor Lacroix openly praised as "anatomically faultless."

They received a long, newsy letter from Marjorie, painting bright pictures of the state of the business, her health, her life in general. She tried to give the impression that she was happy, at least content, but the letter conveyed a wistful resignation throughout that no amount of cheerfulness could conceal. She was lonely. They telephoned her.

"Mother?"

"Wyatt, where are you?"

"In Paris, of course. We got your last letter. We're glad to see you don't mind being a grandmother."

"Mind? I'm looking forward to it."

"How are you?"

"Fine. How are Lucretia and the baby?"

"Both fine." He laughed.

They talked, and she asked to speak to Cree.

Wyatt handed her the phone. "Ask her."

She nodded.

"Marjorie?"

"Lucretia, what a happy surprise this is. How are you? Is he taking good care of you?"

"Best husband in the world."

"Good Lord, don't let him hear you say that. You're feeling well?"

"Very much like an expectant mother, especially when I get up. Marjorie, we want you to come over to visit us. We've plenty of room, you'll love it here, you could use a vacation. Please."

Tempted, Marjorie nevertheless hesitated to accept the invitation.

"She wants to think about it," said Cree to Wyatt.

He took the phone back. "Don't think—just pack your bags."

"All right, I'll come. Yes, I will. But I can't stay long."

"You won't want to leave."

"I miss you two so. I've so much to tell you."

"When can you come?"

"I'll have to make arrangements."

"Start as soon as you hang up. Send us a cablegram, and we'll be there to meet your ship. You don't have to come by way of Southampton anymore, you can go straight to Calais. Have Charles Crowder's office check into it for you. We'll meet you in Calais and take the train back down here. Better yet, I'll rent a car."

"Oh, Wyatt, this is so exciting! I can't wait to see you."

They talked another minute, then said good-bye.

"It'll be good for her to get away from New York," he said.

"She'll stay here, of course, but we can't make her sleep on the settee. We do need another bed, anyway. We never really use the sitting room. We could convert it into a guest room. She'll love the sun shining through the glass door to the garden."

Now that the weather was balmy, Cree spent hours in the garden reading under the catalpa trees. Tubular white flowers splashed with purple and yellow were beginning to bloom. Beyond the trees at the end of the winding gravel walk was a stone wall, on the other side of which was the Séminaire des Missions Étrangères. Bells pealed mornings and evenings, and at dusk the choir could be heard.

"I hope she'll be comfortable here. I hope she likes Paris," he said.

"She will. Not to change the subject, did you take your medicine?"

"Please, I can't stand the taste. I think it's gone rancid."

"Don't be a boob, all medicine tastes bad. If it tasted good, it'd be useless. Take it, don't be such a child."

"Why not? It's fun." He laughed and slapped her on the bottom and ran into the sitting room and out the glass door to the garden. She followed, catching up to him by the trees, circling the largest one, catching him by the sleeve, embracing, kissing. . . .

They didn't hear from Marjorie for almost three weeks. On May 6, a dismal drizzly Tuesday morning, Wyatt was at work in the studio when the knocker sounded. Cree answered it; a uniformed messenger handed her a cablegram.

It was from Marjorie. Cree went into the studio, reading as she walked.

"She's coming on the *Aquitaine*. She's at sea now, due to arrive in Calais on the ninth at eleven o'clock."

"That's this Friday. I'd better see about getting a car."

"I've been thinking about that. It must be three hundred fifty miles round trip. It'll take at least ten hours, and you'll be exhausted."

"We made it up and back to New Hampshire, didn't we? That was closer to four hundred."

"With you and Dink taking turns driving. Why don't we take the train?"

He shrugged. "Whatever you say. I was just thinking of all the luggage. I do wish you'd stop babying me."

"If you took better care of yourself, I wouldn't have to. Did you remember to take your . . ."

"Yes, yes, yes. Come over here, I want to show you something."

On his easel was a sketch of the boy who sold bread on the sidewalk in front of the Bon Marché at the corner. It was almost completed, with only the details of the market in the background yet to be added. At first glance she was struck by the way Wyatt had captured the stoicism in the boy's face, the distinctly unchildlike look, along with the sensitivity of his eyes. He seemed profoundly aware of his lot in life. Cree had never seen him do anything but stand and sell from early morning until dusk every day. He never seemed to have time to play. And yet his expression was that of one who, unlike Roland Robays's old-soldier-turned-defeatist, had not yet resigned himself to his lot and was not about to. His narrow shoulders were squared, his small chin thrust outward; his self-confidence showed through his shabbiness.

"You've captured him; the eyes are magnificent for just pencil. When are you going to paint him?"

"Starting now. I gave him five francs to pose. I'm going to have to get him back, although I don't think his father would let him leave his post. I'll have to work in the street." He laughed.

"Has Professor Lacroix seen this?"

"I told him about it. Cree, I want to submit it to the Salon Exhibition at the end of the month. It's the most prestigious show of the year. I might as well start at the top, right?"

"Your first exhibition."

"Maybe my last."

"Don't be pessimistic."

"Roland's submitting a landscape, of course. It's amazing, everything he does is so good."

"So are you."

"Who knows? Even if I do turn out something half-way decent, even a few things, who knows if I'll get any recognition? I remember back at Yale Ransom Colclough telling us about Van Gogh. Did you know that in his whole lifetime he only sold one painting? To another artist, a woman named Anna Bock, from Brussels. She gave him four hundred measly francs for it. Outside of her, his brother, and a handful of friends he never got a glimmer of recognition. He was a genius, Cree, an incredible talent, but he had to die before anybody knew he was alive. All I want is recognition, to know that you and I aren't the only ones who like what I do."

"What about Professor Lacroix, Roland, your other friends? Wyatt, you're just starting."

"Sometimes I feel like I've been at it a hundred years. Funny, it was always easy until now, no sweating, no straining. Everything I do lately is hard labor. I never dreamed it would be this difficult."

"You go at it much too hard. Sometimes I watch you painting, the look on your face, it's as though you're fighting the canvas."

"No, only myself, my weaknesses, my mistakes."

"How do you feel about yourself now, after ten weeks at the studio? How do you rate yourself against the competition there? Do you think you have what it takes?"

"It's too soon to tell."

She could see in his eyes that he was avoiding a direct answer. Plainly he was refusing to commit himself.

"Are you further along than you thought you'd be? Or not as far?"

"I seem to be making progress. I'm encouraged. Professor Lacroix says nice things."

"Do you think he's being honest or kind?"

"Honest. I think I see what you're getting at."

"What?"

"*The* question. Come December, do we stay or go home?"

"Well?"

He waited a long time before answering, turning toward the east window, folding his arms, and looking out at the houses packed so closely they appeared to be joined, a single sprawling structure, rising to the rain-grayed sky, their chimney pots nudging it.

"I want to stay," he said, in an inflection that hinted there was more to follow.

"So do I."

"If we can."

"What's to prevent us?"

He faced her. "You know as well as I—the company, Mother. The ogre responsibility. It never goes away, does it?"

"What about your responsibility to yourself?"

He gestured, dismissing this. She knew intuitively that he wanted to stay. To leave, to give it up, would be so painful. He was into it now, adjusted to it, living it, loving it. They had talked long enough, she decided. Let Paris and his talent work on him. Both were much more persuasive than she could ever be.

"How old is he?" she asked, nodding toward the drawing.

"Nine."

"He looks like an old man. It's his eyes and the way he frowns."

"You should have seen his eyes when I gave him the five francs. They looked as if sparks were coming out of them. Seriously, what do you think?"

"I told you, I like it."

"You didn't say you liked it, you said that you like his eyes."

"Don't be a boob, I love it."

"Why am I asking you? You love everything, you're prejudiced, you have no objectivity whatsoever."

"Have it your way, then. I hate it."

"I'm not going to finish the background. I just want to get at it."

"Okay, I'll go down to the Bon Marché and see if I can find something for dinner."

She kissed him good-bye, put on her raincoat, took an umbrella, and went out. The rain was beginning to let up, the sky losing its bleak and bleary aspect. Soon now the sun would appear and set the city gleaming. Moving down the tunnel to the gate, she thought back to late January and their arrival, strangers in a strange city that was no longer strange. It had taken them in, opening its heart to them. Out of the vinegar scowl of winter into the bright smile of spring they had come, falling in love with Paris along the way. They would be staying; they would never leave.

Not for as long as they lived.

Chapter Eighteen

Marjorie arrived in a green tweed gaiter-suit and out-rageously wide-brimmed hat trimmed with monkey fur, her eighteen pieces of luggage all but filling the com-partment on the train ride down from Calais and requir-ing a second taxi to follow theirs as they drove from Gare du Nord to St.-Germain-des-Prés and the apart-ment.

The crossing had been mercilessly slow, "as if we were moving uphill all the way! Calm, uneventful, and tedious beyond belief. How many gulls can a person count?" she said with her wonderfully youthful laugh.

She came sailing into the apartment, slipping her gloves off, stopping, turning full circle, taking in every-thing.

"It's adorable. So bright and cozy. Soooooo French!" She introduced herself to Heloise and Abelard, who acknowledged her appearance with brief curious stares. While Wyatt and the driver of the second taxi carried in the bags, Cree produced a cold bottle of Ayala reserved for the occasion and popped the cork. Wyatt paid the man and graciously toasted the guest of honor.

"You look thinner," said Marjorie worriedly. "Are you sure you're all over the flu?"

"Definitely."

187

"Is he?" she asked Cree.

"I am, I am."

"You still look thinner. And pale. Doesn't he, Lucretia? This is delicious, I love *brut*." Marjorie sipped, set her glass down, and sighed exaggeratedly. "Well, Paris, here I am. Let me just get my breath, and I'm all yours. Talking is so exhausting."

Wyatt laughed. "The way you do it. You haven't stopped since Calais."

"You be quiet." Cree refilled her glass. "I love this . . ."

"Ayala."

"But no more, I'll get dizzy. I want to see your studio, Wyatt, and that delightful little garden we passed coming in. I want to see everything."

"Stay right where you are, we'll start with the *pièce de résistance*."

Marjorie questioned Cree with her eyes as he vanished into the studio and came back at once holding a painting under a cloth. With a wide sweep of his arm, off came the cover.

"Da-daaaaaa! Herr Lucas Cranach, permit me to introduce Marjorie Chance."

"How lovely! It's very old, isn't it?"

"About four hundred years. It's an original Cranach, Mother. He's a very famous German painter. Contemporary of Dürer's." He explained how he had found the painting, then he took the front page of the day's edition of *Le Figaro*, rolled it into a cone and, using it as a megaphone, walked her about the studio. Marjorie was impressed, murmuring compliments. She seemed almost awed, decided Cree, especially taken by the half-completed painting of the baker's boy.

On the train coming down from Calais she had plied

the two of them with questions, about Wyatt's health, the studio Gleyre, Paris, and every conceivable aspect of their lives. Now Wyatt took the initiative.

"How's the business going?" he asked. "Still in the black?"

"Oh, yes. I brought along last year's fourth quarterly report and the first quarter of this year's. So you don't have to take my word for it. Lucretia . . ." Marjorie glanced at her appealingly.

"Let me guess," said Cree. "You'd like to take a bath."

"I'd love to." She laughed. "Charles's secretary must have gotten me the last available cabin. It only had a shower, of course, and you know how I adore showers." She grimaced. "Give me a hot tub and plenty of suds tickling my nose."

"I'll go get some towels. Come and see your room. I'll help you unpack."

While Marjorie was undressing, Cree came back to the table where Wyatt was sitting finishing the champagne.

"Have I lost weight?" he asked.

"Your face is thinner. Well, what do you think?"

"About what?"

"Your mother." She lowered her voice. "I must say she doesn't look as good as I'd hoped she would. She's thin."

"She seems okay."

"Oh, she's cheerful and alive, or she's determined to make us think she is, but you look at her, study her when she's listening. You can see the strain."

"We can get rid of it; we'll fill her full of Paris. Show her every shop, every church, every flower, everything. Get her out of herself every waking minute."

"You can't do much, you don't have the time. I'll take care of her."

"Just as long as she doesn't sit around doing nothing."

Marjorie appeared in the doorway of her room in her velveteen robe, her hair turbaned in a towel. She had washed off her makeup; she looked pale and drawn, her eyes darkly circled. Cree could hear the water being drawn in the tub.

"Now let's get one thing straight right off," said Marjorie. "I don't want to disrupt your routines. You have lots to do and you mustn't feel you have to hold my hand and lead me around town."

"If we don't, you'll get lost," said Wyatt. "Whisked off to Marseilles and sold into white slavery."

"Wyatt!"

"There's so much to see," said Cree. "Starting tonight, if you feel up to it. Or would you rather get to bed early?"

"My first night in Paris? You must be joking."

"Mother," said Wyatt, "you're going to be a grandmother."

"I know, but don't go trotting out the rocking chair yet."

She took them to Maxim's for dinner. The purple and gold entrance hall conjured up visions of what Cree imagined St. Peter's in Rome and an audience with the Pope would look like. Up the carpeted stairs they were shown to the Imperiale, where the private rooms were located. The bar was a pompous and somewhat bizarre combination of marquetry and bronze. They sat in comfortable Louis XVI armchairs and sipped iced Sauterne, surrounded by turn-of-the-century elegance and the muffled din of the *beau monde* clientele, the regulars.

Presently the maître d'hôtel approached and led them to a table in the Omnibus under an enormous apple-shaped mirror, one of a dozen identical mirrors that made the room look a square mile in size. Women, beautiful and homely, obese and rail-thin, sat enthroned in their trappings of jewels, lace, and silk. A score of perfumes clashed together. Under the ceiling's incomparable stained-glass window not a single table was unoccupied.

The menu was introduced by the maître d'hôtel, who recommended the saddle of veal Orlov, the caviar and ortolans, and the saddle of lamb. The Mumms flowed as laughter, the clinking of silverware, and the clicking of glasses swirled about them. Marjorie praised every dish, every sip of wine. Her only regret, from the moment they entered to the moment they returned to the sidewalk, was that Maxim's was much too far from New York.

Wyatt went to school earlier than usual the next morning to frame some canvases before class. Marjorie and Cree had a leisurely breakfast, with Heloise and Abelard sharing the croissants. After breakfast, at Cree's suggestion, they took the metro to the Place de la Concorde. She insisted that Marjorie take at least one subway ride during her stay, if for no other reason but to be able to tell her friends that she'd ridden the famed Paris metro. Unfortunately, like every other city, Paris had its poverty, and nowhere was it more evident than underground. Until they were on the train on their way to their destination, Cree did not realize how indifferent she had become to conditions. *Clochards* had invaded every car; most of them were sleeping, taking up two, sometimes three, seats, clutching their liters of *vin ordinaire* and paper bags with their possessions. Beggars, children, and gypsies wandered through the cars. Unreserved seats were hard to find, and at every stop there was a stampede to gain a vacant one. The metro had a unique smell, a mixture of pine-and ammonia-scented disinfectant, stale Gitanes tobacco, and filth blending with the occasional unwelcome reminder that the sewers of Paris lurked behind the tunnel walls.

They emerged to the sight of the Arc de Triomphe du Carrousel. Through the center arch flanked by two smaller ones the famed Egyptian obelisk could be seen rising in the very center of the Place de la Concorde, the site of the guillotine during the Reign of Terror. Here the heads of Louis XVI, Marie Antoinette, Charlotte Corday, and countless others dropped into baskets accompanied by the cheers of the crowd. Beyond the obelisk rose the Arc de Triomphe at the end of the majestic Champs Élysées.

In the afternoon they shopped at the Montogueil market and had a late lunch at L'Escargot. Bright-red banquettes were reflected in mirrors larger than those at Maxim's; the staircase was painted in contrasting green, and there were innumerable potted plants.

Marjorie seemed tireless; Paris was infusing her with energy. She was like a child at the circus, taking in everything with awe and delight, reveling in the color and beauty all about her.

But over coffee she confessed to being lonely. She saw friends often, attended and gave dinner parties, went to the theater, the opera, the ballet, but the hours by herself were long, and the burden of her loss was giving no indication that it might eventually lighten.

"Your marriage is no small consolation to me," she said. "It's easy to see you're happy. So many young people have such a trying time of it."

"Easy to see?" asked Cree.

"In little things. The way you look at him. And vice versa. He surprises me, he seems to have matured overnight. You deserve the credit for that. My dear, you really are meant for each other, hackneyed as that sounds. Sometimes I wonder whether when two people are born they are predestined to meet and fall in love. If they're perfectly suited to each other, they must be."

Cree smiled. It was true, their own marriage was "natural," going as smoothly as a sailboat across a pond. Would it always be this smooth? When the wind rose and the water turned choppy, would they be able to ride it out? Of course they would. If anything, adversity could only strengthen the bond.

Late in the day they found themselves across the street from Studio Gleyre. Cree pointed out the building.

"Let's go in," said Marjorie. "We can watch him."

"I don't know as he'd like that."

"We'll stand where he can't see us. Come on."

An officious-looking little man answered the bell; he was a stranger to Cree.

"We're here to meet one of your students," said Marjorie. "M. Chance. He should be getting out soon." She turned to Cree for confirmation. Cree obliged her with a nod.

The man glanced at his watch and told them they would have to wait another ten minutes. He showed them to a plain wooden bench in the corridor and went away. The doors to the classrooms off either side of the corridor were ajar. They could hear stirring, an occasional cough, a word or two, but no extended conversation. Marjorie went exploring. Peering into the first room, she motioned Cree to join her. It was a class in drawing with about twenty students. Wyatt stood at his easel on the far side. An eerie silence pervaded the room, the students concentrating on their work, Professor Lacroix ambling about, stick in hand, now and then tugging at his mustache, pausing before a sketch, pointing, reacting. Cree recognized Roland's laugh and drew Marjorie away from the door.

"They'll be coming out soon. Maybe we'd better wait out front."

"I want to watch," said Marjorie. "I've waited all my life to see this. Don't worry, I won't make a sound."

Cree went back to the bench and sat down. Class ended, and the students came filing out. Wyatt spotted them.

"Let's see what you've done," said his mother. "Please?"

He swept the sketch behind him. "When it's done. Maybe."

They took a taxi to Rue du Bac, dropping Roland off along the way.

The next day Cree and Marjorie went to the Right Bank to explore the more expensive galleries on Avenue Matignon, the Faubourg Ste. Honoré, and the Boulevard Haussmann. They went into the Galerie Boucher. It was a small, narrow room with an iron spiral staircase leading up to the second level. The walls were a ghostly white, but the interior lighting was superb, and here and there was an interesting painting, including a Matisse, *The Nun*, two Franz Marc horses, and a Bellini landscape—or an excellent copy of one— in fair condition.

There was a table on the second floor that held a number of woodcuts. Cree discovered a pair of Cranachs, one of a knight, the other of a lady, well fed and amply jeweled. At the sight of them Cree had to steel herself to keep from shouting. The woman in charge of the gallery was small, with spectacles much too large for her little girl's face, and hair untidily bobbed. Her eyes snapped about restlessly. Cree got the feeling that she had been robbed and was determined to avoid a second such incident. Every time Cree and Marjorie moved a hand toward a painting the woman stiffened.

"Cranachs, I can't believe it," whispered Cree. Marjorie started to pick one up. "Don't. Don't look as if you're interested."

The woman glided over to them.

"Can I help?" she asked in heavily accented English.

"How much does this cost?" asked Cree, picking up one of the woodcuts beside the knight.

"Ten thousand francs."

"A bit expensive," said Cree as she picked up the Cranach lady, turned, and looked at the woman.

"*Vingt mille,*" said the woman.

"How much?" asked Marjorie.

"Too much, twenty thousand."

"That's . . ."

"Four thousand dollars, Marjorie. Let's just look around."

"Lucretia, if you want them, go ahead and buy them."

"Not for eight thousand dollars. They're only woodcuts, not paintings."

They moved away from the table. The woman stood watching them. The doorbell jingled, and she went back downstairs.

"Aren't they worth four thousand?" asked Marjorie, examining the woodcuts.

"Maybe twice that. But there are thousands of Cranach woodcuts still in existence. See the winged snake? That's his signature. He put it on everything that came out of his workshop."

"So it's genuine."

"It probably is, although he did have two sons and assistants and apprentices, any one of whom could have cut these and added his signature. Maybe the signature is all that's his, if that." She sighed. "Still, I hate to pass them up. Wyatt would have a stroke."

"He doesn't have to know."

"I couldn't do that to him, not with Cranach. He's crazy about his work. Let's take these downstairs and talk to her."

"*Comment appelez-vous cela en français* is about all the talking I can do," laughed Marjorie. "And when they tell me 'what they call it in French,' I don't understand. I have to keep looking in the book." She tapped her head. "Nothing sticks. You speak it like a native."

"You will too."

The woman was talking to a customer, describing the Matisse in glowing terms. It was obviously the centerpiece of the gallery, although Cree recalled seeing dozens of his works around town. Hundreds of Impressionist paintings were available. Virtually every gallery exhibited at least a dozen. The man listened and politely nodded but did not appear interested in buying. He drifted off to browse, tipping his hat to Cree and Marjorie as he passed them.

"*Vingt mille francs,*" said Cree to the woman.

She nodded, smiling, her hands starting up from her sides, as if she were about to rub them together.

"For both."

"*Mais non. Impossible!*"

Cree laid them on the counter. "*Merci.*" She took Marjorie by the elbow and started for the door.

"*Une seconde,*" called the woman. She beckoned them back. She explained that the two woodcuts were rare Lucas Cranachs, with a certificate to prove their authenticity. Rummaging through a drawer, she came up with the certificate, waving it like a flag. She kept repeating that Cranachs were all but unavailable outside Germany since the war.

Cree picked up the knight.

"Fifteen thousand."

"Non, non, non, non, non."

Cree shrugged and put it down.

"Trente cinq mille francs le paire," said the woman.

Here was the chink in her professional armor Cree had been looking for. They began to haggle, each snapping prices at the other. Cree got the figure for the pair down to twenty thousand. To slam the door on the discussion, she got out a check and laid it on the counter.

"Non, non, non, non, non," shrilled the woman, shaking her head. *"De la monnaie seulement!"*

Marjorie eyed her questioningly.

"Cash only," murmured Cree.

Marjorie dug into her handbag, bringing out a thick wad of newly printed thousand- and five-hundred-franc notes, and counted out twenty thousand. Cree was handed the certificate of authenticity, the woodcuts were wrapped, and out the door they went.

They walked to the corner. Cree was barely able to keep from shouting triumphantly. Holding up the package, she kissed it loudly.

"Wyatt, Wyatt, Wyatt. He'll go absolutely wild with joy. What time is it?"

"Half past three."

"The bank's closed. I'll go first thing in the morning and cash a check."

"Nonsense, they're a gift. An investment in fine art. Charles Crowder and Mr. Mayhew, the chief accountant, would approve wholeheartedly." She looked about. "Where to now? Let's go to another gallery. This is such fun. Let's buy a Rembrandt or something."

The moment Wyatt walked in at the door they hurried him to the table and made him sit down. Cree brought in the package and laid it before him.

"What's this?"

"Open it. It's a gift from your mother."

He looked from one to the other. "A painting?" He loosened the string, unwrapped the paper, and looked thunderstruck as he slowly lifted the lady in one hand, the knight in the other.

"Cranachs!"

Jumping up, he threw his arms around Marjorie, squeezing hard.

"Wyatt, you hurt!"

"They're beautiful!" He ran into the bedroom and placed the woodcuts on either side of the crucifixion over the bureau, studied them, changed his mind, and set them side by side above the head of the bed.

"What do you think?"

"Much better," said Cree.

Marjorie nodded. "A knight and his lady ought never to be separated."

Bringing the woodcuts back to the other room, he listened gleefully as Cree and Marjorie described the transaction.

"Did you measure them? They look about ten by six. We have to see about getting them and the crucifixion insured. They're priceless. Oh, say, I almost forgot, something else good happened today. We got the date for the exhibition, the twenty-seventh. It's earlier than I figured, but I'm almost done."

"Don't rush it," cautioned Cree.

"You're going to win!" exclaimed Marjorie.

"I'll be lucky to get hung," he said, laughing. "You should see the Palais, the Salon. There are twenty-four rooms, each one eighty feet square, every wall filled with paintings. Some are huge. What you have to do is get a place on the line."

"What's that?" asked Marjorie.

"At or close to eye level, so you'll be seen. If they hang you up near the ceiling, you're out of luck. The exhibition's supposed to be fantastic. Painters, sculptors, and art writers mingle with the crowd. There's a band, and they serve luncheon every day in the restaurant in the garden below. They announce the winners the last day of the month."

"You'll win," said Marjorie flatly. "I feel it in my bones. Cree, let's have some wine, a toast to victory."

Chapter Nineteen

Wyatt grudgingly admitted he was satisfied with the completed *Baker's Boy*. He had gone to the corner every other day for a week to study his model at first hand, setting up his easel at the curb and catching the boy between customers. The day before the *ministère du exhibition* was to begin accepting submissions he turned the painting in to Professor Lacroix. He had not had a chance to see Roland's landscape, but there it was, standing on the long table against the wall in Lacroix's office, the familiar double R scrawled in the lower right-hand corner, one of a couple of dozen other entries from Studio Gleyre.

He almost gasped at the sight of it, so startlingly different was it from any other landscape he had ever seen. Roland had worked in the woody confines of the Bois de Boulogne, he knew, setting up his easel on the bank of one of the lakes. His subject was a swan, a great chesty cob, its wings folded back, its head erect on its slender, beautiful neck. The water supporting it and the sky above were merely suggested in pale gray and paler blue. The swan filled the canvas, which was larger than any canvas Wyatt had ever seen Roland use, nearly forty inches across, he estimated.

The swan's body provided the outline for the landscape, the rolling hills, green fields, a barn and farmhouse, a cloudless azure sky, the whole bathed by the unseen sun. By deliberately muting the sky and water, he had succeeded in bringing the various greens and browns and other colors vividly alive.

It was a risky painting, thought Wyatt at first, one that invited adverse reaction, even ridicule, on the part of the judges. But considering it further, he decided it was not so much risky as daring. What Roland had done was to elevate realism to a level of imagination that openly challenged the eye. It was absolutely captivating. It would be talked about, of that Wyatt was sure, argued over, would probably be the center of attention of the entire exhibition. If nothing else, it defied indifference.

It was, in his opinion, a masterful painting, an outstanding effort for a student—so good that he wanted to turn around and take his *Baker's Boy*, still under his arm, out of the office, out the front door, straight home. *Avilly*, as Roland had titled his painting, was marvelous.

He sensed somebody standing behind him in the doorway. It was Roland.

"What do you think?" Roland asked, his tone uncharacteristically sober and subdued.

"It's fantastic. You never said a word."

"My surprise. For you, everybody. You can bet the graybeards are going to be surprised. Watch, they'll take one look, haul it down from the wall, and chase me out the door with it." He shrugged. "So I broke the rules. Why not, eh?"

"It's far and away the best thing here." Wyatt set his canvas down, leaning it against his leg. He took hold of

Roland. "It's really great. When it wins you'll be able to peddle it for a fortune. Roland, you'll be made."

"Please, if there's anything I can't stand, it's a friend who refuses to hide his jealousy." He laughed. "Only fooling." He searched Wyatt's eyes. "Seriously, I appreciate your kind words. Wish me luck. What am I saying? Wish yourself luck. Me, I'll pray to Saint Catherine of Bologne, Saint Althea, Saint Luke, all the patron saints of the arts. Enough. Let me see the *Baker's Boy*."

"You don't really want to."

"Stop it." He picked it up, set it on the table in front of *Avilly*, stepped back, and assessed it thoughtfully. "I like it."

"It's nothing, one more portrait, character study, whatever you want to call it."

"I said I like it. You must learn to accept a compliment. You should have more confidence. Look at me, *Monsieur Confiance en soi,* that's me. Did you hear who the judges are going to be?"

"No, who?"

"There are five of them. Paul Poiret, the designer, André Lhote, Armand Duprier, the artistic director of *La Vie heureuse* . . ."

"Oh, my God!"

"What's the matter?"

Wyatt explained. Roland listened, his dark face sympathetic.

"He'll take one look at this, and all his resentment will come welling up."

"How do you know? He may not be overly fond of you . . ."

"He hates me. He took it as a personal affront. He has an ego the size of a Zeppelin, and I stepped on it.

He'll take one look at my signature and rip this to shreds." Picking up the *Baker's Boy*, he slipped it under his arm.

"What are you doing?"

"What do you think?"

Roland snatched it from him. "No, you don't, you're going to enter this, or I'll break it over your head. Forget Duprier. Put him out of your mind. Five judges are going to be judging your work. They're not going to be judging you or how grateful you are."

Wyatt sighed. "Maybe you're right."

"I'm never wrong."

"It's funny. Ever since that night when he blew up at me I've been wondering when our paths would cross again. I never thought it'd be this soon. Wait till Cree hears."

"Why tell her? Why upset her? She can't do anything about it."

Roland took the painting from him and set it on the table.

"There we are, an outstanding work of art, gentlemen." He puffed up his chest pompously and pulled in his chin. "What do you think, *mes amis?*" Wyatt grinned. "Forget Duprier, cross your fingers, and pray to Saint Catherine of Bologne, Saint Althea, Saint Luke, the whole tribe. Come on, let's get out of here."

Chapter Twenty

The exhibition, the first since the beginning of the war, drew mobs of art lovers from Paris and the outlying provinces. People crowded the twenty-four spacious rooms of the Salon from nine in the morning to closing time. On every wall individual canvases were lost to the eye, dissolving into great square splashes of color. To the artist hopeful that the jury would single out his submission for critical praise, the great size of the exhibition was discouraging.

Wyatt went with Cree and Marjorie the first morning. To his disappointment, the *Baker's Boy* was hung well above eye level, an excellent duplication of a Monet landscape all that separated it from the ceiling. Impressionists, Cubists, and conventional portraitists dominated the exhibition. The École des Beaux-Arts alone submitted nearly four hundred canvases.

The Chances did not return the second day or the third. On the fourth day, when the judges were to select the winning entries, all of Paris seemed to be assembled in the Salon. Wyatt, Cree, and Marjorie escaped the crush, fleeing to the garden restaurant just after eleven for an early lunch. Surrounded by lovely flower beds and grassy walks, under the unconcerned eyes of scores of statues, they discussed the exhibition while sipping wine and dispatching a somewhat melancholy *tarte au poisson*. The day had dawned murky, but an hour earlier the sun had broken through and burned away the gray and now spread its gold over the city and the garden. Wyatt had little appetite for his fish.

"I had my fingers crossed hoping I'd get a good spot, just so I could get some sort of reaction. Just be seen, you know? Fat chance."

"I'm sure Professor Lacroix will find out what he can from the judges . . ." began Cree.

"I doubt if he can get near the judges. There must be a hundred and fifty instructors here. This is where the Beaux-Arts has the edge, being the biggest and with the most submissions."

"That's silly," said Cree, "the paintings aren't labeled by school. Something from some little atelier nobody ever heard of could just as easily catch their eye as the best the Beaux-Arts has to offer. Something like the *Baker's Boy*, right, Marjorie?"

"Absolutely."

"I shouldn't have done a conventional portrait. It's just a waste of time, just one more face in the crowd. Not bad, not good, just not any different. Funny, I liked it, I honestly felt there was something there, until I saw Roland's swan."

"How can you possibly compare the two?" asked Cree. "It's oranges and apples."

"I guess. But I know one thing—I'll never submit anything to a circus like this again. We live and we learn, right?"

He went back to picking at his fish. Cree and Marjorie exchanged glances. The crowd was beginning to stream down the stairs into the restaurant, the tables filling around them, the waiters scurrying about. Wyatt caught their waiter's attention, and Cree and Marjorie ordered a sherbet, which they ate in silence.

"Let's go back upstairs," suggested Marjorie.

"The jury should be finished judging by now," agreed Cree.

"If you want," he said, "although frankly I'd rather read about it in the papers."

He laid money on the table. Starting up the stairs, they met Professor Lacroix coming down.

"Here you are. I've been looking all over for you. Guess who's won an honorable mention!"

"Not . . ." Wyatt gaped in disbelief. Lacroix nodded, beaming.

"I congratulate you. Splendid work, splendid!"

"Wyatt!" Cree threw her arms around him. Marjorie kissed him loudly on the cheek.

"I don't believe it," he said. "How could they even find me, let alone give me honorable mention?"

"It's very simple. They looked for excellence and they found it."

"But Duprier . . ."

"Wyatt, you have M. Duprier to thank for it. I spoke to André Lhote. He says they would have passed you by had not Duprier directed their attention to *Baker's Boy*."

"It still doesn't make sense. You can't imagine how upset he was with me."

"With you, perhaps, but what does that have to do with your painting? It's not you hanging on the wall."

Lacroix laughed and drew the three of them to the railing out of the traffic moving up and down the stairs.

"I've come down from the conference room on the third floor. Every teacher in Paris was standing outside the door, crowding around like newspaper reporters after a cinema star. The door opened, and André Lhote emerged. He quieted everybody and read from a paper. First prize, second prize, and ten honorable mentions. Again, congratulations."

"Who won?"

"Somebody from the Beaux-Arts, a portrait of his mistress. I haven't seen it. The jury was partial to portraits this year, except for your friend, the buffoon."

"Roland?"

Lacroix nodded. "He took second prize. You should have heard them spouting over his swan. Come and help me find him." He took Wyatt by the arm. "Let me steal him from you."

"I saw him on the third floor, but that was a couple hours ago," said Wyatt. "I wonder if he knows yet."

"Do you know, this is the very first time Studio Gleyre has placed two students among the winners. The third floor, did you say? Come."

Captured by the professor, Wyatt shrugged apologetically at Cree and Marjorie.

"I'll see you back at the apartment, okay?" he said, then turned and followed Lacroix up the stairs.

"What a pity," said Marjorie.

"What do you mean?"

"I was hoping he'd win."

Marjorie planned to leave on June 2. While Wyatt was outside helping the taxi driver load her baggage, his mother and Cree sat in the garden ready and waiting for him.

"Lucretia," said Marjorie, "it's no concern of mine, of course, and you can tell me to mind my own business, but I've been thinking about your grandfather and your sisters. Don't you miss them?"

"Very much."

"Any idea where they are?"

"I assume Julia's still in California, I don't know where exactly. Livvy and Alec were here during the war, but they must be back in New York now."

"When I get home, why don't I look Olivia up?"

"Would you?"

"Of course. They must be in the phone book. Her married name is White, isn't it?" Cree nodded. "And what about your grandfather? Have you written him?"

"I wrote from New Haven when we first got married. He never answered."

"Would you like me to give him your address here?"

"I'd rather you didn't. He'd never write me, except perhaps to bawl me out for eloping. Even though I'm married, I'm still the baby in the family. But I'd like to get in touch with Livvy. I'd write her now except I can't remember the address of Alec's firm. I miss her so, I'd love to see her and Jule."

"Have you thought about coming back for a visit?"

Wyatt appeared, stuffing money into his billfold. "You could go to New York, sweetheart," he said, "if you want to."

"Not without you."

"It would do you good," insisted Marjorie. "You'd stay at the house, of course."

Cree shook her head. "Maybe some day, not now. Not until the baby's born and grown up enough to travel. When Daddy here can go back to New York and mount a one man show."

"Don't hold your breath," said Wyatt.

Mme. Boulette came to say good-bye to Marjorie and give her a small packet of tea as a going-away present.

Marjorie had stayed four days short of a month. Her

ship, the *Provence*, was scheduled to depart Calais
early that evening. On the northbound train from Gare
du Nord the three of them sat back as the engine puffed
its way out of the station. Through the grimy yellow
window the spires of Montmartre slid slowly by, giving
way to St. Denis and the high-piled scrap heaps that
formed a barrier around the city. Through the suburban
estates they threaded, past miles of unsightly stone
walls isolating small houses attached to poles by long
lines of laundry. The land was as flat as a coin for
miles, the wheat fields stretching to the horizon.

Cree's spirits sagged; she would miss Marjorie. They
had become very close friends. She loved exploring
Paris with her. They might be able to get away next
spring; it depended on Wyatt. She wouldn't go without
him. He might not want to take as long as a month off.
He'd made no mention of it, but she was convinced that
he would go on painting, and in Paris. Where else but
Paris?

The train reached Calais shortly before five. The
platform was mobbed with businessmen and workers
on their way home to St. Pierre, Gîunes, Marck, and the
other towns ringing the city. Calais had suffered prolonged heavy bombardment; the detritus of war was
still evident and the efforts at reconstruction appeared
half-hearted at best.

The *Provence* was taking on cargo when they arrived
at the dock. They boarded and stayed until the bell
rang, ordering all visitors to leave.

"Kiss me good-bye," said Marjorie to Wyatt.

He did so. She hugged him, her eyes glistening. Cree
turned her head, pretending to look at the setting sun to
hide her own tears.

"Be a good boy, take care of her, and when the baby
comes, you help with the diapers and feeding. Your

father did, you know. He was a wonder with you."

"Come back so you can help, too."

"Don't tempt me. Lucretia." She flung her arms around her. "Thank you for putting up with me for such an interminable time. I shall miss you both terribly. I think I'm going to cry, isn't that silly? Wyatt, give me your handkerchief. Never mind, I think I have one."

The bell rang, the whistle overhead hooted. Visitors were moving down the gangplank, turning, waving, blowing kisses.

"Good-bye, Marjorie," said Cree, "we'll miss you. We'll write. I'll keep you posted on the baby. On everything. I hope you have a good crossing."

"I'll be bored stiff. I'm going to spend hours on my French. When you see me again I'll be *une prise étudiante*, just you watch."

They made their way down the gangplank. Within moments the dockhands began removing it, detaching the ship from Calais. Cree and Wyatt stood in the crowd waving as Marjorie leaned over the railing, her wide-brimmed hat securely pinned against the wind. Her face was in shadow, and for a brief instant Cree's imagination substituted her mother at the rail of the *Lusitania* in her favorite navy-blue hat, the offshore breeze threatening to steal the wings and satin fold, loosening twin wisps of blonde hair and thrashing her skirts.

Safe journey, Marjorie, she thought.

Chapter Twenty-one

June arrived, bright and beautiful, giving way to the steaming, sultry days and nights of July. Studio Gleyre was closed during July. Professor Lacroix locked the black and gilt door and ran off to Brittany to visit relatives.

Wyatt continued working, as did Roland and the other serious students. Wyatt and Cree saw Roland and Giselle frequently. Their money problems vanished like smoke in the wind when a collector offered Roland two thousand francs for *Avilly*. It also signaled the end of his career as a sign painter.

Cree went to see Dr. Chabot for her July checkup. His office was the customary shambles. He looked well suited to his surroundings, as if he had slept in his clothes. They sat on stools across from each other; he ran down her record, questioning her. She in turn asked him about Wyatt, why his cough persisted, curious as to why the heat of summer hadn't put an end to it. It would go shortly, Chabot assured her.

He began examining her. He slipped his stethoscope around his neck, listening to her heart, checking her lungs, and listening to the fetus. His expression was bored. How many hundreds of fetuses had he eavesdropped on? She wondered. The question gave way to an idea, an urge to clean up the place. Get Giselle to help her. The two of them could pick the lock some night, sneak in, and tidy up. When he arrived in the morning, shock at the sight would probably give him a heart seizure!

All at once he began moving the bell of the stethoscope from one spot to another, then back. Back and forth, back and forth. He looked puzzled. Fear quickened the beat of her heart.

"Is something the matter?"

He didn't answer her. At length he straightened, dropping the stethoscope clasps down to his shoulders and nodding slowly.

"Two."

"What?"

"Two distinct heartbeats. Madame, you are going to be the mother of twins."

"Are you sure?"

"Listen for yourself." He placed the stethoscope around her neck, adjusting the clasps, put her hand on the bell, and guided it from place to place. She gasped.

"She's a witch!"

"I beg your pardon?"

"Giselle Robays. When I told her I thought I was pregnant she said I was going to have twins."

"Lucky for you. She could have said quadruplets!"

Cree came home to find Wyatt busy converting the guest room into a nursery, painting gamboling lambs, pink-nosed bunnies, and Mother Goose characters circling the room in a parade that crossed the door and caught up with itself by the light switch. When she announced they were going to have twins he was struck dumb, his brush poised in mid-air. Then a smile spread over his face. He whooped loudly, dropped his brush, picked her up, and swung her around.

"Nobody in our family's ever had twins!" he burst.

"Nor ours."

"Two boys!"

"One of each, if you don't mind."

"Oh, that's up to you, of course."

She laughed. "I've as much say as you have."

"How was your checkup? Everything okay?"

"I'm fine. You're the one Dr. Chabot and I are worried about."

He thumped his chest. "I'm a hundred percent." He swept the room with one hand. "What do you think?"

"I love it."

"It's going to take at least three days. I figure about eighty characters. Come on, you can help."

He put her to work opaquing the three little pigs, coloring in their clothing, adding flesh tone. Working together, they brought one whole wall to life and sketched out a second. But after two hours on her feet, Cree was too tired to continue. She lay down on the settee while he fixed a salad for their supper. They ate in the garden, watching the shadows lengthen, and listening to the vespers service of the Séminaire des Missions Étrangères. Afterward, while he continued working in the nursery, Cree wrote Marjorie, telling her the news.

Dr. Chabot's prognosis proved correct; near the end of July a heat wave so stifling that all of the breathable air seemed to have been vacuumed from the city cleared up Wyatt's throat condition completely. Well into August the mercury continued to linger in the high nineties, with the only respite an occasional brief shower. Professor Lacroix came back from Brittany tanned and rested and as energetic as ever. Classes resumed at the Studio Gleyre. Wyatt and Roland and the other students sweated at their easels, praying for the arrival of September and cooler weather. Cree haunted the galleries and antique shops on both sides of the Seine looking for bargains, but had little luck. She did manage to find an early authentic pre-Paris Modigliani, a portrait, according to Roland, one of many that the artist had done of his mother. She was a homely woman who, from the firmness of her mouth and jaw, struck Cree as someone who had never laughed in her life.

Along with the Modigliani she bought two Monets from a gallery on Rue de Monceau which had only that day put up a going-out-of-business sign in its window. Paris was flooded with the works of the long-lived but luckless Impressionist. His beautiful and frequently brilliant efforts had gone virtually unrecognized until he was well into his sixties. Most of his paintings were selling at twenty-five thousand to thirty-five thousand francs, but she managed to buy her two for a combined price of forty-two thousand francs. One was a version of the artist's well-known *Impression, Sunrise*; the other was entitled *Quai du Port* and was a view of a seaside village embankment promenade flanked by acacia and palm trees, resplendent with shimmering light. It was one of a number of paintings the artist had executed on a trip to Côte D'Azur in the company of Renoir. Wyatt was taken by the Modigliani portrait but less impressed with the Monets, although he conceded that they were an excellent investment.

When he himself browsed, he looked for one painter only. He found a second Cranach, a portrait of Cardinal Utterman of Westphalia in fur-collared robe and red hat, his expression phlegmatic. The cardinal's seal located in the upper left-hand corner needed restoring, but in Wyatt's opinion it could be easily brought up to the quality of the portrait. *Cardinal Utterman of Westphalia* cost ten times as much as the unnamed crucifixion, but they were convinced that it was worth every franc.

With this acquisition the Galerie Chance increased its collection to seven properties.

Encouraged by Professor Lacroix, Wyatt entered a still life, one of the very few he had attempted, in a competition sponsored by the Galeria Duval. Out of seventy-three entries, he managed to take third prize. In the same competition a landscape by Roland was awarded honorable mention. Wyatt's own honorable mention in the Salon Exhibition had infused him with optimism. His third prize made him feel, as he put it, like Picasso. He couldn't get over the fact that a still life, a type of painting he had given such little attention to throughout his studies, had won him attention. Two days after learning of his good fortune he was offered two thousand francs for the painting.

He had arrived. His attitude, his suddenly discovered self-confidence confirmed it to Cree, without any overt declaration on his part.

"We're here to stay," he announced happily, walking into the apartment waving the check for two thousand francs. "If you want to," he added quickly.

"Let me think about it," she said, smirking, throwing her arms around him.

October arrived, Cree's eighth month of pregnancy. During the first few days of September she had blossomed and now found herself unable to fit into anything except her two maternity dresses. She could not button her coat and had to walk down the street holding the sides together. She was convinced that her stomach would never again be flat and that regardless of what the calendar said she had been pregnant for at least five years.

Although she tired easily, on the advice of Dr. Chabot she insisted on taking a short walk every evening. Autumn had arrived in Paris, the chilly nights stealing the color from the flowers and lending it to the leaves. October in Paris brought back memories of New Haven, leaves spinning and dancing and skating down the cobblestones on the tips of their curled blades.

On their walks Wyatt held her hand. He had always been attentive; now he smothered her with consideration, treating her as if she were a fragile vase in danger of shattering. As the time drew nearer all he could talk about was what it would be like to be parents, for him to be a father. He had finished decorating the nursery, and they had furnished it with identical cribs and a bassinet and stocked up on diapers and other necessities.

They were passing the Bon Marché on their way home one evening when he began reminiscing about his father.

"He was the world's best. If I'm half as good you'll be satisfied. Being home every other day will help."

"You think you'll be up to washing out diapers?"

"I . . ."

She laughed. "I'll teach you. Seriously, I think you're going to make a first-rate daddy."

"I have a lot to learn."

"Who doesn't?"

"I'm afraid I might drop one of them. I'm afraid of spoiling them."

"We'll both do that."

"I'm afraid of doing something wrong when you're not around. Maybe we should hire a nurse."

"No, thanks. I thought about that, but I don't want one. I don't want some stranger horning in on my pleasure."

"It's not going to be all fun, not changing diapers."

His expression was that of a man called upon to risk his life for a friend, she thought: willing to, but less than enthusiastic over the prospect.

"I wish I could buy a baseball glove for him," he said wistfully.

"Have you looked for one?"

"Frenchmen don't play baseball, sweetheart. Or football. Only soccer. I'll have to ask Mother to send me a glove."

"What's the rush? At least wait until he's walking. Besides, maybe we'll have two girls."

"If that happens, I'll love them just as much as if they were boys," he said determinedly.

"That's very generous of you."

He was suddenly deep in thought, his expression sober; he seemed, she thought, somewhat intimidated by the prospect of fatherhood.

"Two babies," he went on. "It doesn't seem possible."

"It does to me."

"I should have been more careful."

She stopped him. "What's that supposed to mean?"

"You know."

"Don't you want us to have them?"

"Of course."

"Do you really, or is it that as long as they're inevitable, you'll go along with it?—the good sport."

"That's not fair. Certainly I want them." He took her in his arms and kissed her lightly, then passionately. Two children walked by, tittering. She broke from him gently.

"I'm sorry, I shouldn't have said that. It's just that I can't help wondering sometimes. We're so free now. We do what we want, come and go as we please. It's going to be a whole different life."

"It's going to be wonderful. I can't wait to walk down the street pushing the baby carriage."

"Your mother'll be in seventh heaven. It wouldn't surprise me if she showed up on our doorstep any day now."

"If it's a boy and a girl, what will we call them?"

"Wyatt and Marjorie."

"Why not Lucretia? And why does it have to be Wyatt?"

"After your father, of course." She laughed. "And his son. Wyatt Chance the Third. Sounds Ivy League, wouldn't you say?"

"Too."

"Let's not worry about names right now. First let's see what we get."

Wyatt sniffled as a gust of wind flapped the collar of his jacket.

"You're catching cold."

"I'm not."

"You'd better not. Let's go home and cuddle up in bed. I want you to hold me, I want to sleep in your arms all night tonight."

"What's the occasion?"

"I just decided I love you."

"You should. I'm outstanding, exemplary. Did you know that I'm about to become the father of twins?"

"Is that a fact, monsieur?"

His face darkened. "Do you realize it's only about a week now?"

"It could be tomorrow. It could be three weeks."

"Are you okay? Are you . . ."

"Ready?" She patted her stomach. "What does it look like?"

"You know what I mean."

"Psychologically? Yes, I'm ready. Looking forward to it. Oh, I plan to do a lot of screaming and I'm sure I'll come out of it limp as a rag, but you can't imagine what a relief it'll be getting rid of this. It's heavy, you know. When I get back on my feet I'll feel like Pavlova."

That night she fell asleep in his arms. And awoke there in the morning. He slept on, a beatific smile turning up the corners of his mouth slightly. The sun, dazzlingly bright but lacking warmth, filled the room. She eased out of his arms carefully so as not to wake him and, propping herself on one elbow, watched him sleep. His breathing was scarcely discernible; to look at his face, one would think him without a care, contentment personified. In her mind she pictured him when they were first introduced. They were both self-conscious, blushing, stumbling over words, which always seemed to happen when you liked someone at first sight. Then came the long succession of parties and dances at Yale and in the city. He had not aged, but he had matured. He was a man now and soon would be a father. She was confident he would be a very good one, sensitive, considerate, caring, loving; good husbands make good fathers. With his money and the type of people with whom he had associated his whole life, he could have been spoiled and self-centered, self-indulgent. He never had been anything of the kind, which was one of the reasons he had attracted her from the first. But then his father and mother were not at all like that either, not in the least snobbish or pretentious.

Her sister Olivia had her Alec and loved him just as deeply as she loved Wyatt. How lucky she and Livvy were. She wondered fleetingly if Julia had found anyone. It wouldn't be easy for Jule. She was very choosy about whom she went out with; her standards were towering, but then she had a great deal to offer. She was a beauty and bright. Too bright for her own good? There were such girls.

All her life until she'd met Wyatt she had been secretly envious of Julia's beauty. Marriage to him had given her the confidence in herself she'd always admired in both her sisters.

Leaning over him, she drew her finger around his face and kissed him lightly on the mouth and eyes. He stirred and made a sound deep in his throat. She kissed his cheeks and his mouth, more firmly this time, and then under his chin. Again he stirred, his eyelids flickering; waking, he smiled at her.

"I love you, Wyatt."

He held her against his chest, nuzzling her hair. "I adore you, my wife."

"How's your cold?"

He didn't answer; instead he stiffened.

"Good God, what time is it?"

"A little after eight."

He leaped out of bed. "I'll be late for class. Roland's going to be cursing. We'll have to take the subway. How come the alarm didn't go off?"

"I guess we forgot to reset it for a school day."

Whereupon the alarm went off. She laughed and, seeing the uselessness of taking it seriously, he did also.

It was November 3, a Monday. Shortly after he left for school the sun vanished, the sinister-looking clouds came rolling in abundance from over the Vosges Mountains to the east, and rain splattered the city, drilling the cobblestones in the courtyard. The downpour became heavier and heavier until it obscured the trees at the bottom of the garden. Around noontime it let up, but resumed within the hour, and from then on, with the wind up and buffeting it about, it came down in sheets.

She crossed her fingers and fervently hoped it would stop completely before Wyatt got out of school. But when he arrived at around five, he was soaked to the skin. Taking off his shoes the moment he set foot in the door, he poured water out of them. She had already started a hot bath for him and now she practically pushed him into it. While he soaked himself, she poured a kettle of boiling water into the tub to keep the temperature as hot as he could stand it. She insisted he go right to bed, offering to bring him hot tea mixed with lemon and a tot of brandy.

"The bath's enough, I'm fine."

"Wyatt, you can't be too careful."

"Cree, stop babying me." He changed the subject. "We waited about twenty minutes for it to let up," he explained, "then we decided it wasn't going to, so we ran for the subway. It's only three blocks, but that's all it took to get sopping. We both got off at St.-Germain-des-Prés, and I ran home."

"How did you get water in your shoes?"

"Running through puddles, I guess. The corner at the end of the street in front of the market is under water. We must have gotten six inches so far. It's like somebody picked up the Seine and tipped it upside down."

"I'm taking your temperature."

"Cree, I'm not sick. Will you please cut it out?"

"Dr. Chabot's orders are to watch you like a hawk. You were already getting the sniffles. Lie down on the settee, and I'll get the thermometer. And some aspirin."

"Sweetheart . . ."

"Do it."

"Okay, nurse."

His temperature was normal. The rain did not let up until well past midnight. Still awake, Cree heard it stop; he lay snoring beside her.

He woke up feeling fine. She took his temperature before she let him get up and gave him two aspirin. His temperature was still normal. But halfway through breakfast he began coughing, and she had to pound him on the back before he could stop. It left him flushed and sweating. Once more she took his temperature.

It was a hair above 99.

She ordered him to bed.

Chapter Twenty-two

By the time the ambulance that Dr. Chabot had summoned arrived at Hôpital St. Louis, Wyatt's fever had edged above 100 degrees; he was shaking with chills and was complaining of chest pain.

Within four hours of his arrival his lungs were producing sufficient pus for him to begin coughing up thick greenish sputum.

"It's not tinged with blood," observed Chabot to Cree in the corridor outside the ward. Inside, Sister Phillipa stood over Wyatt administering medication. "Let's hope and pray we got him here in time." He shrugged.

"I'm so afraid for him," murmured Cree. "What are his chances?"

Again he shrugged, reminding Cree that the shrug was every doctor's noncommittal response to questions regarding an illness that were beyond his capabilities to deal with effectively. Fear struck at her heart. "Does he *have* a chance? Doctor, how bad is he? I want to know."

"It's too early to say." She could tell by his eyes that he was trying to be kind.

"The influenza caused it, didn't it?"

"Oh, yes. Even with all these months between the

two attacks. There's no mistaking the symptoms, the sudden rise in temperature, his respiration."

"That damned rain!"

"It wasn't the severity of it. An April shower could have done it to him. His lungs are not strong, that made him vulnerable. And pneumonia germs are frequently present in the nasal or throat secretions of perfectly healthy people."

"But he's infected because of his lungs."

He nodded and lowered his eyes to avoid looking into hers. "He's been inhaling the infected mucus into his lower respiratory passages. The lungs consist of five lobes, three on the right side, two on the left. If just one becomes infected, the infection can spread like the plague to the others. But the outlook's not all black. We got him here quickly, Sister Phillipa and I will keep a close watch on him, he's young, strong. What we've got to do is clear up the infection as quickly as we can. The coughing puts a strain on his heart."

"It's much worse than the flu, isn't it? You said it was last spring. Dear God . . ."

"You mustn't upset yourself. Look, you're due to come in in a day or two. Why don't we sign you in now? Maternity has empty beds—we'll get you one, and you can come up and visit him whenever you like."

"Yes, yes . . ."

"But you must wear a mask. It's highly contagious."

"I know, my sister Julia had pneumonia."

"I'll say this about the rainstorm. He had a cold. Damp clothing with a cold can lead to pneumonia. Then, too, I suppose he's been working as hard as ever."

"Oh, he's run down. I've tried to get him to slow down. I thought when he sold his first painting he might, but if anything, he's been working harder. It's ridiculous, rushing the way he does. I don't believe you can speed up the stages of your development."

"Well, he won't even be *thinking* about painting for the next few days." He took hold of her hands, smiling his kindly smile. "We'll get him through the night and by morning we should have a leg up on beating the infection. Pray for him, Lucretia, stop imagining the worst. You're about to become a mother. You mustn't let this depress you, not at this stage. It's not healthy."

There was no change in Wyatt's condition the next morning. He was no worse, but he continued to vomit and complain of feeling miserable. He had no appetite, no desire to talk, he couldn't so much as shift his hands across the sheet. Roland came to visit after school; Cree had phoned him to ask him to tell Professor Lacroix what had happened. Roland was not his customary ebullient self. Concern darkened his face as he sat by the bed making friendly small talk. Unintentionally he deepened her pessimism.

Dr. Chabot did not get to the hospital until late in the afternoon, showing up shortly after Roland left. Sister Phillipa informed him that the patient's temperature had risen to 104. Over the next two days it hovered there. At eleven o'clock on the night of the third day Cree felt her first contraction. It was like cramps, only much more severe, and even more so as they began coming with regularity. Chabot was summoned from a card game, arriving redolent of cigar smoke and cognac, all smiles and premature congratulations. By the time he got to the hospital Cree had been removed to the labor room. Her contractions were now coming five minutes apart.

Chapter Twenty-three

The moon sent its pallid light through the tall curtainless windows. The only sound in the ward was the rhythmic breathing of the patients. Wyatt dozed, his temperature still at 104 degrees, his beleaguered lungs filled with congestion. His pulse continued to quicken, his breathing was rapid, shallow, difficult. He was only dimly aware of the pain in his side, caused by the onset of pleurisy.

Sister Phillipa wiped the sputum from his mouth and nose and repositioned the ice poultice on his side. She had just finished sponging him. Turning to the night table, she tested the hypodermic syringe and prepared to inject digitalin. Then she changed her mind and put the needle down. She glanced down at him, pursing her thin lips and shaking her head sympathetically. She was, she realized, merely going through the motions of helping him do battle. The poultice appeared to ease the pain of his pleurisy, but the digitalin was ineffective. Nor was there any other medication that might help him. She could only make him as comfortable as possible—and pray to St. Luke. After she had given him the medication, she put the syringe down again and folded her hands in prayer.

Cree emerged from the gray gauze of sleep exhausted, scarcely able to summon enough strength to lift her eyelids. The birth experience flashed across her fuzzied mind in a jumble of images. Once again she imagined herself straining in labor, obeying Dr. Chabot, pushing, pushing.

Now at each of her breasts was a slender red baby— her son, her daughter, both sucking hungrily, eyes tightly closed, tiny fingers flexing. Chabot stood over her smiling; two nurses were at the foot of the table, both beaming.

"Congratulations, Lucretia," said Chabot.

"How is he?"

"Holding his own, doing okay."

"When did you see him last?"

"Just a few minutes ago. I have Claude Mercerou, one of the orderlies, running back and forth between here and the third floor while I'm down here. Sister Phillipa is with him. I'm going back upstairs now. Again, congratulations. You have a fine, handsome, brawny boy and a beautiful little girl who is going to look just like her mother. Both perfect. We've given you something to help you sleep. Close your eyes."

With each word his voice reached her from further away, his tone hollow, as if he were speaking from the far end of a pipe. And the light over her head went out as the curtain fell, tangling her in its folds. She slept.

When they brought him to the hospital, despite his malaise, his rising fever and chills, his pulse had been full. Now, with the interruption to pulmonary circulation, he had become weak, seemingly immune to the digitalin, to any cardiac stimulant. He breathed with difficulty, fighting for air like a drowning man, drowning in his own fluids. Dr. Chabot stood beside the nurse. It was morning; sunlight pouring through the east windows whitened the polished floor. Chabot pulled the screen closer to the foot of the bed.

"He's getting worse. His breathing, his fever, the pleurisy." He sighed. "It looks like meningitis. It's frightening."

"Sir?"

"In all my experience I have never seen acute pneumonia cause such rapid deterioration. Like lightning."

"He's worn out," she said resignedly. "He's used up all his strength. Shall I give him more digitalin?"

"No."

"Strychnine then?"

"No, no, no. His heart wouldn't stand it."

"What can we do?"

Chabot shook his head and, looking up, beckoned the orderly standing by the corridor door. "Bring a new ice poultice, hurry."

"Yes, Doctor."

Cree woke to discover that her babies had been taken away to the nursery. She yawned and glanced about the room.

"Appelez le médecin vite," she said. "Dr. Chabot."

"Qu'avez-vous?" asked the nurse solicitously.

"Il n'y a pas. Vite, s'il vous plaît! Quickly."

"Oui, madame."

She hurried out. After moments that seemed like hours Chabot came shuffling in.

"Is something the matter?"

"How is he?"

"Doing all right." His head bobbed determinedly, as if to add conviction to his words.

"Better? Worse?"

"Holding his own."

"I want to see him."

"You can't get up, it's much too soon."

"I can be wheeled to the elevator, taken upstairs. Please."

"Later, perhaps."

"Now, please. I want to see my husband!"

His face seemed to fill with pain, his eyes suddenly suffused with it, the muscles of his jaw and around his mouth tightening. He was holding something back. What else could it be but the worst? They stared at each other.

"Something's happened," she said. He took hold of her wrists. The anguish in his eyes revealed his sorrow. "Dear God, no!"

"I am so sorry," he said quietly, "so very, very sorry."

Chapter Twenty-four

Cree stood in the studio looking about: at a sketch of a house bundled in shrubbery, at a half-completed nude, twisted tubes of paint, his brushes, his stained and splattered taboret, his palette, empty frames. She picked up his worn palette knife, turning it over in her hand, catching sunlight on the blade. She imagined he was there, felt his presence, saw him standing at his easel, squinting, scowling hypercritically at his canvas.

Six days had passed. And nights, when her grief lay heaviest upon her, and the question "Why?" came and went unanswered again and again and again. And she yearned to die, to escape this incubus, until she remembered that she could not die, for now she had babies, responsibility, and there was no choice but to go on. Dr. Chabot had prescribed laudanum to help her sleep. It helped, but then, too, soon morning came, and the next battle in her war of survival would begin.

The babies kept her busy—her beautiful son and daughter, his seed come to life. Giselle Robays had dropped by and at the moment was in the kitchen heating broth.

"It's ready, Cree."

They sat down at the table. Heloise and Abelard cooed softly, almost hesitantly, Cree thought, as if reluctant to disturb her. Dear little birds, keep your love alive, keep each other.

The broth, chicken with onion and parsley and other herbs, smelled delicious. But she had no appetite. She forced herself to eat. Giselle talked and talked with the obvious intention of preventing her from brooding. She went on about the babies, the weather, everything she could think of to keep from falling silent. Dear, sweet, caring Giselle, stuck with this emotional invalid, Cree mused dejectedly. Was the condition curable? Not likely, not now, not soon.

She had no more tears left, the last of them having been shed just before she'd gone to bed the night before. She had soaked her pillow. Now she could no longer cry. She wished she might reach inside her chest, remove her heart, hold it in front of her, and gently knead it, gradually work the anguish out of it, cleanse it.

Wyatt had been buried in the cemetery on the plateau of Méry sur Oise, sixteen miles north of the city. She had visited the grave that morning; it was the first time she'd been out of the house since the funeral four days earlier. Roland and Giselle had gone with her, the three of them taking the train. It had rained all morning. Standing over the grave, on which the headstone had not yet been installed, she could only stare down at the mound of unsettled earth and the rain splashing upon it—stand and stare, not uttering a sound, for a minute, two, then turn and walk away. Now she found herself wishing she had prayed, had given silent voice to words of comfort for his soul. But she had not, she couldn't, unable as she was wholly to accept the fact that he was buried there at her feet and would lie there forever.

Returning to the city and to St.-Germain-des-Prés, coming out of the subway station and walking to Rue du Bac, they had passed a little church wedged between two large buildings on the Boulevard Raspail. The rain had let up, the sun was out, and the city glowed and glistened under the bright November sky. The windows in the housetops looked like shimmering, flashing diamonds. Standing out from the checkerboard pattern of the roofs, gables looked as if they were preparing to leap into the sky.

A wedding party was coming out of the church. The bridegroom was gangling, too tall for his suit, his collar too large for his neck, his Adam's apple bobbing nervously. He seemed frightened and dazed. He held a bouquet of rosebuds, gripping the stems so that the flowers tilted downward. His bride, much shorter than he, looked self-possessed in comparison, serene, smiling and nodding to the friends, relatives, and well-wishers who formed a gauntlet, flinging rice and voicing congratulations, as the bride and groom came down the steps. The bride wore a tiara of white blossoms and she carried roses set in embroidered-edged white paper. At the curb they got into a horse-drawn *fiacre*. The onlookers waved and shouted farewells, and the horse clopped off.

Cree and Giselle and Roland had stopped to watch. May you both live happily ever after, Cree had thought.

She was almost done with the broth when the phone jangled. It was the overseas operator—Marjorie came on the line. Cree sighed inwardly and shook her head at Giselle.

"Lucretia? I hope I'm not interrupting anything. I had to call. I've been on pins and needles wondering what's happening."

"I've just got home from the hospital," Cree lied. "I was going to call you. Everything's in chaos here. Marjorie, we have a boy and a girl."

"Marvelous! I'm so happy for you both."

"Wyatt and Marjorie."

"Marjorie? How flattering. Tell me all about them. Are they beautiful? What a question, of course they are! Does he look like Wyatt? Does she look like you?"

"Everybody seems to think so."

"You sound absolutely exhausted. It's no wonder. You two must be so proud. I bet Daddy's bursting his buttons. You tell him for me, ride high while he can, now start two o'clock feedings and washing out diapers. No, I'll tell him myself, put him on. And don't let him hang up, I'll want to talk more to you. Isn't this exciting!"

"He's not here at the moment, he's over at a friend's and won't be back until late."

"Shame on him, running off and leaving you to do everything. Tell him I said he should be ashamed." She laughed. "No, just tell him I called and congratulations and I wouldn't be at all upset if he sat down and wrote me a line now and then. Oh, I know all he does is work, but my dear, you really must make him pitch in and help. You're going to have your hands full with two. I did with him alone." Again she laughed. "Bless him, I can just picture him changing diapers. I'd give my eyeteeth to see that. The new daddy. Oh, but we can talk about him anytime. Tell me all about my grandchildren. What a shock, I'm a grandmother! Twice. I do wish I could see them. I came over too early. I should be there now to help."

Cree described the babies, consciously striving to keep her tone cheerful, to avoid any suspicion that something was wrong. Marjorie talked and talked; it was nearly forty minutes before she said good-bye. Cree cradled the receiver and turned to Giselle, her eyes misting.

"Poor woman. I've never lied to her before, but I couldn't tell her, I just couldn't."

"Of course not."

"I'll have to write her. Tonight. It's better, the phone is so damned impersonal."

"Can't it wait a day or so? You're tired."

"I ache all over I'm so tired." She dropped into her chair, her eyes fixed on the soup bowl. "Giselle, Giselle . . ."

Giselle put her arm around Cree's shoulder. "Would you like more broth? I can heat up what's left."

"No, thanks. It was delicious, but . . . Oh, Giselle, why did I do it? Why?"

"You couldn't tell her over the phone."

"Not that. This." She flung out her arm. "Coming to Paris. It's my fault, you know, all my doing."

"What are you talking about?"

"I was the one who hounded and hounded him until he changed his mind and agreed to try it. If I'd kept my mouth shut, we'd still be in New Haven. He'd be finishing up his junior year. If I hadn't forced him to come, this never would have happened. He'd still be alive, don't you see?"

"That's crazy!"

"It's true."

"You didn't force him to come. Nobody forces his sort to do anything, any more than I could force Roland. He came because he wanted to, because he knew in his heart he had to. If you'd never said a word about it, he still would have come sooner or later."

"No!"

"Cree, he was an artist. There's no way you can keep people with talent from expressing it, not unless you chain them in a dungeon. He would have come over even if you were dead against it. He would have quit his college and gone into painting full-time. And ended up here. How can you say you forced him?"

"I feel so guilty."

"Only because you want to."

Cree stared as if she couldn't believe her ears.

"I know," Giselle went on. "How can I say that? I'm not trying to be cruel, but you're doing what many do in the same situation. You loved him, he's gone, you want to blame yourself. You're like the husband who's lost his wife in childbirth. He blames himself for making her pregnant. You let Wyatt go out without buttoning his coat, you let him skip breakfast. He should have taken a cab from school the day it rained, and you blame yourself for not being there and insisting on it."

"You're right, I do think there were many things I should have done and didn't. I do feel guilty, I can't help it."

"It's absurd. You took better care of him than he took of himself. And you can't blame Paris, who's to say he wouldn't have caught pneumonia at the college? There's flu and pneumonia all over the States."

"I guess. What time is it?"

"Almost eight thirty."

Cree got up. "I have to check on them."

The babies were asleep, Wyatt sucking his thumb hungrily. She kissed them. The night light cast a soft glow over the Mother Goose characters. They actually seemed to be marching to silent drums and bugles. She went back to the kitchen. Giselle was drying the soup bowls and putting them away. Cree laid her hand on her arm.

"You needn't stay. I'll be all right. Not that you're not welcome, but I hate to think of you leaving Roland alone night after night on my account."

"It's good for him for a few nights. Keeps him from taking me for granted." She winked and grinned and glanced about. "Besides, I like coming here. I like your corners. Every time I go into one I don't have to duck my head, as I do in the garret. Are you going to write that letter?"

"Tomorrow. I wouldn't be able to keep my eyes open tonight."

"Why don't you go to bed? I'll stay and keep an eye on things. Till midnight, at least."

"I dread writing that letter. It'll be impossible. How can I tell her?"

"You'll find a way. You're good with words."

"It might be better if I wrote to Charles Crowder. Ask him to tell her." She shook her head. "No, I can't put it on him, it's my job."

"But perhaps it would be easier if she heard it from him."

"I don't know. I'll wait to decide when I'm not so tired."

"Do you plan to stay in Paris or will you go home?"

"Home?" She held up her hands. "This is it. There's nothing to go back to New York for. I couldn't go back to living with my grandfather. And I wouldn't want to live with Marjorie—not that I don't love her, she's the kindest human being I've ever known, but the two of us would be like two old maids in perpetual mourning, consoling each other, living in the past. Strange, it was just about this time a year ago that his father was killed. It's scary, as if it was all scheduled." She sighed.

"Two lives for two lives," said Giselle. Cree looked at her, puzzled. "Two people you love die. Two you love come to take their place, two beautiful babies. Cree, in all this nightmare have you stopped to realize that you're the mother of two beautiful, perfect children? How I envy you."

"Do you? I'm sorry, I'm the last woman in the world you should envy."

Chapter Twenty-five

Cree would not leave Paris, but she could no longer tolerate the apartment. The walls were beginning to close in on her, assailing her with reminders of Wyatt's presence. It was as if he had gone out and would be back shortly. Putting his materials and equipment away in a closet, hiding them from view, taking everything out of the studio, helped not at all. She continued to see him everywhere: standing at his easel, lounging on the settee, sitting in the garden under the bare catalpa trees, in the nursery bending over the cribs and talking to the children. And he was in bed beside her, within reach of her hand and her lips. Lying in the darkness, she imagined she could hear his measured breathing.

When the estate was settled and she came into her inheritance, she decided to move and found exactly what she wanted almost immediately.

She received a letter from Olivia with welcome news. No sooner had she finished reading it than she sat down and wrote to her.

Dearest Livvy:
   Congratulations to you both! I hope it's twins. Mine keep me so busy I rarely get a chance to sit

down, but I adore them. I love being a mother.
Nothing in the world beats it for satisfaction. Keep
me posted, and take very good care of mother-
to-be.

In answer to your question as to what my plans
are: I've come to love Paris. In spite of what
happened, I still feel at home here. I don't see
how I could feel so much at home in New York.
Paris seems to have the same effect on everyone
who comes here. So I'll be staying. I can afford
it—I got a letter from Charles Crowder in Monday
morning's mail. My inheritance amounts to just
under six million dollars. Isn't that preposterous?
Most of it is still on deposit in banks in New York.
The rest is in our account here in the Bank of
Paris. I don't deserve it. I feel guilty. The last
thing I want is to be wealthy. I guess I just never
thought about money the way others do. You,
Jule, and I never really had any of our own, in
spite of our silver spoons.

I miss him so, Livvy. I feel utterly drained; I
have no energy, no drive. Getting out of bed in the
morning is hard labor. It's as if I were waiting
for something to happen, for a magician to touch
me with his wand, and whoosh—it's out of my
system. A magician or something or somebody to
snap me out of it so I can go back to living. Everybody tells me it's normal, going through the
doldrums, feeling so lifeless. But I'm getting fed
up with it. It's even changing my outlook. I used
to think Paris was the most spectacular city in the
world, lovely beyond description. It still is, of
course, but not through these eyes. I just don't see
the color, I don't smell the flowers, the birds don't
sing, the seminary bell on the other side of the

wall doesn't sound the same. It used to be music, now it's just a jarring sound.

Thank God for the children. They're healthy and happy and growing up so fast they seem to change from day to day. I'm sending the latest snapshots. You'll have a shoeboxful before long. Roland Robays, Wyatt's best friend over here, who studies at Studio Gleyre, has promised to do a portrait of them on their first birthday. I can't wait.

I do hope all is well with you two, that Alec's law firm is prospering. There's no need to ask if you're happy. Do you ever see Grandfather? I'm sure you do, being only ten blocks away. I still haven't heard from him and long ago decided not to write him again. Still, I miss him. I can't help wondering how he looks, how he's feeling, if he's still as cantankerous as ever. Of course he is, what a question! One of these days you and Alec ought to put Mrs. Bates up for sainthood. Oh, oh, I hear crying. Somebody needs changing.

Back again. I'm glad you had lunch with Marjorie. Isn't she darling? I miss her, I miss you all, but if I ever left Paris, I know I'd regret it. We were so happy here when Wyatt was alive. Oh, to be young, dedicated, ambitious, and roughing it in St.-Germain-des-Prés! As I say, I still love it, even if the glow has dimmed. I keep telling myself it's only temporary. I wish you and Alec could come for a visit. Marjorie's promised to come back next spring.

I'll have plenty of room for you. I went house-hunting yesterday and found an adorable place in Montmartre. I'm hoping the change of scenery will do me good. Wish me luck.

I love you both and I hope it's a girl. Or a boy. How I love mine!

Much love,
L.

Two days before the year turned into the new decade Cree moved into a house on Rue de la Boëtie, a five-story, yellow-brick building trimmed in white, with a massive door surmounted by a peaked and intricately carved lintel. The jaws of a ferocious-looking Bacchus clasped a brass knocker. Window boxes below each of the windows sat empty, awaiting the flowers that would emerge with the warmth of spring. A brick walkway led from an iron gate to the stoop. The foyer within ended at the foot of an impressive staircase distinguished by plinths and cornices in pearl gray; the wall beside it was hung with violet-colored paper in long stripes of unequal widths, and there were coffee-colored double doors at each landing. The entrance hall was painted garden-green and off to the left was the dining room. Two enormous rooms on the second and third floors were to serve as the gallery for her art collection. The rear of the house looked out upon a wilderness of winter-withered plants and leafless trees. A stone path meandered through the garden, and there was a mirror in the fence at the far end, which created the illusion of all but interminable depth.

Across the street and two doors up at number 23 was the studio of Pablo Picasso. Cree had seen him from an upstairs window shortly after she had moved in. He was big and broad-shouldered, with a massive chest, and wore his beret at a confidently jaunty angle. His face hung loosely, like a pudding, and his complexion was bone-white. She followed him with her eyes as he walked with his head down and his hands thrust deep into his pockets. A lovely house in what promised to be an interesting neighborhood, she thought, turning from the window.

Giselle insisted she hire a nanny to help her take care of the children. The nanny's name was Margaret Willis. She was English, educated, refined, a lady in every respect. She was almost fifty and looked even older. Age had begun its relentless assault upon her pretty features, etching a hundred lines, which appeared to fade when she smiled and her lovely green eyes lit up. Interviewing her for the position, Cree found her pleasant, unusually personable, and professional. Her credentials were excellent. She had worked for an English couple in Paris for eight years. The husband, a career soldier, had recently been posted to India. Not wanting to leave Paris, admittedly shuddering at the thought of Bombay, Margaret had reluctantly given notice.

Cree also hired a housekeeper. Like Mme. Boulette, Mme. Simone Ratelle was a war widow. She was a slender, quiet, nervous woman; Cree immediately felt sorry for her. In spite of her frail appearance, she turned out to be a tireless worker, as conscientious as Mrs. Bates, priding herself on keeping the house immaculate.

Moving out of 110 Rue du Bac proved the tonic Cree needed to restore her flagging *joie de vivre*. Even though the days were marching toward the heart of winter, the sun suddenly seemed to shine more brightly, the city seemed more dazzling, the hard grayness of the season seemed to soften. Even more helpful than ridding herself of the apartment was suddenly finding herself surrounded by good neighbors. The area was an enclave of amity. She could not leave the house without meeting one or another of her neighbors, exchanging greetings, and chatting. It was like a friendly rooming house *al fresco*.

Routinely, she stayed at home in the morning to be with the children and attend to her correspondence, answering letters, paying bills, and taking time to pore through *Art International, La Revue du Louvre, XX Siècle*, and the *Gazette des Beaux-Arts*, looking for news of the latest acquisitions, sales, and scheduled auctions. When the children took their afternoon nap she generally went out to follow up what she'd read about in the morning. And throughout the rest of the winter into spring and summer she worked at building her collection.

The time was propitious. In the postwar economy prices were inflated, but good to excellent paintings, now and then even a masterpiece, came on the market. One had to be lucky. Timing was extremely important. She would never be as fortunate as she had been when she'd bought her Monets, arriving at the gallery barely minutes after the going-out-of-business sign was put in the window. But she worked hard at it and did well for herself. She was by instinct a shrewd bargainer and became shrewder with experience. Into her hands came no fewer than seven Cranach copperplates, nine more woodcuts, and four paintings. Among the paintings was one that, although extraordinarily expensive, she considered the prize of her collection, the so-called lost painting of 1545 depicting hares catching and roasting hunters.

One of the four paintings was the work of Lucas Cranach the Younger—an oil on copper, *Christ and Adulteress*, depicting the Savior zealously defending the adulteress, the two of them surrounded by angry citizens. Besides the "lost painting," Lucas Cranach the Elder's canvases including a tempera-on-paper painting of two dead cedar waxwings suspended by their necks from a nail. It was a grim, even odious, subject, in Cree's opinion, but it was a Cranach original, was available, was in quite definite contrast to his religious and mythological subjects, and she could not resist buying it.

The fourth painting was from the artist's later period: his *Lucretia*. Roland Robays had discovered it in an obscure but interesting little gallery on the Right Bank. He called to tell her about it, and before the day was out, it was hers.

It was dated 1535. The quality of the painting was superb, suggesting that only Cranach himself could have executed it. And it was in good condition. According to legend, Lucretia, a Roman lady, was raped by the son of the tyrant Tarquinius Superbus. Informing her husband and father and exacting their oaths of vengeance, she then stabbed herself to death. Lucretia's fate was a subject that had inspired many artists of the Renaissance. The lady personified the highest and most enviable human virtues—courage, dignity, and honor—and her death was considered heroic. However, Cranach had treated it melodramatically, apparently intending to stir the onlooker's imagination as opposed to his sympathy. He had set off her half-naked body with fabrics lined with soft, fluffy fur; her fashionable hairstyle was resplendent with highlights and detail, and the glow of her golden chain and her jewels emphasized the contrast between the rounded forms of her breasts and face and the sharp blade of her dagger. In essence, the picture could be criticized as superficial, but in its own way it was interesting. Cranach's wealthy patrons delighted in just such portraits, and he had produced many.

But there was only one *Lucretia*. Cree was overjoyed to get it and wasn't in the least bothered by the fact that the artist had portrayed her namesake in the act of suicide.

Cree sold the furniture from the apartment on Rue du Bac and set about furnishing her house. It offered splendid possibilities. The fourteen-foot walls in each of the two upstairs galleries featured exquisite eighteenth-century *boiserie* from La Remise du Soleil washed in three pastel shades, with arched, mirrored panels and tall windows serving to soften the *boiserie* geometry. She furnished the living room, dining room, and upstairs rooms with period pieces and had the sofas, daybed, skirted tables, and windows done in a variety of fabrics from Clarence House.

For her own bedroom on the fourth floor she bought a huge four-poster, a Louis XV *lit à la polonaise*, with two hundred yards of gauze flowing down from a baldachin. Unbleached muslin filtered the light through the windows, and Louis XV *fauteuils*, a trictrac table, a nineteenth-century Beauvais tapestry, and a Louis XV commode completed the arrangement.

Apart from her new Cranachs, she acquired a Teniers, an early Rubens, and one of Goya's eleven cabinet pictures, originally done for the Academy of San Fernando in Madrid and imbued with a singularly tragic intensity.

When she was not at home or out haunting the galleries, she made new friends with an ease that astonished her. At a party given by Mme. Duvivier, who held court in a thirty-room monstrosity of a house on the corner of Rue de Courcelle and who wore the most bizarre clothes Cree had ever seen, she finally met Picasso, along with Paul Poiret, whom she found one of the most congenial, good-hearted men of talent she had ever known. He was in his early forties, a big man, with perpetually twinkling eyes and dark hair slicked back and stuck to his scalp in a "patent leather look" like Rudolph Valentino's. He dressed impeccably. He had no choice but to do so, being the world's foremost designer of *haute couture*. He chain-smoked cigarettes and tossed off brandy with the ease of a thirsty runner swigging ice-water. Three years before, he had set up the painter Raoul Dufy in a textile design studio on the Avenue de Clichy. He was a personal friend of practically every prominent painter in Paris and, according to Mme. Duvivier, was beloved by everyone who knew him except his competitor and professional archenemy, Coco Chanel.

Picasso also proved fascinating. In October of the previous year, just before the war ended, looking for more space and wishing to be close to Paul Rosenberg, his principal dealer, he had moved into 23 Rue de la Boëtie. He sat in a circle of nine people, with Cree and Poiret opposite him, regaling the gathering with a description of the sloppiness of his studio. The room was filled with Gitanes smoke contributed mostly by Pioret and Mme. Duvivier, whom Cree had yet to see without a cigarette hanging from her Cupid's bow lips.

Cree studied Picasso. Nature had roughed out his face with six vertical lines angling downward from his eyes, nostrils, and the corners of his lips. His dark eyes were restless, his mouth sardonic, on the verge of a sneer, as if it were crammed full of insults waiting to be spewed forth. But this was deceiving, for he was not an insulting man. He was hard on one person only— himself. Cree found him as admirable in his own rustic and avowedly bohemian way as Poiret was in his cultured way. Picasso talked with his hands, his voice rolling low in his throat, except when anger colored his cheeks or amusement lit up his hangdog eyes. Listening to him and to those around her laughing at his description of his work habits, it came back to her that when Cubism was barely more than an untried concept, a new direction not yet explored in the ateliers of Montparnasse, this man had taken it in hand and given it meaning and stature, imposing it first upon Montmartre and in time upon the rest of the world.

The conversation drifted from the condition of his studio to a subject that could all too easily be debated for hours on end: the artist's attitude toward his art. Cree remembered Giselle asking her how Wyatt felt toward his art: Was he sincere? How deep was his commitment? Poiret had raised the question, and Picasso answered it by saying that never in his life had he set out to produce "a masterpiece."

"On the contrary, my only aim is to put all that I love or hate into the canvas."

His methods verified this assertion. Discarded odds and ends went into his sculptures, many of his paintings had been done on dirty pieces of cardboard, and there were times when, finding himself short of materials, he had used discarded paper for his gouaches.

All evening long the conversation centered on art—questions, discussions, arguments, even an impromptu lecture by Rodrigue Lemeux, a little-known Impressionist, on the politics involved in getting one's works exhibited.

Little did Cree realize when the party was over that it was to be a night she would hold precious in memory, marking as it did the beginning of a new life for her.

Chapter Twenty-six

The months fell from the calendar, the seasons changed, changing the face of Paris—the lady's face, but not her heart. The city was too full of joy, of music and desire and love and even a little madness to allow room for pessimism. Great days were arriving, the last days of the magnificent Ballets Russes, the days when the music of Honegger and Milhaud filled an appreciative people's souls, the heyday of Nijinsky and Pavlova, Josephine Baker's moment in the spotlight. These were glorious times, when living in Paris was a prize to be coveted.

The twins were growing up, becoming young man and young lady, soon to start school. Life was changing for Cree, in style, in routine, in innumerable ways. Regretfully, she saw less and less of Roland and Giselle. He had become successful, very successful for an artist only two years out of school. He was so busy working he rarely had time to socialize. But even though the wolf had been dismissed from the door permanently, Giselle also continued to work. As she explained to Cree over lunch at L'Escargot, it was either work or stand behind Roland and watch him paint.

True to her promise, Marjorie came to visit in the spring of 1920, staying six weeks. Olivia and Alec could not come. Cree continued writing to Olivia and to Julia, who, after a brief but extraordinarily successful career in movies, a turbulent marriage, and a divorce, had grown disillusioned with Hollywood and returned to New York with her daughter Claudia.

Paris became gayer, more exciting, enchanting. Each year with the arrival of spring, the city seemed to become even more dazzling than the year before. Styles were revolutionized. Paul Poiret, Gabrielle Chanel, Charles Worth, Jeanne Lanvin, and other dictators of fashion joined their geniuses to liberate women from the cocoons of cloth that passed for stylish attire, baring flesh, revealing the figure, assaulting the eye with color and design. Hemlines climbed. The theatergoing public waxed ecstatic over a production called *L'École des Cocottes*, in which the performers wore short-skirted chemises made from gold and silver lamé. A makeup trick five thousand years old—the smudge under the eye—was rediscovered and became the rage. The stylish woman wore her hair short and as straight as a boy's, with her hairline at the back carefully clipped and shaved. Huge earrings fashioned of imitation gemstones tested the holding power of her earlobes.

Observed Paul Poiret in exasperation, "Now women look like nothing so much as the undernourished boys one sees working in post offices."

In November of 1925, two days after the twins' sixth birthday, Cree received a letter from Charles Crowder. She was having breakfast, gazing out at the rain-ravaged garden, dispirited by five sunless days. She heard the postman's ring. Simone brought the letter to her.

Noting the return address, she hesitated just long enough to let the adder of fear touch her heart. The last time Crowder had contacted Wyatt had been to tell him that his father had been killed. It was so predictable; practically every time one heard from one's lawyer it was bad news. In her haste to open the envelope she tore the letter. Flattening the pieces, holding the torn edges flush, she read:

Dear Mrs. Chance:

It is my unhappy duty to inform you that your late husband's mother has been taken seriously ill with cancer. Her physician, Dr. Stabler, has told me that he does not expect her to live.

You will undoubtedly be hearing from her, if you have not already. She will probably avoid any allusion to her condition, but I felt that you should know about it. If I hear anything further from Dr. Stabler, I'll contact you at once.

Again, I'm sorry to be the conveyor of such tragic news. Please permit me to extend my deepest sympathy.

Sincerely,
Charles Crowder

She crumpled the letter, closed her eyes and attempted to absorb the news. Poor, poor Marjorie. Chance—the family was fittingly named; father, son, and now mother doomed before their time. It was so dreadful, so horribly unfair. She called to Simone, who came at once, beaming, then abandoning her smile at the sight of Cree's expression.

"Oui, madame?"

Maggie Willis came up behind Simone, also noticing the look on Cree's face.

"Bad news?" Maggie asked.

Cree handed her the letter. "I have to call the Compagnie Générale Transatlantique," she said, as Maggie read in silence.

"Will you take the children with you?" Maggie asked, as Simone brushed by to get the telephone directory.

Cree pondered. "I should, she'll want to see them. You'll come too. Simone can take care of things here on her own. Would you mind coming?"

"Whatever you say." `

"I'd be lost without you. And when we get there I've a feeling I'll be running around every day. I want to see my sister. Maybe even my grandfather." Simone came back with the directory. Cree riffled through it.

"Let me call," said Maggie, "you'll want to start packing."

"Poor Marjorie, almost since the day Wyatt and I got married it's been all downhill for her. I hope to heaven we can get passage right away, get there in time. Poor woman."

Chapter Twenty-seven

The *Provence*'s captain rarely pressed his ship to its top speed of twenty-two knots; in consequence the crossing was infuriatingly slow for Cree. Day after day, in spite of the frigid wind, she paced the deck as if urging the vessel to greater speed. She cabled ahead for Charles Crowder to meet them. He was there at the dock, as lugubrious-looking as ever, struggling to smile, only partially succeeding. He drove them to Marjorie's house and dropped them off, apologizing for having to get back to the office.

Janice, the maid, greeted them at the door.

"How is she?" whispered Cree.

Janice was about to answer when Marjorie called from the living room.

"Is that you, Lucretia?"

She was sitting before the fireplace under her portrait, clad in a plain white silk day dress with a small brooch pinned at her breast; she wore no other jewelry. On her lap was a plaid robe and around her shoulders a straw-colored knitted wool shawl. Cree nearly gasped aloud. Marjorie looked eighty years old. The loss of weight had drained the beauty from her face, and her complexion had a waxen hue, which the color of her shawl only emphasized. Her eyes seemed much larger, as if the rest of her face had shrunk around them; they were lusterless and suffused with weariness. Bracing herself on the arms of the chair, she tried to get up. Cree hurried to her, kissed her, with one hand gently kept her sitting.

She introduced Maggie Willis and Wyatt and Marjorie. Wyatt bowed stiffly; he wore his dark-brown worsted suit with knee socks, a white shirt, and necktie. His hair was combed like his grandfather's, parted in the middle and slightly curling at the ends. His sister wore a black velveteen bloomer dress. Her blonde hair was pinned up in the front and reached down to the small of her back in a V. Her grandmother held up her arms. The twins hesitated, looked at each other, and ran to be held. She hugged and kissed them and beamed happily.

"My darlings, my darlings, Grandmother's been aching to see you and hold you." She held her namesake at arm's length. "She looks just like you. And you can see Wyatt in his face, in his eyes. How was your crossing?"

"Smooth," said Wyatt.

"Choppy," said his sister.

Marjorie laughed. "Which?"

"Don't ask," said Cree. "They can't even get together on black and white. It was so peaceful around the house before they learned to talk."

Once more Marjorie seized them, eliciting a squeal from her granddaughter.

"Come along," said Maggie, holding out a hand for each of them. "We must change our clothes." Janice had appeared. Maggie followed her out, Wyatt pausing to look back and smile at his grandmother and blow her a kiss, which his sister promptly began chiding him for.

"It's so good to see you," said Marjorie, taking Cree's hands and searching her eyes. "Five years is too long. I should have gone every spring, just dropped everything and climbed aboard the first ship." She shook her head slowly, her expression wistful. "When I think of all the things I should have done and didn't get around to over the years, all the plans that were never carried through. We live by calendars and clocks, and yet life can be so frightfully disordered; impulse just takes over. We move from day to day, blissfully oblivious to the fact that it can all end at any time. And you haven't done half the things you wanted to do or ought to have done." She shrugged. "Then suddenly . . ."

"Please, Marjorie."

"Oh, it's all right now. It wasn't before, but now I can handle it. Really. Dr. Stabler told me day before yesterday that I have about two months. He didn't want to tell me. Getting it out of him was like pulling teeth. I badgered and badgered the poor man and finally broke him down. When he told me, I nearly fainted, even though I had assumed that I didn't have much time left. Two months. Early in February. I despise February, I always did. I think it's everybody's least-favorite month, that's why they made it so short. I'm sorry, I must sound grisly, sitting here running on about it so."

"I understand, I do."

"It's just that I can't see any sense in brooding, feeling sorry for myself. I'm not suffering, I'm comfortable as can be, Janice takes good care of me, friends come to visit. My sister Meredith will be dropping in. She comes every day, bless her heart.

"I look back on my life and weigh the good against the bad. I can't complain, Lucretia. I've had a good life, a wonderful husband, the finest son a mother could have, and the best daughter in the world." She squeezed Cree's hand. "Life's been good to me." She smiled. "And Christmas is coming. We'll sail through the holidays with all flags flying. With you and the children here, it'll be the happiest Christmas ever."

"We'll make it the happiest."

"Dear Lucretia, when I got your cable I whooped like a football fan at the winning touchdown. Ask Janice if I didn't. You should have heard me. It wasn't very dignified."

She rattled on. Cree struggled to contain her tears. What a perfectly splendid human being she was. What nobility, what courage. She staunchly refused to let death intimidate her.

Aunt Meredith arrived shortly before tea. She was five years older than Marjorie, her face creased, her skin mottled. The fingers of her right hand curved slightly, as if she were preparing to take hold of a glass. She had been drinking. Her watery, pink-rimmed eyes were slightly glazed, her breath smelled of stale liquor. Prohibition appeared to have had no effect whatsoever on her habit—her husband, the bottle, as Wyatt had once said.

Cree had last seen Meredith at Wyatt's father's funeral; she liked her, in spite of her habitual petty complaining, her pessimism, and occasional displays of childishness. In times of stress she could always be counted on to lend her strength and support.

While Marjorie visited with the children, Meredith took Cree into the study to talk. The room was little changed from when Wyatt and Charles Crowder had had their talk, when she had passed by the partially opened door and overheard part of the conversation. The dominant piece of furniture was a leather-topped desk, which was complemented by studded leather-and-oak chairs and bookcases that completely concealed two walls. They sat across from each other.

"How have you been, Lucretia? How is Paris?"

"I love it."

"I don't blame you. Still, it's a pity you're so far away. Marjorie misses you dreadfully. She's always talking about you and the children." She frowned. "I'm sure you noticed, she's very bad, poor dear, getting worse."

"At least she's not in pain."

"Is that what she told you? She's fibbing. Stabler is giving her pills for it." She spat out the word disdainfully. "But they don't help. It's been a rugged four weeks. Of course, you know Marjorie, the iron lady. She wouldn't admit she was suffering if her life . . . Oh, dear. Charles met you at the dock?"

"He drove us here."

"Did he happen to mention anything about the business?"

"No. What about it?"

Meredith sighed. "I need a drink." Getting up, she pulled the bellcord. "I guess he didn't say anything because it's not the best news to welcome you home with. Not on top of Marjorie's illness." Pursing her lips thoughtfully, she lowered her eyes as she returned to her chair. "Lucretia, the company's on the brink of collapse."

Cree sucked in her breath sharply. Meredith nodded.

"How? What's happened?"

"Outsiders have been systematically draining it. I don't know the particulars, but as I understand it, it all started about three years ago. Business began falling off. Charles told me it was as if it was being chipped away with hammer and chisel. You know that Wyatt's father had very capable people with him. They've been trying to fight off the wolves and managed to for a while, but lately . . ." She shook her head. "Marjorie doesn't know, she doesn't suspect a thing. You mustn't say a word."

"I won't."

Janice tapped lightly at the door.

"Scotch and soda, Janice, please." Meredith looked at Cree.

"I don't want anything," Cree said.

Janice withdrew, closing the door. Meredith pulled her chair up close, laying one hand on Cree's.

"I feel you should know. It's your problem, too."

"I'm glad you told me. Please go on."

"As I said, outsiders have been draining it, taking away the accounts one by one."

"How can they?"

"According to Charles, it's the usual way you go about taking over a company. You pilfer the accounts, get it into the red, then step in and buy it for a song."

"Who are these 'outsiders'?"

"That he didn't say."

"I'll talk to him."

"I'm sorry, Lucretia. It all falls on your shoulders, I'm afraid."

"I appreciate your telling me."

"Marjorie won't be around much longer." She sniffed and took out a handkerchief, touching the corner of her eye and her nose. "I suppose there are some who'd say, so what? Why bother trying to save it? What difference does it make now?"

"It makes a great deal of difference to me and to my son. Even if I didn't have children, I wouldn't stand by and do nothing to stop it."

"I only wish there was something you could do."

"I have a lot of money, Meredith."

"I don't know if money can help. That's the problem, I really just don't know the ins and outs of it all. I wish I could be more helpful. Talk to Charles."

"First thing tomorrow."

Janice reappeared with Meredith's drink.

"Excuse me," she said to Cree, "tea is being served in the living room."

Cree phoned Olivia and then Julia, two tonics to lift her spirits. Talking to them did just that. They both insisted she call Mrs. Bates and tell her she would be bringing the children over that evening. Cree was less than enthusiastic over the prospect of facing Grandfather after so many years. He had a long memory. When his feelings were injured, he was a long time recovering. She told Olivia she'd think about it. Later, speaking to Julia, she capitulated, deciding that there was nothing to be gained by being obstinate about it. Marjorie's condition would be keeping her in New York for the next two months at least. She and Grandfather would have to face each other sooner or later.

Finally Cree called her grandfather's house. Cora, the maid, answered the phone and put Mrs. Bates on.

"Lucretia! Is it really you? I don't believe it!"

"How are you, Mrs. Bates?"

"Wonderful now, top of the world. How are the children, the twins? I've been dying to see them, and you; all of us have."

"Even Grandfather?"

"Absolutely." Cree laughed. Mrs. Bates lowered her voice. "He'd love to see you, I know he would. He just got home from the office; he's upstairs in the study. Shall I put him on?"

"No, no, no. Don't even tell him I called. It's better if I just walk in. Livvy and Jule will be there for moral support. He won't dare castigate me with them standing by. Just be sure he stays home after dinner. We'll be coming at eight."

"It'll be so good to see you. Seven years. It's been like seven centuries."

"Julia will be bringing Claudia. It's hard to believe I've never even seen her. Or Olivia and Alec's daughter, Jessica."

"Don't you dare come without the twins. His Nibs'll have a fit if you show up without them. So will I."

"He'll have a fit anyway; he'll probably take one look at me and start throwing things."

"Nonsense, he'll be delighted to see you."

"Don't bet on it. And don't tell him I'm coming."

"Why don't you come earlier, for dinner?"

"I'd like to, but I don't want to run out on Mrs. Chance." She told her briefly about Marjorie's illness. Mrs. Bates clucked sympathetically.

"How dreadful."

"We'll be there on the dot. I can't wait to see you."

They finished talking, and she hung up. A family reunion: unbelievable. A while ago she would have laughed in the face of anyone even hinting at such a possibility. She glanced at her watch. In a little more than three hours she'd be walking up the steps to the double doors of 1 East Sixty-first Street, ringing the bell of Shackleford Castle, to be greeted by Mrs. Bates and the maids and raising her eyes to the sight of Grandfather looking down on her from the second-floor landing.

Chapter Twenty-eight

Cree greeted Olivia, Alec, and little Jessica loudly in the foyer. In the years that she and Olivia had been separated, Olivia had come to look remarkably like Mother, thought Cree, the same ash-blonde hair, high cheekbones, flawless complexion, and Mother's beautiful aquamarine eyes. Alec looked the same, with his dark, tightly curling hair, dark complexion and eyes, and gentle, kindly manner that was almost bashful. They greeted her and the children, Alec picking up first Wyatt, then Marjorie, swinging them about, setting them both shouting, bringing Grandfather to the top of the stairway,

"Look what the cat dragged in," he muttered, the corners of his mouth pulling up in a quick and deliberately vague suggestion of a smile.

"Hello, Grandfather."

"Hello, yourself." He started down the stairs. He looked the same, Cree thought—rugged, powerful, his torso stretching the material of his suit, his light-blue eyes twinkling. He moved easily for a man in his early seventies, as light on his feet as anyone thirty years younger.

"How long has it been?" he asked. "Ten years?"

"Seven, and you know it," interposed Olivia.

"Last I heard from you, Lucretia, was that cold-blooded telephone call out of the blue."

"The last you heard from me was a letter explaining."

"I don't recall any letter."

"Because you never read it."

"Now, hold your horses, young lady . . ."

"Both of you!" burst out Olivia, coming between them as he reached the bottom of the stairs and started toward them. "Let's not start. Let's have a pleasant, enjoyable family reunion."

"Where's Julia?" Grandfather asked Olivia, pointedly ignoring her admonition.

"Coming."

"She'd better bring Claudia. Last time she didn't."

Wyatt and Marjorie had fled to the front room at the sight of their great-grandfather bearing down on them with a scowl on his face and a belligerent tone. They stood in the doorway watching him, their eyes big, their expressions so grave that Cree almost burst out laughing.

"Hello, there," he said.

"Hello, sir," said Wyatt.

"Oh, now, that's a good start," responded Grandfather. Stooping, he held out his arms. "Come say hello properly."

Both hesitated, looking at Cree. She nodded slightly.

"Come on," he urged, "you don't need permission."

They came to him; he hugged them both. "And what do you call yourselves?"

"I'm Wyatt Chance the Third and this is my little sister, Midgy."

"Marjorie!" shrilled Marjorie, glaring at Wyatt.

"It's a pleasure to meet you," he said, shaking their hands. "How old are you?"

"Six going on seven," said Marjorie.

"And how old do you think I am?"

"A hundred?" asked Marjorie.

Everyone laughed, with one exception. "Do I look a hundred? I'm seventy-two."

The doorbell jangled. It was Julia with her husband Lloyd Rush, one of Alec's law partners, and little Claudia. Julia gave Cree a long hug. Suddenly the foyer erupted with chattering, everyone talking at once. Wyatt chased Marjorie, stopping short to stare at Claudia, then at Jessica, both of whom were appraising his sister. Julia touched Cree on the arm to get her attention.

"Look at Wyatt and Claudia and Jess."

"She's beautiful," said Cree, "she looks just like Mommy. And Jessica looks like Alec. They're both so cute; no wonder he's staring."

"Claudia's a handful. How in the world do you manage with two?"

"With help."

Grandfather ushered them into the front room. Drinks were served. He dandled one of his great-grandchildren after another on his knee and spoke in low tones with Alec and Lloyd. Cree talked with Olivia and Julia, watching her grandfather out of the corner of her eye. He appeared to get along well with Alec and Lloyd. She glanced about. The years hadn't changed Castle Shackleford one whit. She couldn't imagine coming back to stay. It was as gloomy as ever, infested with memories, happy, painful, warm and wonderful and black, like invisible wraiths floating about.

"Lucretia?"

"Yes, Grandfather?"

"Where are you staying?"

"At my mother-in-law's on Park Avenue."

"I hear she's ill."

"She's not expected to live."

"That's a shame. Damned unlucky, that family. But see here, if it gets inconvenient, you and the children are welcome to stay here. I'd certainly enjoy having you."

He was bending; the somewhat sour look on his face betrayed how he felt. It was always a yeoman effort for him, and the beneficiary of his generosity was always obliged to recognize that a certain amount of strain was involved for this particular benefactor.

"That's sweet of you," said Cree, "but I should stay with her."

"She's ill."

"I wouldn't want to hurt her feelings."

"You two get along?"

"Of course. I'm very fond of her."

He grunted; her answer seemed to disappoint him. "Well, the door's open if you want to use it. You don't have to if you don't want to."

As gracious as always, she thought, smiling inwardly. "Thank you."

They stayed very late, the children yawning as they started out the door. It had been a happy reunion, far happier than Cree would have thought possible. She was the last to leave. At the door he made her promise that she'd come back with Wyatt and Marjorie as soon as she could.

"No more than a week, or I'll come get you. I like the way that boy says sir."

The next morning Cree left the house immediately after breakfast with Marjorie and the children to make the rounds of the banks that held portions of her inheritance on deposit. She filled out the forms necessary to transfer the money to the Banque National de Paris.

Charles Crowder was waiting for her at the Palm Court in the Plaza Hotel for lunch at twelve thirty. A string quartet was working its way through one of Debussy's "Images." The dining room was only half-filled; at most of the tables were ladies in twos and fours who had been out shopping. The Palm Court was too cathedrallike to suit Cree, the ceiling much too high. Voices carried too far, unless you put your heads together and whispered. The stiff-backed waiters in their white jackets sped about, the music swelled to a crescendo and finished with a flourish. Then the tempo picked up ˉnoticeably as the quartet went into Strauss's *Tales from the Vienna Woods*.

"Mrs. Chance, so nice to see you again so soon," said Crowder.

The headwaiter seated them in a corner, whisking the Reserved sign from the table and brushing away a nonexistent crumb.

"It was very kind of you to pick us up at the dock," she said. "I know you're busy."

"Never too busy for old friends. I was glad to do it, to meet the children. And I'm glad you called me," he added, his tone tinged with sadness. He shook his head slowly. "It never rains but it pours. What exactly did Miss Meredith tell you?"

Cree related her conversation with Meredith. He nodded his way through it. Laughter broke out at the next table, and she suddenly wished they were in the study at the house or in his office, anyplace where they might close the door. The four women at the next table seemed to be enjoying themselves immensely. The laughter subsided; the waiter brought the women their check. Cree finished what she had to say.

"That's pretty much what's going on with Chance and Company," he said gravely.

"Who are these damned scavengers?"

He avoided her eyes, pretending his attention was drawn to the musicians.

"There's really only one scavenger. I do wish I didn't have to tell you."

"Don't bother, I think I know. Good God."

Crowder nodded. "He's behind it, with help from his friends. Of course, it goes back to that run-in he had with Mr. Chance over the Dorchester Building years ago. Did you know about that?"

"Yes."

"He's a ruthless man, your grandfather, if you don't mind my saying so."

"I don't mind the truth, Mr. Crowder. What he wants he takes, the devil take anybody who gets in his way. I don't believe this," she mused aloud.

"I beg your pardon?"

"Last night we had a reunion with my sisters at the house. All evening long he was as innocent as a lamb, playing with his great-grandchildren, without so much as a sheepish glance in my direction. When Meredith told me, I should have known it was he."

"The saddest part of it is that to men like your grandfather this sort of thing is strictly business."

"Of course. That's the way they justify anything they do, no matter how heinous it might be, how disgusting. The Dorchester Building was the germ of it. He enjoys nothing so much as getting even."

"It happens he's also an uncommonly shrewd businessman. The technique is quite simple. Concentrate on what you want, wreck it, buy it up for peanuts, then put the pieces back together again."

"He's not getting away with it."

"I'm afraid he has. If something isn't done, and quickly, the company is his. If it isn't already."

The waiter's shadow fell across the table. He proferred their menus.

"May I recommend the Dover sole?" he said.

"Will you give us a few minutes, please?" asked Crowder.

"Certainly, sir. Take your time."

He glided away.

"You think it's too late?" asked Cree.

"It's very late, down to days."

"I don't care if it's hours, he's got to be stopped! And I'll stop him. I have nearly six million dollars. I'll put every red cent into the fight, if need be. What are my chances of winning?"

"It's possible the major accounts might be persuaded to come back."

"Who can persuade them?"

"I'd be willing to try. It started as a trickle, the sort of thing easily ignored in the rush of everyday business. Now the dam's burst. People simply don't want to do business with a financial house that has money problems. Who can blame them? A financial house is really only a glorified bank, and when confidence goes out a bank window, the depositors come running in the door after their money." He frowned. "There's something else."

"More good news?"

"No, a thought. More of a last resort. We could sue

him for tampering. It would be practically impossible to prove. I'd be amazed if we could. You see, he's not doing his mischief directly. It's all done through friends. But bringing him into court would make him look bad. The newspapers would have a field day. In which case, he might think twice about it and back off."

She shook her head. "Not him. You don't know Hiram Shackleford. He couldn't care two pins what the press thinks of him, any more than his friend Henry Clay Frick or J. P. Morgan did. His only concern is getting what he wants.

"This time he's not going to. I'll stop him. Hire whomever you need to help. Do whatever has to be done. Keep all the bills, don't send them to the house. Marjorie's not to know anything about this. I'll see that you get all the money you need. If we don't get the business out of his clutches and back on its feet, I'll never be able to look in the mirror again. Mr. Crowder, I owe everything I have to my husband and his family. And I owe them this. My grandfather can't get away with this. He wins and wins, he's so used to winning he doesn't know how to lose. This time he's going to, if I have to stay in New York for the next two years!"

She stood up.

"Where are you going?"

"Downtown to his office. I'm sorry I have to desert you. May we have lunch tomorrow? We'll have a lot to talk about."

"Lunch, yes, of course." He seemed suddenly confused.

"If you're going back downtown, why don't we share a taxi?"

"By all means."

He was staring, rising slowly, tentatively from his chair. He seemed not only taken aback but even a little frightened of her. She only hoped she'd have the same effect on her grandfather.

Chapter Twenty-nine

"My, my, my, what a sight for sore eyes. And don't you look exquisite, just exquisite!"

Exquisite was Miss Myrna Dell Foley's favorite adjective. Myrna Dell Foley was Cree's grandfather's private secretary, a somewhat frazzled-looking bleached blonde well into her fifties, partial to severely tailored black worsted outfits that always looked like uniforms to Cree. But the woman's smile was genuine; she was gracious and good-hearted. The happy martyr, Livvy called her, in reference to her twenty-odd years in Caesar's employ. Myrna Dell Foley was a phenomenon. She never mislaid so much as a cancelled stamp; she could type one hundred twenty errorless words a minute and was a paragon of efficiency in everything save hairstyle, makeup, and wardrobe.

She shook Cree's hand with both of hers. "It's so good to see you. I was sorry to hear about your husband." She clucked sympathetically. "To think you're the mother of twins. It seems only yesterday you were toddling around this office bumping into the furniture. Twins, no less. They must make you terribly happy."

Terribly, thought Cree. "They do."

Taking her gloves off and handing her coat to Myrna Dell, Cree surveyed the office. It was three times the

size of her grandfather's study at home and ten times as
cluttered. How either he or Myrna Dell could find anything in such incredible disarray was beyond Cree.
Stacked on his desk and on a long oak table set against
one wall was the accumulated paperwork of all the
years he'd been in business. A partially opened drawer
in one of two six-drawer wooden file cabinets bulged
with papers. How often she had heard him boast that
he never threw anything away. And quite obviously
Myrna Dell didn't dare to.

He owned the building, 161 Broadway. Shackleford
Real Estate occupied the entire eighth floor. But though
his subjects were back at their desks after their half-
hour lunches, Caesar himself had not yet returned.

"He's across the street with Mr. Fulton. Fulton, Hed-
ley and Brazinski—they handle all our insurance. I'm
afraid he won't be back for at least half an hour."

"I can wait."

"You're welcome to, of course, but it may be closer
to an hour. When those two get to chinning . . ." She
blushed slightly through her powder. "I mean to say
they like to talk, especially at lunch."

"Don't worry about me. I can wait as long as it
takes."

"Is there anything I can help you with?"

Cree started to say no, then hesitated. Myrna Dell, as
securely entrenched in her grandfather's confidence as
any confidential secretary on Wall Street could be, must
know about his insidious campaign to bring down
Chance and Company. Cree was tempted to question
her, but thought better of it at once. It wouldn't be
fair to push her into a corner.

"I don't think so," answered Cree, "but thanks
anyway."

"I was just on my way up to the tenth floor to see Mr. Hazeltine in Payroll. Would you mind terribly if I left you alone?"

"Not at all."

Mind? She'd love to be left alone.

"He should be back before me. Before I go, can I get you some coffee or a cup of tea?"

"No, thanks, I'm fine."

Myrna Dell handed her the morning *Times*. "Maybe you'd like to look at the paper."

She left, humming "Yes Sir, That's My Baby." Cree watched the door close and was about to begin searching for evidence to confirm what Charles Crowder had told her when she abruptly changed her mind. Fighting fire with fire was one thing, but her conscience wouldn't approve of her taking advantage of her grandfather's absence to poke through his papers. If he walked in and caught her, there'd be the devil to pay. She'd be better off getting out of him what she'd come for. She would never get him to admit he was out to destroy Chance and Company, but if they talked about it long enough, he might slip up and say something to confirm it. As if she needed confirmation!

Bringing the newspaper with her, she went into his private office, leaving the half-glass door open two inches. Sitting at his desk, she began reading. The headline announced that Great Britain, France, Belgium, Italy, Poland, Czechoslovakia, and Germany had finally ratified the Locarno treaties. John T. Scopes, who had been convicted and fined for teaching evolution in the public high school in Dayton, Tennessee, had had his sentence set aside. A Scottish inventor, John Logie Baird, announced that he had successfully transmitted human features over something called television.

She put the paper down and phoned the house. Janice answered.

"Can I speak to Maggie?"

"Yes, ma'am, she's right here."

Maggie came on. "Where are you?" she asked.

"Downtown. I won't be home for a couple of hours. How are the children?"

"Bickering, as usual."

"Over what?"

"You don't really want to know," said Maggie, laughing.

"How's Mrs. Chance?"

"She's taking a nap. She seems terribly listless."

"Keep the children quiet, Maggie, even if you have to lock them in separate rooms."

"I'm way ahead of you."

"See you in a little while, probably around four."

She hung up and went back to the newspaper. But almost immediately her attention wandered back to her grandfather and their impending confrontation. An idea came to her. Pulling open the drawer in front of her, she took out a scratch pad, scissors, and a bottle of Slater's Paste. She sat about drawing letters of the alphabet, cutting them out, arranging them in order, and pasting them over the *Times*'s headline. She was just finishing when she heard the outer door open, and her grandfather walked in. He lifted his eyes in surprise.

"Well, look who's here. Little late for lunch, aren't you?" He looked about. "I see you didn't bring my great-grandson."

"You've another great-granddaughter, too, you know. They're both home."

"I gather Myrna Dell's upstairs with that nincompoop Hazeltine." Cree nodded and started to get up. "Sit, sit, no need to go running off."

"I'm not running anywhere." She indicated the straight-backed chair in the corner. "I'll sit there, if you don't mind."

He shrugged. Taking off his suitcoat, he hung it next to his overcoat on the fumed-oak costumer's stand in the corner opposite the chair. Pulling up his shirtsleeves two more inches above his garters, he plumped down behind his desk.

"What's on your mind?"

"I want to know about Chance and Company."

She had hoped that firing it at him immediately would cause his expression to change; it didn't. She had never known anyone with such uncanny control over his reactions. He should have been an actor, she thought. He continued to stare, a glare intended to intimidate her, throw her off balance at the start.

"Chance? What are you talking about? What am I supposed to know about them?"

"A lot, from what I hear."

"What exactly do you hear?"

"That you're trying to take over."

He scoffed. "Hogwash! Who told you that, that shyster lawyer Crowder? He's full o'prunes."

"Is he really?"

"You bet your boots he is! That's the dizziest thing I've heard in weeks."

"You've been systematically luring away their major accounts, bleeding and bleeding them until now they're on the verge of bankruptcy. I'm curious, what's your schedule? When do you take over?"

"That's nonsense. You don't know what you're talking about. You can go back to your friend Crowder and tell him I said he's a goddamned liar. And shut his big mouth and keep it shut, or I'll slap him with a damned libel suit!"

"You've set up a dummy corporation, Wilton and Butterworth, to do your dirty work for you so nobody can accuse you of being involved. But you're involved all right, up to your ears. You're pulling the strings, don't deny it. You must be very pleased with yourself."

"He's lying in his teeth, I tell you. You can get him and sixteen other shysters, they can dig until their elbows fall off, they'll never find my name associated with any effort to wreck Chance or any other company."

"You're not listening, as usual. Forget about Charles Crowder. I don't need him or anybody else to convince me you're involved. All I have to do is look in your eyes when you deny it. You and your phony indignation. You've been waiting years to ruin the company. Too bad I came back to New York when I did. That's the one thing you didn't expect, isn't it? Bad timing, terrible timing. I showed up just in time to throw a monkey wrench into the works. That's exactly what I'm going to do if you don't drop this whole disgusting business. If you don't call off your dogs, I'll make you wish you'd never heard of Chance and Company. I'll haul you into court and stop you dead. I've got nearly six million dollars; if you make it necessary, I'll spend every dime to fight you." She stood up.

"Wait just a minute."

"Are you going to drop this thing or not? I don't want any song and dance, just a simple yes or no. Well?"

"Sit down, goddamn it!"

Reflex action, years of experience obeying his commands, restored her to her chair.

"Now then, Missy, if you think you're going to accomplish a damned thing going to law other than to make a public spectacle of yourself, you're sadly mistaken. For the last time, nobody in this world can tie me to Chance and Company in any way, good, bad, or otherwise. Nobody. If it's going down the drain, it's too damned bad, but it's no fault o' mine. I don't know whose it is, and what's more, I don't give a good goddamn. But I can see by your face you don't believe me, so go right ahead, waste your time and squander your money, but don't say you haven't been warned."

"I'll need lawyers, of course. I'm sure Alec and Lloyd Rush would be happy to represent me."

"Don't be daft. There isn't a decent lawyer in this town would take on anything as flimsy as this. You're trying to catch smoke in your hand."

"We'll see." Again she rose to her feet. "As soon as I've talked to Alec and Lloyd I'll contact the newspapers. They should have a field day with this one. I can picture the headlines."

Reaching for the folded copy of the *Times*, she opened it, laying it in front of him. His eyes widened at sight of the mock-up headline.

GRANDDAUGHTER SUES TO PREVENT HIRAM SHACKLEFORD'S TAKEOVER OF CHANCE AND COMPANY. WIDOW ALLEGES PLOT TO WRECK FIRM. PROLONGED COURT BATTLE LOOMS.

"Good-bye, Grandfather. As the old saying goes, I'll see you in court."

She had gotten her coat on; arranging her muffler, she put on her hat and started out the door.

"You're crazy, you haven't a leg to stand on!"

She slammed the outer door behind her. She could hear him bellowing her name. The elevator arrived seconds after she pressed the Down button. She got on; the door slid closed behind her. The elevator stopped at the fifth and third floors to take on passengers going down. Reaching the lobby, she emerged and started for the revolving door and the street.

"Lucretia! Lucretia, hold on."

He had run down seven flights of stairs! His face was red, and he was puffing hard. He caught up with her.

"What are you running off for? Let's talk about it."

"What is there to talk about? Either you give me your word here and now that you'll call a halt and let the company get back on its feet, or I'll . . ."

"Lucretia, you've got the whole thing wrong, you've got me wrong. As God is my witness." He paused, glancing up and down the lobby. Taking hold of her sleeve, he pulled her out of the line of traffic. "I just don't know if I can persuade the men behind the thing to back off," he said quietly.

"Why don't you stop? You're the only one who has to back off. There *is* nobody else. What do you take me for, a moron? You're amazing, you'd rather lie than breathe. Why don't you try telling the truth for once in your life, just for the novelty of it?"

"You'd be very, very foolish to bring the newspapers in on this."

"Don't think I won't bring in Livvy and Jule. If you don't like it, countersue. When I tell them, I wonder who they'll side with? And when the dust clears, I wonder if you'll ever see any of us or our children again as long as you live!"

Away she walked.

Chapter Thirty

It has been said that there are infrequent occasions in the bullring when even the bravest, most ferocious bull will hesitate to attack a matador. Aficionados of bull-fighting claim that in such instances the creature hesitates because of something it sees in its adversary's eyes. Whether Hiram Shackleford saw something in Lucretia's eyes that gave him pause, or whether the cause was all her threats bound together like a Roman fasces, he began to have second thoughts regarding his decision to bring down Chance and Company.

He considered the consequences and changed his mind. It was not even necessary for Cree to bring the matter to the attention of Olivia and Julia, much less the newspapers. Two days after she walked out of the lobby of 161 Broadway, Charles Crowder telephoned to tell her that Wilton and Butterworth had ceased meddling in the affairs of Chance and Company. With Cree's financial help the company began to retrench and there were early indications that it would soon regain its former stability and prominence.

Marjorie Shackleford never knew what had very nearly happened to the company. On the night of February 2, with Cree and Janice keeping vigil by her side, she died in her sleep in her room in Flower Fifth Avenue Hospital. She was buried beside her husband. Two days later Cree, Maggie Willis, and the twins left New York on the *Espagne*, reaching home on the twenty-second.

Without a war to absorb its attention, mankind made do with news of less moment. The Assembly of the League of Nations at Geneva unanimously admitted Germany to the League and to a permanent Council seat. Gertrude Ederle swam the English Channel, and Rudolph Valentino arrived in Paris to attend a charity premiere of his film *The Black Eagle*. The Eiffel Tower nightly displayed a huge red flame at the top and heraldic designs in electric lights up and down the pylons on two sides. The dates 1889–1925 were spelled out in electric lights, and enormous white stars with golden tails shot dizzily back and forth, their cometlike trails forming letters running vertically down the Tower. Parisians and visitors from the provinces alike stood gaping in awe, reading one of France's best-known names:

CITROEN

Commented the newspaper *Le Figaro*: "Every artist and art-lover in Paris becomes ill at the sight."

Cree bought a car, not a Citroën, but a bright-yellow Renault, with a landau roof, gleaming brass doorhandles, and a hood and radiator shaped like the muzzle of some mythological beast. The year 1926 gave way to 1927. Civil war broke out in China and a somewhat timid and short-lived revolution in Mexico, and six hundred United States Marines and several ships of war were dispatched to Nicaragua to protect

American interests when a revolution erupted there. Germany's ailing economy collapsed, and Socialists rioted in Vienna. A general strike followed the acquittal of Nazis for political murder in Germany, and Leon Trotsky was expelled from the Communist Party in Moscow. Colonel Charles A. Lindbergh flew solo non-stop from New York to Paris. He was greeted at Bleriot Airport by wildly cheering crowds and became the hero of the decade.

In the United States Ruth Snyder and Judd Gray were convicted of the murder of Mrs. Snyder's husband Albert, the art editor of *Motor Boating*. The first talking picture, *The Jazz Singer*, was released, catapulting Al Jolson to overnight stardom.

In the year that followed, Ruth Snyder and Judd Gray were executed in the electric chair at Sing Sing Prison. The civil war in China came to an end. Premier Chiang Kai-shek established the Nationalist government at Nanking. The Kellogg-Briand Pact was signed, outlawing war. The pact failed to include any provision for the enforcement of its praiseworthy decision. Admiral Richard E. Byrd set off on an expedition to Antarctica.

In 1929 the world reeled from the effects of the Great Depression, which brought severe unemployment and economic chaos. The United States stock market collapsed. Leon Trotsky was expelled from Russia.

The following year in London the United States, Great Britain, and Japan signed a naval disarmament treaty. The Nazi Party made substantial gains in elections in Germany.

In 1931 England enacted the statute of Westminster, designating Canada and Australia independent dominions. With the overthrow of King Alfonso XIII Spain became a republic. Japan invaded Manchuria. President Hoover proposed a one-year moratorium of war debts. In the United States Al Capone was sent to prison for tax evasion and Admiral Byrd returned after three years at the South Pole

The year 1932 saw the Nazis sweep to victory in elections in Germany, gaining two hundred thirty seats in the Reichstag. Famine swept across Russia. The United States protested against Japanese aggression in Manchuria. Amelia Earhart became the first woman to fly the Atlantic solo. The Lindbergh baby was kidnapped and murdered.

In 1933 Japan conquered Manchuria. Adolf Hitler became chancellor of Germany and was immediately invested with dictatorial powers. In Berlin the Reichstag was set afire. Nazi terrorism and boycotts against Germany's Jews became ever more prevalent.

In Paris, at her brightest and most beautiful with the arrival of spring, Germany and its political turmoil seemed much further away than merely across the border. By now the Great War, the war to end all wars, had been pushed back deep into memory, if not forgotten altogether by many. The Depression had taken its toll of the economy of France. The franc had shrunk to a small fraction of its value in 1920; it was now worth less than three American cents. But during the early- and mid-twenties Cree had invested wisely, patiently adding to her treasures until her collection had become one of the finest private collections in Paris.

Over the years she had continued to correspond with Olivia and Julia, and even her grandfather. She sent pictures of the twins as they grew up and received in return pictures of Claudia and Jessica. Olivia and Julia came to Paris twice, in the spring of 1927 and again in the summer of 1930, when they brought Alec and Lloyd and the girls.

Maggie Willis left Cree's employ in 1932, shortly after the children's thirteenth birthday. Her departure was inevitable. They had grown out of their need for a nanny. The parting was amicable. Cree couldn't help but wonder what went through a nanny's heart when she left one family to begin all over with another. How painful it must be. Was it something one got used to? If she were a nanny, she would never be able to. It would tear her heart out.

As the thirties fell away, she enlarged her circle of friends, but she was unable to meet a man who measured up to Wyatt. He had been her first love, and as time went on, it seemed more and more likely he would be her only love. She often wondered if she was guilty of setting her standards much too high to be met by any man. Or was the explanation even simpler, that she just wasn't interested? She saw Picasso frequently. They often had drinks with Mme. Duvivier and other neighborhood friends at his studio or at Paul Rosenberg's house. Cree herself often entertained. The multitalented and incredibly versatile Castilian had long since deserted Cubism for his first series of still lifes, which in turn was interrupted by a fling at Expressionism, exemplified by the violently deformed figures of *The Dance*. He also flirted with Surrealism. His output continued to be enormous, paintings pouring from his brush. No other artist, living or dead, had ever produced such a prodigious amount of such varied and powerful work.

Paul Poiret grew fatter and less active. He and Cree were with a group of friends enjoying drinks at the Ritz one afternoon when the chair he was sitting in suddenly shattered under his weight. At once he declared that he was going on a diet. He managed to stick to it for nearly an hour, until the pastry cart passed through and a magnificent Napoleon caught his eye. Even before peace had been declared his arch-competitor, Coco Chanel, had wrested the *haute couture feu de projecteur* from him. In the process she had become a force and a legend, perfuming the world with Chanel No. 5, creating a bathing suit for women that complemented nature's endowments instead of concealing them, designing a basic little black dress easily imitated which sold by the millions, fashioning fake jewelry by the metric ton. Even her enemies conceded that she was immensely talented. She was in addition ambitious, wealthy and successful, imbued with personal attractiveness to those who idolized her, and incomparable charm. Paul Poiret disliked her with the intensity of a fanatic. Cree met her only once. She came away with a very definite opinion of the lady. In her view Chanel may have been the equal of any man and often his superior in the jungle warfare of the fashion industry, but she had paid the price. It had taken from her her womanliness; she was hard, her eyes steely, her manner much too self-assured.

Wyatt had grown into the image of his father, the same dark-red hair, sparkling brown eyes, height and build. And he had his father's easygoing nature. However, he lacked his father's fierce dedication—to painting or anything else. His sister no longer resembled Cree as closely as she did when she was a little girl. Her hair, although blonde like Cree's, had darkened a shade, and her features had become more like Julia's. She had the same doe eyes and perfectly sculptured face, and her body, although only two years into pu-

berty and yet to be fully developed, promised to duplicate Julia's lovely figure.

At the twins' fourteenth birthday party Marjorie announced that she wished to be called by her middle
name, Sabrina, complaining that Marjorie was too
pedestrian a name for her liking. She loved Sabrina;
with all due respect to her late grandmother, Marjorie
was boring and "much too American." Naming her
Sabrina had been a last-minute decision on Cree's part,
made in deference to Cree's own mother's fondness for
giving her daughters Roman names. Cree had listened
to Marjorie Sabrina's recounting of reasons for wanting
to change, decided that it was, after all, her daughter's
name and right to change it, and had given her reluctant permission to do so. At the time, however, she
herself decided that she'd never get into the habit of
calling her by her middle name. Wyatt proved predict-
ably uncooperative, taking pains to call his sister
Midgy, knowing that it infuriated her.

The two got along better as they got older. Their
bickering ebbed discernibly, to Cree's and Simone's relief. They attended Lycée Branage. Sabrina was an excellent student, generally at or near the head of her
class. Wyatt was bright, but given to daydreaming and
occasional horseplay. Every so often he would come
home with a note from a teacher or the *proviseur* complaining about his behavior. The note was never necessary. Cree could always depend upon Sabrina for a full
report. He would be forbidden to play soccer for a
week or longer or his radio would be taken from him or
permission to drive his mother's Bugatti coupé denied
him.

Neither he nor his sister gave any indication of artistic talent. Neither could draw as well as Cree. Wyatt

was a sports fanatic, devoted to soccer in particular and to swimming. Sabrina loved music; she studied piano and could play uncomplicated pieces quite well. She was also one of those few fortunate females who looked good in anything and she did some modeling for Madeleine Vionnet and Paul Poiret. Her children were the music, the heart and substance of Cree's life.

In brazen defiance of the Versailles Treaty, Hitler set about rearming Germany. The specter of a second world war suddenly stained the horizon. But the French were convinced that the Maginot Line was impregnable. The Germans would never be so rash as to attack it. There wasn't enough artillery in the world to dislodge the French Army from its concrete.

In 1935, while the former paperhanger was building the *Wehrmacht*, his new ally, Mussolini, former teacher and newspaperman, now Duce of Italy, invaded Ethiopia. Mussolini succeeded in subduing the all but defenseless Ethiopians only after a surprisingly difficult struggle. One year later, in continuing defiance of the Treaty of Versailles, German troops marched into the Rhineland. When civil war erupted in Spain the same year, Hitler came to the aid of the fascist leader General Francisco Franco with tanks and dive-bombers. Italian troops joined Franco's forces.

In 1938 the German dictator forced an *Anschluss* of Austria and Germany. Shortly thereafter, he declared his intention of annexing the Sudetenland of western Czechoslovakia, citing historical fact that the inhabitants were overwhelmingly German. Open war now appeared imminent.

The possibility that the bank robber in Moscow and the paperhanger in Berlin might pit their armies against each other and destroy themselves was a straw that was eagerly grasped by some British and French leaders. The sorry experience of 1914 was a lesson few seemed willing to value. Words continued to speak louder than actions in London and Paris.

On a Saturday morning in June of 1937 Wyatt Chance came home late from a soccer match. His mother asked what had detained him. He quietly told her that he and some of his friends had stopped at the recruiting office on the Champs Élysées and joined the army.

Chapter Thirty-one

Cree went wild with anger. She and Sabrina had been sunning themselves in the garden, waiting for him to come home so that the three of them could go to lunch at Mme. Duvivier's just down the street. Jumping up from the stone seat, Cree flew at him, grabbing him by the wrists.

"Are you insane!"

Sabrina, down on her knees weeding the impatiens, could only gape in astonishment.

"He's kidding, he's just trying to scare us."

"Midgy, I enlisted, I really did." Freeing himself from his mother's hold, he took her hands in his.

"It wasn't on the spur of the moment. I've given it a lot of thought. It makes sense. If I don't join up, they'll draft me anyway. This way, I take the written examination and I can go into officers' training."

"I can't believe you'd do such a thing without even consulting me!" said Cree.

He released her hands and began kicking the dirt at his feet aimlessly.

"Why bother? You'd only have said no. You know you would have."

"She's right!" added Sabrina. "You must be out of your mind."

291

"Why do we have to argue about it? It's my life. Why can't I do what I like with it? Everybody's joining, practically all my friends. Do you want everybody in the neighborhood pointing at me and calling me a slacker? No, thanks!"

He continued to try to justify his action. The years suddenly rolled away in Cree's memory. All at once she was surrounded not by the garden but by walls and windows and Wyatt's first paintings—the front room of the apartment on Whitney Avenue in New Haven. Wyatt was speaking, stumbling through his explanation of why he had joined the Students' Army Training Corps without telling her his intention. It came back as clearly as if it had just happened. The present situation mirrored the memory almost perfectly. The difference was the fact that when his father had joined the Corps the bloodshed in Europe was all but finished. Now the Germans were poised on the brink of shattering the fragile twenty-year peace, preparing to start all over. And he would be in it. Her thoughts flew forward. They would send him to officers' training school, he would graduate a second lieutenant, and by that time war would have erupted and he would be assigned to the front. She would hear from him now and then, then nothing, not a syllable.

Until the telegram from *le ministère de la Guerre*.

"You're not listening to a word I'm saying!" he snapped indignantly.

"I don't have to, I've heard it all before. I know it by heart."

He stared at her blankly, puzzled.

"Never mind," she went on, "it's not important. It was very stupid of you, Wyatt, stupid and inconsiderate."

"What choice do I have?" he shouted. "I can't start college. None of us can now. By enlisting, at least I get to pick which branch I want."

"Which is that?" asked his sister, sitting down beside Cree on the bench.

"I haven't decided."

"You'd better think about it quickly."

"Why don't you mind your own business? I don't need your advice." He softened his tone. "Mother, can't you at least try to see it from my point of view?"

There was a long silence as Cree mustered her thoughts. The breeze bowed the flowers, wafting their assorted sweet scents through the garden.

"I'm trying to, honestly." She shrugged and looked away at the house next door and the two thrushes playing about the chimney pots. "You're right about one thing, you don't have much choice; it's really Hobson's choice."

"What's that?"

"Hobson ran a livery stable. When a customer wanted a horse, he invariably gave him the first one in line. There was no choice; take it or go without. Join up or be drafted."

"Exactly!"

She got up, put her arms around him, and kissed him. Then she held him from her with one hand, brushing the hair from his eyes with the other.

"You're just a child," she said.

"Mother . . ."

"All right, all right, it's done, there's nothing any of us can do about it. My God, just thinking about it makes me ill. When do you leave?"

"Monday morning," he said quietly.

Sabrina gasped. "So soon?"

Cree very nearly groaned aloud. Her heart was wrenched. In that moment the certainty that he would leave and they would never see him again blotted out every other thought. If only they could all just pack up, rush to the docks, and take the first ship to America. Put three thousand miles between them and the guns and blood and destruction.

Too late, too late.

Chapter Thirty-two

On September 1, 1939, Germany invaded Poland. Within forty-eight hours Britain and France declared war on Germany.

Overwhelmed by fifty-six German divisions and fifteen hundred *Luftwaffe* planes, including Stuka dive-bombers, the antiquated forces of Marshal Edward SniglyRidz capitulated in twelve days. Poland was smashed like an egg. There followed a period of inactivity, broken only by a brutal Soviet attack against Finland, an effort to secure strategic border areas. The lull came to an abrupt end in April, 1940, when Hitler's *Wehrmacht* invaded Denmark and Norway.

Long before the two Scandinavian countries fell, Cree came to a decision. The message was strikingly clear; all of Western Europe stood vulnerable to Axis aggression. When Sabrina came home from school one Friday afternoon, Cree met her at the door. Sabrina started to smile a greeting, then shifted her eyes, looking past her mother at the three suitcases standing in the foyer.

"Are you going someplace?" she asked.

"No," responded Cree, "you are. I called your Aunt Olivia in New York this morning, then went to the

Compagnie Générale Transatlantique and bought you this." She held up a ticket. "You're sailing for New York at six ten tomorrow evening."

"I'm what?"

"I want you out of here. I want you where you'll be safe."

Sabrina brushed by her and stood next to the bags, her arms folded, her jaw set stubbornly, her eyes blazing.

"I'm not going!"

"You are, and we're not arguing about it."

"I can't possibly go, I have an exam on Monday. You can't just uproot me and push me onto a ship."

Cree took her by the arms. "Darling," she said softly, "I don't want you to go, but you must, don't you see? When France and England go to war, as they're certain to in a few days—God help us, even a few hours—all of a sudden it'll be 1914 all over again. Only worse. If you don't leave now, you won't be able to go. I was very, very lucky to get you passage; as it is, you'll be traveling second class. Every ship out of Calais is packed to the gunwales. And the *Normandie* may be the last to leave. The government's certain to announce a ban on passenger travel. The Atlantic's already crawling with U-boats."

"I can't leave you, Mother. Please don't make me."

"I'll be fine."

"You won't. I'd be worried sick sitting over there, wondering what's happening to you, to Wyatt. It's a crazy idea. Why do I have to run away like a scared rabbit? I want to do my part, help in some way. Everybody else is." A thought brightened her eyes. "I could be a nurse's aide like Aunt Livvy in the last war. I'm almost as old as she was then. She came over here all by herself. I don't even have to leave home. I could volunteer and get into a hospital right here in the city. So could you, we could work together."

"Darling, it's all arranged."

"Without even asking me."

"Yes, unfortunately. Sabrina, you're going, and that's all there is to it!"

"What are you getting all upset about? I've never seen you so nervous."

"Never mind. Darling, you'll love New York. You'll be with your cousins Claudia and Jessica, you'll make new friends—"

"I don't need new friends. I like the friends I have. Besides, I'll be homesick as hell!"

"That's enough!" Cree turned away. "I know it's unfair of me to spring this on you out of the blue, but everything's happening so fast. We have no choice." Turning back, she put her arms around Sabrina. They hugged each other.

"You'll be all alone," Sabrina said.

"Nonsense, your brother's here in Paris; we'll be seeing each other all the time, just like now. He's not going anywhere."

"How do you know for sure?"

The thought prompted a fresh outburst. She pulled free, glaring. "I won't go!"

"You will, if I have to tie you up and stuff you in a trunk. We'll say no more about it. Come upstairs, I want you to go through your drawers and see if there's anything I missed that you might want to take along."

Sabrina left, glowering and fighting back tears. Cree fought back her own as she followed her onto the ship to get her settled in her stateroom, calm her down, and try for the dozenth time to assure her that it all made sense, that everything would turn out all right. But she had small success convincing her.

Later, as she stood in the crowd waving, the tears came in abundance. And with them a tug of regret. If only Wyatt were standing alongside Sabrina, if only he too were looking down and waving. And if only a miracle happened and the boiling cauldron that was Europe threatening to overflow into full-scale war did not do so.

Having graduated from St. Cyr, Wyatt was commissioned a second lieutenant and assigned to the 104th Intelligence Unit, to his mother's delight and relief. The 104th was based in Paris. Cree counted her blessings: He would not be going up to the front, he would not be under fire, they would continue to see each other often. Unit headquarters were on the Boulevard des Invalides on the other side of the Seine.

She had to concede that he did look dashing in his uniform; in short order he had taken to life in the service like a beaver to water.

What the newspapers had come to call the Phony War—eight months of marking time, polishing bayonets, and fighting fierce battles on maps—came to a sudden end on May 10 of the following spring. Hitler attacked Holland, Belgium, and Luxembourg. Within eighteen days Belgium had surrendered unconditionally. Holland and Luxembourg fell like dominoes, exposing the entire Allied left flank. Through the hole thundered the *Wehrmacht*, decimating thirty-six British, French, and Belgian divisions and smashing the northwestern Maginot Line.

Within weeks the British were driven back to the sea

and the French army, considered the finest and best-equipped in Europe, was reduced to remnants. German tanks rattled about unopposed less than twenty miles north of Paris. Those finding themselves in the path of the invader fled, clogging the roads and train stations, heading for Paris, then south.

But in Paris itself the people remained steadfast in their belief that France would never yield, her routed army would reassemble, the British would return in force, the Germans would be thrown back. Meanwhile refugees flooded the city, their cars, their carts, their backs piled high with their belongings. Food stocks dwindled, public utilities were strained to the utmost. Most of the shops and other places of business were closed; barge-loads of refugees filled the Seine. Vehicles vanished from the streets as supplies of gasoline were used up or diverted to the suddenly flourishing black market.

Cree had had no word from Wyatt in four days. He usually telephoned her every day, if he could not get away from his duties, but call after call to his unit elicited no information as to his whereabouts. The man answering the phone kept repeating that he knew of no Lieutenant Chance, that the commanding officer had not yet returned, and that he was the only one in the office at present. In desperation, on the morning of the fourth day, June 10, Cree drove to the Boulevard des Invalides to find out what was happening. The office door was locked; nobody was around. She returned home to find Pablo Picasso sitting in the living room waiting for her. He had just come back from Royan on the right bank of the Gironde in Charente-Inférieure. He had left Paris the day the Germans marched into Poland the previous September. He looked tanned and rested, but the melancholy look in his dark eyes filled Cree with fear.

"I thought you'd gone for good," she said.

He shrugged his massive shoulders. "I tried." He grinned. "It's like leaving a mistress you're fond of. Abandon her, and you feel guilty. Everybody keeps telling me to go to America or Mexico, but I can't. Never mind me, what about you? The roof is about to fall in, and here you sit pretending it will all go away. A true Frenchwoman. We all have blinders on."

"I have to stay, with Wyatt in the army."

"What army? It's scattered to the four winds."

"I haven't heard from him since Thursday. His unit just picked up and left. Why didn't he let me know?"

"Maybe he couldn't. For reasons of security. I don't know, what do I know about the army? But he must be all right."

"I wish I knew for sure." She suppressed a shudder. "Can I get you a drink?"

"No, thanks. I can't stay, I just wanted to see how you are. I bumped into Claudette Duvivier coming over from the station. She says she's taking her cats, locking up the house, and going south. You'd be smart to go with her, though it'll take you weeks, the roads are so clogged. You should have seen the train coming up from Santes. I had to stand all the way. Everybody going and coming, nobody seems to know where or why. I guess being on the move gives people a sense of security, although why it should is beyond me."

"I'm staying put."

"What about your paintings?"

"They're staying where they belong, on the walls."

"That's not very smart. The Germans are coming.

They're closer than you think. Don't be surprised if that idiot Reynaud declares Paris an open city. They'll take everything that isn't nailed down. The sons of bitches are very thorough. I've already packed my best stuff off to Royan. You'd better do something, and fast. Doesn't your cellar have a dirt floor?"

"I refuse to bury Lucas Cranach!"

"Well, don't be surprised if they march him out the front door and you never see him again. With your Modigliani and your Vermeer."

He rose.

"Don't go," said Cree, "let Simone make you something to eat."

"No, thanks. I have to go around to Paul Rosenberg's. He's leaving, he should have left months ago. Every Jew in his right mind has left, but he's been all this time squirreling away his inventory, splitting it into twos and threes, hiding pictures here and there." He stared at her. "I wish you'd change your mind."

"About leaving? No. You're staying, why shouldn't I?"

"Stay, then, but you'd better do something about your collection. The Ministry of Information has gagged the radio. Nobody knows where the Germans are or when they'll come goose-stepping in. But that booming you hear up beyond Aubervilliers isn't thunder." He shook hands. "Good luck, Lucretia. If you need me for anything, I'll be home this evening. I'm staying in Paris, even if Schicklgruber himself comes marching up the street!"

He left. Cree went upstairs and stood in the gallery studying Cranach's crucifixion. Picasso was right, she had been negligent. She would be foolish to leave her paintings up. Still, burying them in the cellar wasn't very clever. If the Germans knocked on her door, that would be the first place they'd look.

There had to be a better place.

She went back downstairs and telephoned the 104th headquarters again. The phone rang and rang; nobody answered.

Chapter Thirty-three

The week of waiting proved to be the longest of Cree's lifetime: waiting for the Germans to march in, waiting for word from Wyatt, wondering what had happened to him, where he was, why he hadn't contacted her, imagining the worst.

As the sun rose to greet Friday, the fourteenth, it revealed a seemingly endless procession of slate-colored trucks carrying infantrymen sitting ramrod-straight, holding their rifles upright between their knees, and staring straight ahead. Down the boulevards north and east of Notre Dame rolled the trucks into the silent city. At the intersections German military police skillfully directed traffic with batons bearing large red discs. Men, women, and children stood in doorways and in front of shuttered shops, watching and weeping. Panzer and Tiger tanks rumbled into view following the troop trucks, their heavy treads pounding the cobblestones; motorcycles darted about like beetles on burning sand; staff cars flaunting swastika flags attached to their front fenders carried stony-faced officers to their destinations. So coldly methodical and flawlessly orchestrated was the arrival, it appeared that every phase of the entire performance was controlled by an unseen master director pushing buttons at a giant console.

Lining the curbs, looking on, were the police in their kepis and brass-buttoned, dark-blue uniforms, clutching their white batons, awaiting orders from the Germans.

At Napoleon's red marble tomb in the Invalides, under the highest dome in the city, a squad of men began systematically to remove every German flag, each one the symbol of a German defeat in 1914.

Along the main boulevards detachments of infantry were directing firemen who were taking down the French tricolor and replacing it with the swastika. Before ten o'clock in the morning a large swastika could be seen flapping in the breeze above the Arc de Triomphe, and identical flags had been raised over the Senate and the chamber of Deputies.

After the troops came a host of men in civilian workclothes, who set about covering every advertising sign, every wall, with pro-German propaganda posters.

"Abandoned people, put your trust in the German soldier!"

In the words of British Major-General Sir Edward Spears, it was "as if all the sewers of France had burst and their nauseating mess was seeping into the beautiful city like a rising flood of abomination."

Friday, the fourteenth. A day destined to be marked in the minds of men for all time, a dazzlingly bright, incomparably beautiful day in June, when the shadow fell, and the heart of Paris was crushed under the jackboot.

Chapter Thirty-four

On June 22, eight days later, France formally surrendered. Representatives of the victors and the vanquished assembled in the same clearing in Compiègne forest, north of Paris, where Marshal Ferdinand Foch had dictated terms to Germany in November, 1918. The identical railway car, kept since 1918 as a museum piece, was trundled out of its shed for the obsequies. It was a lovely day, the skies cloudless, the sun daubing the oaks and beeches with silver. His pasty face wreathed with a gloating grin, Hitler stood with Goering and his aides while General Wilhelm Keitel, his Chief of Supreme Command, read the conditions to the French delegation. Keitel had not yet reached the bottom of the first page when Hitler became impatient and walked out of the musty Pullman car, followed by Goering, Hess, von Ribbentrop, and the assembled high-ranking officers.

The armistice provided that German troops would occupy more than half of France, including the entire Atlantic coastline.

For days Cree had been telephoning everyone she knew, trying to trace Wyatt's whereabouts. The 104th and every other army unit stationed in the city had vanished like a covey of quail at the sound of a shot-gun. Most of those with whom she spoke were convinced that Wyatt and everyone else in Paris in the service had gone underground, joining the Resistance. This opinion was invariably expressed in a tone that seemed to take it for granted that she should be relieved, pleased, and proud. Her only reaction was apprehension. It took hold of her heart and refused to let go. She awoke each morning not knowing whether he was dead or alive, where he was, what he was doing. The dreaded presence of the Germans all around her, the coldly efficient manner in which they governed the subjugated city, the repeated warnings from loud-speakers, on posters, and over the radio that any opposition to their policies, any violation of curfew, would be dealt with harshly, only intensified her concern for Wyatt. He was rash, fearless, and zealously patriotic, a combination of character traits that could too easily get him into the kind of trouble from which he'd never be able to extricate himself.

No sooner had the Germans moved in and taken over than the people of Paris began to retaliate in subtle and clever ways. Staff cars suddenly refused to start, spark plug wires were cut, rotors were missing. Officers and men were kidnapped and found in culverts and ditches and abandoned barns outside the city with their throats cut and the Cross of Lorraine marked on their foreheads. The bodies of two drunken SS colonels were discovered floating in the Seine. The generator in the basement of the Hotel Crillon, which had been taken over by General von Studnitz, commander-in-chief of the occupation forces, was disabled, and it took three days before power was restored. The sabotage was effective, frustrating the Germans and lifting the Parisians' morale. In retaliation, the enemy tightened the screws. No longer were those caught out after curfew lectured and sent on their way or held overnight in jail. Now they were taken out and shot.

Cree stayed at home on the phone most of the time, trying in vain to find out something about the 104th. Picasso dropped by every morning to see how she was; he continued to caution her about her collection. She finally hit upon an idea for protecting it. She telephoned Roland Robays, who sent around four of his students. They glazed the paintings and then painted still lifes over them. The oranges, apples and pears and bowls and pitchers were scarcely works of art. But on the other hand they weren't all that poorly executed. They were precisely what she wanted them to be—of little value. It wasn't the cleverest ruse ever devised for discouraging would-be confiscators, but she preferred it to burying everything in the cellar. Too many people knew of her collection. Tongues wagged readily. If the Germans came looking for Cranach and Modigliani, it would be stupid to show them bare walls. Covering her paintings with still lifes was a long shot at best, but she could think of no better alternative.

She was home alone one afternoon, having sent Simone out to the greengrocer's, when the doorbell rang. The sound sent an icicle up her spine. She had to clench her fists and hold her breath to get control of herself. At the door was a German lieutenant, no more than eighteen, blond, handsome, and frigidly aloof. With him were two enlisted men. The lieutenant demanded her radio; a three-wheeled Opel truck parked at the curb was piled high with radios. She obliged and was given a receipt for the radio signed by an Oberst Henzel. Before leaving, her visitors also disconnected her telephone.

That night she had another visitor. She was upstairs,

looking over Roland's students' handiwork, deciding that they showed promise just as Roland's and Wyatt's early works had, when Simone answered the door.

Cree stiffened. But it wasn't Germans this time, it was Giselle Robays. They embraced.

"Cree, we need your help."

"Is something wrong?"

"We didn't know who to turn to. Listen to me, we've brought eight children with us. They're Jewish. Roland and I know their parents. He's hiding with them in your garden. We've got to get them out of the country. We can do it, we can get them to the right people, but it's going to take time to make the necessary arrangements. They have to have someplace to stay tonight. Tomorrow around eleven o'clock we can get them on their way."

Cree sensed that she was gawking at Giselle as she listened. Giselle stopped speaking and took hold of her as if to shake her.

"You must hide them in your cellar. Or up in the attic, wherever they'll be the safest."

"No."

"Cree!"

"If the Germans come, the cellar will be the first place they'll look. They'll search every room, even the attic. Don't look at me so, I'm not refusing to help, I'm just trying to explain. We wouldn't be able to hide a postage stamp in this place."

"Where then?"

"I know! Claudette Duvivier's house down at the corner. It's closed up. She's gone, but she must have left the key with one of her friends. Simone!" Simone came running from the kitchen. "*Appelez M. Picasso. Dépêchez-vous!*"

Simone flew out the front door and across the street. Cree started toward the kitchen, Giselle following.

"Let's get them in here."

"Turn out the light," said Giselle. "What's so special about the house on the corner?"

"It's about a hundred years old. It was built by a smuggler or a fence, somebody dealing in stolen goods. There's a secret chamber off the cellar about as big as this kitchen. There's a passageway that leads from it to the gazebo in the backyard. And a trapdoor in the floor of the gazebo."

"Do we need the key? Can't we get in through the trapdoor?"

"No, there's a door into the room. It has to be opened from the inside. We have to get into the house."

Roland brought in the children. The oldest was only ten, the youngest, his sister, just old enough to walk. The boy held her in his arms, his eyes wide and fearful. The same worried expression masked all their faces. And Roland was very nervous, clearly out of his element in conspiring to outwit the Germans. After Giselle had introduced Cree to the children the two women put out glasses of milk and cookies, which Simone had baked that morning. Simone returned with Picasso. He was in his pajamas and a bathrobe, which made him look like a brown bear from the wilds of the Canabrian Mountains of his native Spain.

"Claudette didn't give me her house key," he said. "I think Paul Poiret has it. Let me call him."

"Not on my phone," said Cree, "they cut it off this afternoon."

"Mine, too," he said. "I keep forgetting. Six times I've picked it up. It's dead as a fish. I know that lately Paul's been working nights at the textile design studio on Avenue Clichy. I'll go over and see if he's there."

He came back in less than an hour, waving the key triumphantly. By then the children had eaten, and Cree and Giselle went about bedding them down in the hidden room in Mme. Duvivier's house. The following night Roland loaded them into a borrowed florist's van and drove them to their rendezvous. There they boarded a small boat, which carried them down the Seine and out of the city to the coast, where a British trawler waited to take them to England.

The morning after they'd left, a Sunday, Picasso came to see Cree. He was desolate. They sat in the garden under the stark white sun. Simone brought them coffee and raisin *tartalettes*. From high in the apple tree came the twittering of a red-faced swallow, and the flowers danced as the breeze circled the garden.

"It's started," he grumbled. "The Gestapo's showed up. The slimy bastards are filtering through the city like a virus, searching houses, piling trucks full of loot. They have lists—very thorough, our Aryan friends. They know exactly where to go and what to look for."

"They've got a lot of territory to cover," said Cree. "Maybe they won't be as thorough as you think."

"They've got all the time in the world. Besides, they're Germans, they don't know how to be lax. You'd better be prepared for the worst, my friend."

"Well, I can't show them bare walls!" snapped Cree. "I could end up in a concentration camp."

"They'll see right through your apples and oranges. They know what you own. If they don't, there are enough collaborators around to tell them. Did you hear that one of the lift operators in the Impériale has reputedly been here since '33? They're saying half the waiters in town are transplanted Huns. I believe it—

nobody listens in on conversations better than a damned tip-taker. You can't trust your best friend these days."

"I know I'm taking a chance."

"You should have shipped them out with Sabrina."

"I should have." She sighed, nibbling on a *tartalette*. Suddenly she flung it into the phlox in frustration. "I never dreamed they'd some day march in and take over. Who did? All any of us has ever heard was how powerful the French Army was, how formidable the Maginot Line."

His concern for Cree's collection proved well founded. Shortly after lunch two moving vans with Cologne license plates pulled up outside Paul Rosenberg's gallery in the Rue Faubourg St. Honoré. Every single painting and *objet d'art* remaining was removed.

The rape of Paris had begun. Reich Marshal Hermann Goering, with no fewer than eight magnificent homes at his disposal, had appointed Walter Andreas Hofer, a Berlin art dealer, his agent and adviser in what was to ultimately be termed history's most ambitious campaign of confiscation of art on the part of a single individual.

Earlier, in Poland, Holland, and Belgium, Hofer and his assistants had made a pretense of dealing fairly with the people whose works he coveted, but whenever anyone balked at his terms the paintings were simply seized.

The Rosenberg Task Force, named for Alfred Rosenberg, Germany's Cultural Minister, arrived in Paris and set up headquarters in the Salle du Jeu de Paume in the corner of the Tuileries Gardens near the Place de la Concorde. The Task Force speedily set about systematically plundering the homes of Paris's Jews. By order of Goering himself, thirty-eight thousand houses were sealed and emptied of their contents, which were then stored and catalogued. Within three weeks more than twenty-one thousand works of art were seized and inventoried, including five thousand paintings, twenty-four hundred articles of antique furniture, and more than five hundred tapestries, among them the famed Gobelins tapestries, dating from the late seventeenth century. Into Goering's pudgy, greedy hands came oriental weapons, Renaissance sundials, alabaster vases, Beauvais and Gothic tapestries, and several altar pieces, including the French Passion and Crucifixion of the fifteenth century.

Even the Louvre was not exempt from the Reich Marshal's depredations. When the collections belonging to Jews had been seized, the gangs of plunderers turned their efforts to those of Christians.

One afternoon an old acquaintance came to Cree's door, reintroducing himself with a smile and a ludicrously deferential bow. Armand Duprier had aged considerably since she had last seen him twenty years earlier. He was shrunken and slightly bent, and arthritis had appropriated his little body; he moved with difficulty and obvious discomfort. His once-flourishing mustache now drooped pathetically, and its jet-black color had given way to gray, which appeared on the verge of yielding to white. But his snapping black eyes were as piercing as ever. He had a painting wrapped in butcher's paper under his arm.

"May I come in, madame? It is extremely important we talk." He looked up and down the street, as if fearful they were being watched.

For a moment Cree was speechless, conscious only of mixed emotions. She had never particularly liked him from the moment Professor Colcough introduced him; still, she had no reason to think ill of him. For all his bluster and threats he had never done Wyatt any harm. On the contrary, it was he who had gotten him his honorable mention in his first exhibition. She stood aside to let him enter and invited him into the living room. Duprier seemed disturbed.

"I have to leave Paris, or it'll be my skin. I'm getting out tonight. I'm trying to get rid of everything I own." He began unwrapping the painting. "This came into my hands some years ago. It's not one of my favorites. I'm not much for German painters, but when it came my way I grabbed it as an investment."

It was a Cranach, a self-portrait done in late middle age. The artist was strikingly handsome, with dark eyes, straight hair combed forward and whitening at the ends, and a prematurely white mustache joined to a beard that came down to two points. She had never seen such sensitivity in the eyes of any painter on canvas.

"It's genuine," said Duprier. "It cost me a fair sum, I can tell you. Will you buy it from me?"

"Why don't you take it with you?"

"I'm already planning on taking fourteen works. Make no mistake, I'd love to take everything, but it's impossible. Look at it, isn't it magnificent? What is it worth to you?"

"Nothing, I'm afraid. I could buy it from you, and tomorrow or the next day the Gestapo would show up at my door and take away everything."

"Surely by now you've gotten rid of your collection."

"In a manner of speaking."

"You've sent your paintings abroad?"

"No."

"But they're safe."

"No safer than anyone else's."

"You must buy this. You can have it for a fraction of what I paid for it. Name any price. I'm a desperate man. I hear you have a good head for business. Take advantage of me, do, I beg you." He held up the painting. "Have you ever seen a finer self-portrait in your life?" Standing up, he held it against the wall. "It could be the centerpiece of your collection."

"M. Duprier . . ."

"Armand, please, we're old friends."

"In ordinary times I wouldn't hesitate to make you an offer, but these are not ordinary times. I'm sorry, I can't possibly buy it. Who in his right mind is buying anything these days?"

"Then take it." He came to her, thrusting it into her hands. "Keep it with your Cranachs. Some day, when this nightmare is over, I'll be back to claim it and pay you what you ask for taking care of it. At least I'll know it'll be in good hands."

"You're not making sense. It's as vulnerable to confiscation with me as it is with you."

"But you said your paintings are safe."

"I said no safer than anyone else's. I've had them glazed and still lifes painted over them. I'm praying that when the Germans come after them they'll be in a hurry and pass them up."

"But they already know you have Cranachs. Won't they suspect?"

"Probably. Undoubtedly. I'm more or less resigned to losing everything. So why in the world would you want me to take this?"

He ignored the question, running off at a tangent.

"That's ingenious, painting over another painting. I recall hearing about a fellow-countryman of yours, a certain Bullard or Bullfinch, something like that. He was in Italy a while back. He found a Titian. Unluckily that very week Mussolini decided to declare all of Italy's paintings national treasures. M. Bullard was stuck; there was no way he could get his Titian out. He went to a fourth-rate artist, had him glaze the painting and cover it with a portrait of Il Duce. Brilliant, no? He sailed through Customs. One inspector even complimented him on taking a portrait of Mussolini to America. When he got back to New York he sent the picture out to a restorer. Two days later he got a phone call. The restorer told him he had removed the portrait of Mussolini all right, and the glaze covering the Titian. But there was something wrong. Digging deeper, he had found something under the Titian. You'll never believe what it was, another Mussolini! Isn't that priceless? It's a true story. But of course under your Cranachs nobody's going to find Hitler."

They talked further. She gave him a glass of burgundy. He left with his treasure, visibly disappointed, but no longer pressing his plea that she take care of it for him.

Closing the door, she leaned against it and thought the thing through. It was absurd. Why would he come to her in the first place? Why come to anybody? There wasn't a house in the city that wouldn't be ransacked sooner or later. Had he acted out of impulse? No. He may have been erratic at times and short-tempered, but he was much too bright to make any sort of move without first thinking through to its consequences.

Had he come to check on her? On her collection? To make certain it was still in Paris? She sucked in her breath sharply. She had told him it was! She had told him as well that instead of caching it somewhere she had had the paintings glazed and covered with still lifes.

"Damn!"

Come to think of it, he hadn't even asked her; she'd told him voluntarily.

The plunderers arrived the next morning shortly before nine o'clock. Herr Hofer came in person: a short, balding, fussy-looking man whose head sat in his starched collar like an egg in its cup. A tic laid siege to his left eye, and shaking his outstretched hand was like taking hold of a fish. He was, however, extraordinarily polite, standing with his derby between his chubby pink hands like a servant awaiting his birthday pittance from his master. With him was a sour-looking SS *Obersturmführer*, who stood as if he had a steel rod in place of his backbone.

"Permit me to introduce Lieutenant Balzar, madame. May we come in and have a word with you? I promise we won't take much of your time."

She led them to the living room. Hofer glanced about, his eyes narrowing and bright with admiration. His companion conducted himself like a robot, acknowledging his introduction to her with a bow, and sitting with his elbows at his hips and his cap held in front of him like a salver.

"What a lovely home," murmured Hofer. Simone appeared, her cheeks pale, her lower lip quivering slightly.

"Will you have coffee?" Cree asked.

"No, thank you, madame. With your kind permission we will get down to business. It has come to the Cultural Minister's attention that you have in your possession a number of paintings. As you may or may not have heard, the Rosenberg Task Force has taken on the backbreaking job of cataloging and caring for works of art belonging to the city as well as to dealers and individuals. The program is being carried forward at a tremendous sacrifice in time and manpower in order to insure the protection and proper care of priceless works of art. I don't have to remind you that these are parlous times. Saboteurs are everywhere. Only last night the bronze statue of General Mangin in the Place Denys-Cochin was tipped over and smashed by vandals. The army is doing its best to maintain law and order, but we cannot guarantee that people's priceless possessions will not be stolen or damaged. Now that the war is all but over, you will rest easier knowing that your own collection will be in safe hands. You will, of course, be given a receipt for each painting and informed where your collection is to be stored. At any time, providing you obtain written permission from any officer with the Task Force, you will be allowed to visit your treasures. Reich Minister Goering and Cultural Minister Rosenberg are committed to preserving the priceless heritage of art. Your Cranachs, your Modigliani portrait, your Vermeer street scene, couldn't be in better hands."

"Cranachs? Mo—?"

"*Lucretia,* a *Crucifixion, Cardinal Uttermann of Westphalia, The Lost Painting, The Birds,* and *Christ and Adulteress,* by Lucas Cranach the Younger. You'll be delighted to know that Reich Marshal Goering shares your love of Lucas Cranach's work. None of these modern painters for him. He thinks the Impressionists are a bunch of fakes. But Dürer, Altdorfer, Cranach, all the good Germans, he idolizes." He snapped up from his chair, the lieutenant rising with him. "Now, may we see them?"

"Herr Hofer, you're welcome to see my paintings, but you won't find any Cranachs or Vermeers or Modiglianis. They are in America, in New York City with my daughter."

"One each only of the latter two. Please lead the way."

She showed them both galleries, her eyes riveted on Hofer. Her heart felt as if it were shrinking inside her. Had he believed her? It terrified her that he not only knew she owned Cranachs but was able to recite the titles from memory.

Why delude herself? It was all over. He barely glanced at the last three pictures. He seemed in a hurry to get on to his next victim. To her astonishment he said nothing—not a word.

They stepped out into the hallway, and her heart thumped so loudly she was afraid they could hear it, even though they were standing ten feet away. Hofer was about to set his left foot on the top stair when he changed his mind and, going back to the left gallery, took down the painting nearest the door. Cree's heart crumbled.

It was the Vermeer, concealed by a painting of six yellow apples in a glass bowl.

"With your permission, may I borrow this? I'll see that it's returned to you shortly. You have my word on it as a gentleman."

"Certainly."

"Thank you. You needn't bother to show us out, we know the way. It's been a distinct pleasure meeting you. And once again may I say your home is lovely? As you are yourself, madame." She turned away.

Simone shut the door behind them. She was pale and trembling. Cree sank against the wall, struggling to relax. Locking the door, she turned to Simone and told her to pack her bag and go to her sister's place across the river and to stay there until she got word to her.

There was going to be trouble, she said, and added that she herself was getting out and taking her paintings with her.

Chapter Thirty-five

Picasso and Paul Poiret had dropped in to say good-bye to Cree. Simone had left, loudly voicing her displeasure, insisting that Cree was "forcing me to desert her." Cree had helped her pack and had driven her to her sister's apartment at Place Blanche.

Cree made supper for Picasso and Poiret. The conversation turned from a discussion of Hofer's visit to Paul Rosenberg.

"I saw him this morning," said Picasso. "He's about ready to kill himself. He had a huge inventory on hand. Even working day and night, he wasn't able to get halfway out of town before they swooped down on him and finished him off. The tears were rolling down his cheeks when he told me about it. All his life he's worked like a mule, and in two hours they destroyed him. God, how I hate the sight of them, stinking Huns!"

"Did they get anything of yours?" Poiret asked, his napkin tucked in his collar, his soup spoon poised just under his chin.

"About thirty paintings and forty or fifty drawings." Picasso shrugged. "*C'est la vie.*"

"*C'est la guerre, mon ami,*" said Poiret, and resumed his attack on his *crème de volaille.*

"They'll be coming back here tomorrow for the rest of my paintings," said Cree. "I'm getting out tonight."

"Of course, you realize that little *serpent à sonnettes* Duprier set you up."

"With my cooperation. Hofer didn't swallow that business for a second about sending my Cranachs to New York with Sabrina. What I don't understand is why he only took the Vermeer? Why not everything?"

"He's playing games with you," said Picasso. "He's a sadistic son of a bitch. He'll be back with your Vermeer all cleaned up, brand you a liar, and toss you to the wolves. That's more fun than taking everything away on his first visit."

"Don't listen to him, Lucretia, he's only trying to scare you."

"He's right, that's why I'm getting out while I can."

"Why not hide your collection in Claudette's secret room?" inquired Poiret. "Seriously. Pablo, you still have the key I gave you."

"I don't see how I can take them with me," said Cree.

The doorbell sounded. It was Giselle. Cree dragged her inside and slammed the door.

"Not again!" Giselle's face fell. "Oh, my God, your timing is marvelous."

"I'm sorry, Cree, we've gotten into this business and we can't seem to get out."

"How many this time?"

Giselle lowered her eyes. "Thirty-two," she said quietly.

"Thirty-two?" Picasso and Poiret had come up behind Cree. Poiret still had his napkin tucked into his collar and spread over his paunch. She introduced them to Giselle.

"They're out back with Roland and a man named Douglas Archer, an Englishman."

Picasso looked puzzled. "An Englishman is helping Jewish children to escape?"

"What's strange about that?" asked Poiret. "Is Churchill anti-Semitic?"

"This time we have a small problem," said Giselle.

"I'd call thirty-two kids a pretty big problem." Cree held her hands against her cheeks and shook her head slowly. "Well?"

"We don't have any boat. And they have to get out tonight. The Gestapo is breathing down our necks." She looked at Picasso and Poiret pleadingly.

"What about your barges?" Cree asked Poiret.

"*Amour, Delices,* and *Orgues.*" He grunted and began tilting his head back and forth, his multiple chins drawn up and deeply furrowed.

Picasso snickered. "Tell them. You're a little late. He had all three sunk yesterday. Opened the cocks and zoomph, zoomph, zoomph."

Giselle groaned. Poiret was scratching the side of his face and ruminating. "They're only partially submerged. I did it so the Nazis wouldn't get their hands on them. Before they were sunk, I had the engines covered with thick layers of grease to keep them from rusting. There's a little damage to the engines. I wanted to make it look like sabotage."

"Can one of them be refloated?" Cree asked.

"All three can."

"We only need one," said Giselle, "if it's big enough."

Cree nodded. "They're huge. Any one of them could hold a hundred people."

"They're party barges," explained Poiret. "*Amours*

is the biggest. It shouldn't take long to pump her out and fix her up."

Giselle brightened. "Douglas can repair any damage to the engine. He's very good at fixing things."

Picasso started toward the door. "I'll go get the key to Claudette's house. We'll hide the kids like the last time."

"I don't think we should bother," said Giselle. "It would be for such a short time. We've got to get out before curfew." She glanced at the kitchen clock worriedly. "I hope they can get the barge floated by eleven."

"Easily," said Poiret.

Cree guided Giselle toward the kitchen. "Get them in here and up to the top floor. Maybe you'd better stay with them and keep them quiet. Paul, take Roland and Douglas to where the barge is, okay?"

"Under the Pont des Invalides." He laughed and elbowed Picasso in the arm. "What do you think of this? Poiret, the hero of the Underground."

Picasso snorted. "It's about time you did something for your fellow Frenchman."

"For your information, señor, I did plenty in the last war."

"You weren't even in the army."

"I was in the quartermaster corps. I helped win the war. I standardized the cut of army overcoats and saved twenty-four inches of cloth per coat and four hours' labor per finished garment. And what did you do in the war, my son? Any war? Camouflage mules?" He laughed and slapped Picasso on the back, jolting him forward and eliciting a glare.

Douglas Archer and Roland stood on either side of the children filing in from the backyard. Archer stood well over six feet, more than a foot taller than Roland.

His dark-brown hair gathered at his forehead, tumbling partway down it. He smiled easily and often. After Giselle introduced him to Cree they stood talking to each other. He lived in a sixth-floor walk-up on Rue du Bac in St.-Germain-des-Prés. Cree recognized the house from his description. She told him that she had lived at 110 for almost a year. He was a free-lance journalist who had tossed a coin and thereby made his decision to stay when the Germans marched in. He was writing a "Diary of Occupation," as he called it—a working title. To her surprise he told her that more than seven thousand Englishmen were still in Paris. Giselle and Roland interrupted them.

"We got them all into your bedroom and the one across from it," said Giselle to Cree. "They'll be okay until the barge is ready and we leave."

"I'm going along."

"There's no need."

"I want to help."

"It could be dangerous. Besides, you've already helped."

"Damn!"

"What is it?" asked Roland.

"My paintings. I can't leave them here. Hofer's sure to be back before we get back from the coast."

Picasso waved away her concern with his massive hand. "Don't worry, I'll hide them in Claudette's secret room. You two ladies can help move them while you're waiting for the men to come back. With three of us working, it shouldn't take long."

Chapter Thirty-six

The kitchen clock read 10:32. The men had been gone almost two hours. Cree, Giselle, and Picasso had removed Cree's collection to Claudette Duvivier's secret room.

The three of them sat waiting at the kitchen table.

"You really shouldn't come with us," said Giselle, covering Cree's hand with her own. "It's going to be touch and go getting to the barge. If we're stopped . . ." She shook her head and looked away.

"I'm coming, and that's all there is to it. It's only six or seven blocks from here. There's no moon, no stars. If we keep the kids in groups of three or four, each group within sight of the one ahead, we can all dodge into doorways or down alleys or under stairs if we have to."

"It's crossing the Champs Élysées," said Giselle. "It's the widest damned street in the world. Once we get to the Grand Palais it shouldn't be hard, but the Champs Élysées scares me."

"Whatever you do, don't run," declared Picasso. "Don't do anything to attract attention. That looks suspicious."

"Thirty-two children and four adults out for a stroll

at eleven at night can't look anything but suspicious," said Giselle glumly.

"Act nonchalant and keep your eyes peeled. You'll make it."

"If we don't, the kids are finished. Us, too. They'll ship them off to Germany and stick the four of us in front of a firing squad."

Cree swallowed. "They wouldn't shoot us."

"Oh, no? Getting caught smuggling Jewish children out of the country is worse than high treason in their eyes."

"We'll make it. Stop worrying."

Two minutes later Poiret, Roland, and Douglas walked through the front door. Douglas's hands were black with grease. Cree gave him soap and a towel. Poiret was carrying two large cartons, his fat face spread in a mischievous smirk.

"What do you have there?" asked Giselle.

"While these two were doing the bullwork I had a bright idea. I drove over to Avenue Clichy. Next door to my textile design studio is Bojany Theatrical Costumes. Lucien Marquet, the owner, is a friend of mine. He always works nights. I saw the light on and got you these." Setting the boxes on the table, he opened one, then the other. Each contained a nun's habit. "Wimples, crucifixes, rosary beads, the works. I guessed at the sizes. Congratulations, both of you, on taking the veil. This way, you can march the kids in a double line from here to the barge, two Sisters of Passion of our Blessed Lord bringing their students back from Saint-Augustin. Just make sure nobody's wearing a yarmulke." He laughed. "Brilliant, no?"

Cree and Giselle threw their arms as far around his bulk as they could, hugging him and kissing him loudly on his cheeks.

"Get dressed," said Douglas, wiping his dripping hands with the towel. "We have to get moving. We'll go on ahead and have the engine started and be ready to cast off when you get there."

Cree glanced at Picasso.

"Go, I'll lock up for you. When you get back, stop in and I'll give you your key."

"I'll give you the keys to the Bugatti, too, in case you need it. Pablo, would you please keep an eye on the house?"

"I will, stop worrying. What will you do when you get back?"

"Leave Paris, I guess. When Hofer comes back and finds the paintings gone, he'll be furious. I don't want to cross swords with him. I'd rather just get out."

"We can discuss it when you return."

Giselle had taken both habits and started up the stairs to change.

"Hurry," she called to Cree. "We have a long night ahead of us."

Chapter Thirty-seven

As any English Channel-bound crow flies, from Paris to the mouth of the Seine between Honfleur on the left and Le Havre on the right is about a hundred miles, but the *Amours*, following the exaggerated twists and turns of the river, had to cover almost twice that distance. The route from Paris to below Rouen was particularly tortuous. The vessel's top speed was only eight miles an hour, and it wasn't until nightfall of the following day that they came within sight of the Channel. A British trawler was waiting, prearranged signals were exchanged, and the children taken on board.

The entire adventure had been far less hazardous than Cree had imagined, the only close call coming off Quevilly, when Douglas sighted a motorcade of German troop trucks dusting up the highway. Their passing was ignored and, removing their collective hearts from their throats, they settled back and endeavored to relax. Sisters Giselle and Lucretia had marched the children in a double line across the Champs Élysées without so much as a pause at the curb, the boulevard being all but empty of traffic at such a late hour.

On the voyage back, they struggled against the current. Nearing Honfleur, they put in out of sight of the docks. Cree, Giselle, and Roland disembarked, and Douglas opened the cocks and sank the *Amours* at Paul Poiret's orders. They returned to Paris by train.

Cree went straight to Picasso's studio. He answered her ring, his face collapsing at the sight of her.

"Everything go all right?" he asked.

She nodded. "What's happened? My paintings!"

"Sssssh." He glanced up and down the street, then lowered his eyes. "They came early this morning and broke your front-door lock. The hullabaloo woke me up. Hofer had a dozen uniforms with him. I'm afraid they made a terrible mess of your house."

"I don't care, as long as they didn't get the paintings."

Once more he lowered his eyes.

"Pablo," she whispered, her throat tight with tension.

"When they didn't find them in the house they went straight to Claudette's. Like damned retrievers right for the bird. They know you two are friends. They know everybody's friends with everybody else in this neighborhood. They knew about the hidden room. I love Claudette like a sister, but she does run off at the mouth. I went over after they left." He shook his head and studied the toes of his shoes. "I'm sorry, there was nothing I could do."

Cree sat down heavily on the stoop. "And we thought they'd be safe there."

"Nothing's safe anywhere." He fished in his pocket and brought out her keys. "I'll go over and help you straighten up."

"I was stupid. I have nobody to blame but myself. I should have shipped the lot out months ago. When Sabrina left."

"It's all spilled milk now." He studied her, his eyes

filled with sympathy. He put his arm around her shoulder. "I'm so sorry."

"Twenty years' collecting down the drain. *Heil* Hitler, *heil* Goering. Where did they take them, do you think?"

"To the Salle du Jeu de Paume, Task Force Headquarters."

"Where do you think they'll store them?"

"I doubt if they will. The Cranachs, at least, will go straight to Germany. Goering has residences in Berlin and three castles—Carinhall, in the Bavarian Alps across from Hitler's own place, Veldenstein, near Nuremburg, and Mauterndorf, not far from Berchtesgaden." He put his arm around her consolingly. "I know it doesn't count for much, but at least in Goering's hands they won't come to any harm."

"That fat, filthy thief!"

"Come, come, you mustn't talk so about our distinguished Reich Marshal, Herr Art-Lover *extraordinaire*."

The house was a shambles. Cushions and bedclothes, drapes and carpets had been slashed with bayonets. There were bulletholes in the ceilings upstairs, and Cree's beautiful antique trictrac table had been smashed into kindling with a rifle butt. Every mirror in the house was shattered, and gaping holes had been poked in the walls in the living room and dining room. Cree and Picasso were picking up downstairs when a loud knock sounded at the front door, reverberating through the house. They exchanged worried glances.

"It sounds like our friend is back," said Cree. "Maybe he forgot something."

Picasso had moved to a front window and with his back to the wall peered out from behind the torn curtain.

"German soldiers, eight, nine, ten of them."

"What the devil do they want?"

"You'd better answer the door."

Standing before her was a good-looking young man in the now familiar single-breasted green-gray uniform of the *Wehrmacht*, a coal-scuttle helmet on his head, the insignia of a major on his epaulets, and the German eagle-and-swastika emblem over his right breast.

"Guten Morgen."

"Wyatt!"

He grinned and marched in, followed by his men. Throwing her arms around his neck, she kissed him fiercely.

"Where have you been? Why didn't you get in touch? What have you been up to? I've been out of my mind with worry. What in God's name are you doing in that disgusting getup?"

"Making life difficult for your friendly neighborhood Teuton." He glanced about as he removed his gloves. "What hit this place?"

While she told him what had happened, he and the others shook hands in turn with Picasso.

"You're right, Pablo," said Wyatt. "They must have taken everything to the Rosenberg Task Force Headquarters. Let's go. We have a truck parked at the corner." He started toward the door.

"Wait," said Cree, "I'm coming with you."

"Me, too," said Picasso.

"No, Pablo, I don't want you getting into this."

"Mother, you stay here. I'll be in touch."

"I'm coming, damn it! Don't argue, we don't have time."

He started to protest, thought better of it, and motioned the others toward the door. He had his hand on the knob when the bell rang. Everyone stiffened. Once more Picasso moved to the window.

"It's all right. It's Douglas Archer."

Cree let Douglas in and introduced him to Wyatt, hurriedly explaining what had happened. He too insisted on accompanying them. Wyatt was becoming impatient.

"We'll follow you in my car," said Cree. "We won't be in any danger."

"Okay, okay."

"You still haven't explained what you're doing in that uniform," said Cree.

"I took it from the former owner." His men laughed. "We've been assigned to disrupt German operations in and around the city. Last night we blew up an SS radio truck on the Rue de Turbego. What a sight!"

"Wyatt, that's dangerous. If they catch you in that uniform, you'll be shot as a spy. All of you. You can't even speak German."

"*Ja. Nein. Ich verstehe.* That's all I need to get by. A couple of these fellows speak it like Berliners. They do all my talking for me." He brought out a monocle, slipping it over one eye, and pulled himself up arrogantly. "Officers don't involve themselves in petty conversations. Come on, if you're coming. Let's get over there before they start moving the stuff out."

Chapter Thirty-eight

The canvas-covered truck pulled to a stop opposite the entrance to Task Force Headquarters in the Salle du Jeu de Paume, a formidable-looking, two-story building. Cree parked the Bugatti a block behind the truck, turning off her engine just as a familiar figure emerged from the building. Armand Duprier.

"There he goes," she said, "the deceitful little traitor. I'd like to wring his puny neck!"

Douglas grinned. "Friend of yours?"

She drew in her breath sharply, clenching her teeth and following the little man with her eyes, staring daggers at him as he made his way down the street with a smug, self-satisfied expression on his face.

Wyatt and two of his men got out, crossed the street, and entered the building. Cree and Douglas waited. A German army truck passed by, followed by a mud-caked staff car. A dark-blue Peugeot pulled up at the entrance, and four civilians emerged and went inside.

"Gestapo," murmured Douglas, "either that or collaborators like your friend."

Presently Wyatt and the others reappeared. He came over to the car, his face dark with disappointment.

"Oh, oh," said Cree.

"Bad luck," he said, leaning in the window. "It came

337

in, all right, but they've already taken everything away. Direct orders from Goering."

"Well, that ends that," said Cree.

"No, it does not. Don't give up so easily. Your paintings are in a truck with other loot heading for Nancy. One of my men spotted the plate number on the dispatcher's sheet. They left about an hour ago." He looked at his watch. "We'll go after them. With any luck we'll catch 'em before they get to the border. You go on home. I'll phone you."

"Just get into your truck and get going," said Cree. "We'll be right behind you."

"No, you won't, damn it. Mr. Archer, take her home, please. Mother, I promise you we'll get your paintings."

"All right, all right," she snapped irritably.

"I'll be calling. Does anybody still have a phone on our block?"

Douglas was writing down his number. He handed the slip to Wyatt. "We'll be at my place."

Wyatt walked off. Cree started the car.

"He's right, Lucretia. There's absolutely no point in following them. It could get sticky."

"It could."

The truck started off, reached the end of the block, and turned left. She watched it vanish before following it around the corner.

"What are you doing?" he asked.

"If we stay back far enough, they'll never see us. If you don't want to come, just say so. I'll let you off at the first metro station we pass."

"Never mind," he said wearily. "I'd hardly let you go running off by yourself. Still, it's extraordinary."

"What?"

"Every day that goes by, something new pops up to keep me from my typewriter. If it isn't kiddies, it's

Cranach. Lucretia, do slow down, you're getting much too close to them."

Leaving the city, they ran into unusually heavy traffic, but once they gained the eastbound road dividing the countryside between the Marne and the Seine, they began to make better time. They headed for Nancy, in Meurthe-et-Moselle, which was two hundred nineteen miles distant and on the railroad line to Strasbourg, approximately eighty miles further east. Their chances of recovering the collection would be excellent if they caught up with the truck before it reached Nancy. But once the paintings were transferred to a train they would be whisked through Strasbourg and across the German border to Kehl in no time.

Over the lush and gently undulating plateau of Lorraine they sped, down a highway carrying little save military traffic. The speedometer needle held at sixty, the miles peeled away, but there was no sign of their quarry. They followed Wyatt's truck into Nancy, entering the *ville vieille* late in the afternoon and following the signs to the railroad yards, which were situated on the southwest side of the city. When the truck stopped at an intersection, Cree boldly pulled the Bugatti alongside it, leaning across Douglas and calling up to the driver. Wyatt was sitting beside him.

"Do you still think you can stop them?" she asked.

"Oh, for God's sakes!"

"Head for the railroad yards. We'll be right behind you. Maybe we can catch them loading the paintings."

"You head for the station! Check on all trains heading out for Strasbourg, freight and passenger. We'll check the yards and meet you in front of the station in half an hour."

"No. It'll only take a few minutes to find out about

the trains. You stay in the yards. We'll find you."

"Have it your way, but if this turns into a fight, you're going to be sorry you bothered."

A dozen horns were honking behind them. Off drove the truck, Cree slipping into the lane behind it.

"He'd never show up in front of the station," she grumbled. "He'd just light out after them. You watch."

"Lucretia, he's right, you know, about this developing into a near thing."

"I can't worry about that. I didn't come all this way to go home empty-handed."

German uniforms of every rank swarmed about the station, lending the impression that it was under heavy guard. Cree stopped across the street from it.

"I'll go in," said Douglas.

"I'll come."

"No!"

She read the seriousness in his eyes and shrugged.

"I didn't come all this way for the ride," he added, getting out.

She watched him cross the cobbled street to the main entrance. A guard stopped him. She held her breath. They talked briefly; he went inside. The second hand of her watch carved its way through a minute, two, three. He came walking toward her.

"There's a freight leaving in about two minutes."

"Oh, my God . . ."

They circled the station and drove into the sprawling yards just in time to see Wyatt's truck pulling out in pursuit of a five-car train flying twin swastikas on its front plate. The train was moving slowly away from the loading platform.

"Didn't I tell you he'd duck out of meeting us?"

"Lucretia, don't be ridiculous. Isn't it more important he keep his eye on your collection?"

"Can he, I wonder?"

"I imagine so. There must be a road of some sort paralleling the tracks."

They followed the truck out of town. The road ran parallel to the tracks, but there was no indication of how long it would continue to do so. The truck was picking up speed, easily passing the slowly moving train. The locomotive's stack belched cinders and dirty white smoke that stained the clear sky. Within minutes the truck was more than a mile ahead, speeding through pastureland broken here and there by isolated groves of beeches, pines, and maples and ponds dotting the green velvet countryside like fragments of a mirror. Far ahead the Col de Severne could be seen, guarded by adjacent peaks of the Vosges. Beyond them lay Strasbourg and Germany.

The pastureland was giving way now to widely spread forests as the road began to climb. Behind them the train rolled on, carrying Cranach and Modigliani and Boucher and Monet. Cree tried to ignore the disheartening realization that once the train passed over the Col de Severne, her treasures would be lost.

"They should have stopped them back there in the yards," she said wistfully, "in the midst of loading."

"Maybe they didn't get there in time. Even if they did, shooting would have alerted all those men in and around the station. He obviously plans to stop them up top somewhere."

"How? With what? What if we get there and find the road's two or three miles from the tracks and there's no possible way to get to them in time? We'll all be standing there helpless, watching the damned thing roll right past."

"Lucretia, stop being so pessimistic. Have a little faith. He knows what he's doing."

She fell silent; there was nothing she could think of to say. The road was climbing sharply now, heading straight up to the Col. There was one thing in their favor, she reflected. The train would have to slow to a crawl to make the grade and the summit, which would give Wyatt and his men added precious time. Now the twin peaks were no more than two miles distant. The truck was slowing, the driver shifting gears for the third time, she noted. She, too, shifted, sacrificing speed for power. Douglas glanced behind them.

"I can't see the train anymore for the bloody trees."

"Oh, Lord, I just thought of something. He wouldn't be so foolish as to dynamite the tracks, would he? The train's so short the whole string would go up. And come down and smash to . . ."

"That's it, keep thinking positively."

Before she could respond, the truck pulled over to the side and stopped. Men rushed out, weapons in hands, and ran into the woods. Wyatt got down from the cab.

"Stay here," he called. "There might be shooting."

"Wyatt . . ."

He waved and disappeared around the front of the truck, following the others into the woods.

"Come on," said Cree.

Moments later Douglas was leading the way through a thick grove of wind-whipped maples and pines. The land sloped upward. He held back branches for her, cautioning her to duck every so often. He was scowling and muttering to himself. She had difficulty suppressing a smile. He was such a good soul, trying so hard to be helpful, in spite of his frustration over her obstinacy. From the time they'd left Paris she had refused to go along with almost everything Wyatt had asked of her.

They could make out the cliff rising on the other side of the tracks. Reaching the edge, she looked at the tracks below and started down. Douglas pulled her back.

"This is far enough. We can see the whole bloody show from up here. Let's just belly down and wait, shall we?"

She nodded. Down below, six of Wyatt's men were already busy piling boulders, dead logs, anything they could find to build a barrier. Two other men were setting up a .45 caliber machine gun and tripod between the tracks.

The muffled sound of the locomotive struggling up the grade could be heard in the distance. The barrier completed, the men dispersed, climbing the rises on either side, taking up positions thirty and forty feet above the tracks.

They waited. The wind funneling down from between the peaks moaned like a creature in pain, rustling through the pines and doubling over the weeds lining the roadbed below. Then they saw the smoke; the train climbed into full view, moving sluggishly at less than five miles an hour. The shooting started, rifle fire coming from the opened doors of the second and third cars and from the end corners of the caboose. Cree watched as one of Wyatt's men clutched his stomach and toppled from his perch high above the tracks. The others returned fire, the machine gun up the line sending a steady stream of bullets into the cab walls on both sides, keeping the engineer and fireman inside and neutralizing the two guards riding with them. The train shuddered to a stop just short of the barrier, whooshing, clanking loudly. The attackers dodged the fire from the cars and concentrated their own on the open doors.

One train guard and then another were hit and fell forward onto the roadbed apron.

The engine started up, sand dropping from the sandbox in front of the dome, the driving wheels spinning, catching hold. The train moved backward. Several of Wyatt's men rushed the caboose vestibule, firing mercilessly, driving the Germans inside. Suddenly, just as the train was beginning to gather steam, a sniper at the top of the rise hit the engineer. Letting go of the throttle, he pitched forward at an angle, falling over the windowsill on his stomach, the weight of his body carrying him all the way down into the weeds. Shots poured into the cab from both sides, killing one of the guards and sending the fireman to his knees, screaming.

In minutes it was over. The soldiers emerged from the train, their hands clasped on top of their helmets. They looked dumbfounded. German against German?

The Frenchmen assembled and herded them, nineteen in all, into the caboose.

"They're not going to kill them, are they?" asked Cree.

"I doubt it. Why would they?"

"Wyatt!" she called.

Wyatt's men were climbing aboard the train to search for the stolen artwork. Running down to the tracks with a clattering of loose stones, Cree rushed over to Wyatt.

"What will you do with those men?"

"Let them walk back to Nancy or on to Strasbourg, whichever they choose." He indicated the locomotive cab. A man was smashing it with a sledgehammer. "Train service is out for the rest of the day."

"Lieutenant!" A burly private was calling down from the doorway of the third car. *"Les voici."*

Wyatt cheered triumphantly. "We did it!"

Mother and son threw their arms around each other. Douglas came up, all smiles, and began pumping Wyatt's hand.

"Congratulations, well done."

"We'll help carry them to the car," said Cree.

"Maybe that's not such a good idea, Mother. Think about it. Why take them back to Paris? Your friend Hofer will only come after them again."

"How will he know we've recovered them?" Her eyes drifted to the caboose. She nodded. "I see what you mean."

"Where would you take them?" Douglas asked Wyatt.

"South, down over the border into Switzerland. To Basel or Allschwil. They'd be safe there for the duration. It's less than a hundred miles from here."

"How will you get across the border?" Cree asked. "They'll search the truck. They'll take every painting. What difference is there between losing them to Goering and to the Swiss?"

"The Swiss wouldn't confiscate them, not if we can prove we're with the Resistance, which shouldn't be difficult. We have friends we can count on in Basel."

"It does sound practical, Lucretia," said Douglas.

"I suppose. I would like to look at them for a minute before you load up," she said quietly. "No, on second thought, maybe it's better I don't. You have Douglas's number. When you get back to Paris, call if you can. Get in touch some way. I won't sleep a wink until I hear from you."

"You will, I promise."

They kissed good-bye. A corporal came up; in his hand was a list of the paintings.

"Il n'y a pas de Vermeer."

"The Vermeer," said Cree. "By now it must be hanging on a wall in Carinhall. The pig. Better somebody burn it then it fall into his fat hands."

Douglas and Cree climbed back up the cliff and made their way through the woods, heading toward the Bugatti. He got behind the wheel.

"Wait," she said, "just until they finish loading the paintings."

"It'll be some time. Then they're going to have to bury the dead."

She nodded. "Yes. Let's go home."

Chapter Thirty-nine

The war wound on. On D-Day, June 6, 1944, 176,000 Allied troops were put ashore on the Normandy coast under the protection of 11,000 aircraft and 600 warships. Very soon the tide of battle began turning dramatically. By September two million Americans were fighting in Europe. In the East the Red Army invaded Poland, launching a powerful offensive against the Germans along an eight-hundred-mile front. The "Thousand-year Reich" was caught in a vise that quickly began to close. The end came swiftly. On May 8, 1945, Germany's surviving generals surrendered the remnants of their battered armies and their country to the Allies.

Cree and Douglas Archer had left Paris two days after returning from the Vosges mountains, delaying their departure only until word came from Wyatt that his mission had been accomplished and that he was back in the city. He was no longer wearing a German uniform, however; he and his men had prudently discarded their disguises in favor of civilian clothes before tackling a new assignment.

Cree and Douglas went with Picasso to Royan. Cree begged Simone Ratelle to go with them, but she was reluctant to leave her sister. One month to the day after

Cree and Douglas arrived in the little resort town, he offered her his mother's ring; she had already realized that her fondness for him had ripened into love, and she joyfully accepted his proposal. They were married, with Picasso serving as Douglas's best man.

After the signing of the armistice agreement, all three returned to Paris. Within a week Cree's collection was returned to her intact and restored to the walls of the two galleries in the house on Rue de la Boëtie. Wyatt returned home, proudly displaying the Ordre de la Libération, awarded him personally by General de Gaulle.

The day after Wyatt came back, all three sailed for New York to bring home Sabrina.

Chapter Forty

The reunion was all that Cree could have wished for and more. Sabrina, Julia, Claudia and Jessica, Alec White, and Lloyd Rush were all there to meet them. One familiar face was missing. Cree could barely make herself heard above the din of the crowd of disembarking passengers and those who had come to meet them.

"Where's Livvy?"

"She's at the house with Grandfather," said Julia.

"What's the matter?"

"He had a stroke last night. Dr. Bingham is with him now."

"How bad is he?"

Julia shook her head. The joy of the reunion suddenly dimmed. Alec drove Cree, Douglas, Wyatt, and Sabrina to the house on Sixty-first Street, the others following in Lloyd Rush's car. Coming home, Cree suddenly felt like a child again, coming home from school to change her clothes and have a glass of milk with freshly baked cookies in the kitchen with Mother and Mrs. Bates. Mrs. Bates had been dead seven years, her place taken by Myrna Dell Foley, retired from the office, haggard-looking, but still determinedly bright and cheerful.

Cree kissed her on the cheek fondly and introduced

Douglas and Wyatt. Olivia appeared at the landing upstairs.

"Cree."

Cree ran up the stairs to embrace her.

"How is he?"

"He's dying."

"Dear God."

"Cree, he's ninety. Oh, he's fighting it tooth and nail. Dr. Bingham says in all his years of practice he's never seen anyone like him."

"Can I see him?"

"Of course."

He lay staring blankly, his eyes rheumy. For a moment Cree could not see whether he was breathing. The sheet covering him seemed to lie so perfectly still. Dr. Bingham, standing on the other side of the bed, nodded a greeting. He had given up—Cree could see it in his expression. Standing over her grandfather, she looked down at him pityingly.

"Grandfather."

A glimmer of recognition brightened his eyes. His lips moved as he tried to speak, but all that came out was a succession of soft, slurring sounds.

"Don't try, please."

She kissed him on the forehead, covering his hand with her own and aimlessly adjusting the sheet under his chin. Olivia touched her arm. She led Cree and Julia out of the room and closed the door softly. Cree could feel tears coming.

"Let's go into the study," said Olivia. "There's something I have to show you."

She sat on a high stool. "Last night, when it happened, Myrna Dell called Dr. Bingham, then Jule and me. He was here when we arrived. Grandfather was coherent. But all he could talk about, according to Bingham, was how badly he felt about his past, the things he'd done, the enemies he'd made, his sins."

Rising from the stool, she drew open the middle drawer of the desk and brought out a small black book with a brass lock.

"What's that?" asked Cree.

"His diary. The lifetime record of his sins, from what I gather."

"Haven't you read it?"

"I can't find the key."

"We can break the lock," said Julia.

Olivia nodded. "We could. The question is, do we or don't we? It's our decision."

Cree held out her hand; Olivia placed the book in it. It barely covered her palm and outstretched fingers.

"All his sins, the mass of guilt he's accumulated over a lifetime. Set down, chapter and verse. Amazing. Why would he do such a thing?"

Julia eyed her questioningly. "To clear his conscience? At least try. Put it down on paper and get it out of his system. He might even have considered it an act of expiation of sorts. He may have hoped that one or all of us would some day read it and be shocked out of our skins. And condemn him."

Cree shook her head. "I doubt if there's anything in here that can shock me or any of us."

"But Jule's right," said Olivia. "He wants us to know everything. He loves us, and if we react in horror and condemn him, we'd be punishing him, don't you see? He wants to be punished. He wants to pay for his sins."

"Do either of you want to read this?" Cree looked from one to the other. "I don't." Her sisters shook their heads.

"I don't think anybody should see it," said Julia. "I say we destroy it." She poked through the drawer and found a packet of matches. Breaking the lock on the book with a letter opener, she ripped off the first two pages, crumpled them in the ashtray, and set them on fire. They passed the book around, adding one page after another until all that was left was a mound of ashes.

"Let's look in on him before we go back downstairs," said Olivia.

They walked out into the hallway. Dr. Bingham was coming out of Grandfather's bedroom. He paused, his hand on the doorknob. Cree could see by his expression that it was all over. The three of them joined hands, finding strength in one another.

And started down the stairs.